* * *

Once The Wing reached the proper elevation, Stan placed his hand on the throttle, ready to pull the levers back and leave America behind. But a sixth sense of sorts that he'd developed back in his street crime days stayed his hand. He turned around in the pilot's seat to see two men standing behind him, just watching his actions.

Stan laid eyes upon the one in a painfully familiar uniform. "*You*! Just what does it take to kill you? *Who are you*?"

"I am THE SKYMAN," the costumed man said, cracking his knuckles, "and you're sitting in my seat!"

* * *

If pulp magazines ever make a comeback, Morris' Skyman may become the new Doc Savage!

— **Roy Thomas**, writer, editor and comics historian

The Original

Skyman

Battles

The Master of Steam

By

Brian K. Morris

Based on the Columbia Comics

and

ACE Comics characters

created by

Vincent Sullivan

with

Gardner Fox and Ogden Whitney

A fully-authorized **ACE Comics** Presentation

In cooperation with

Rising Tide Publications

Copyright © 2016 by Ronald J. Frantz and Brian K. Morris

Executive Editor: **Ron Frantz**

Cover by **Pat Boyette** with **Ogden Whitney**

Back Cover Illustration: **Ogden Whitney** (from *Big Shot Comics #1*, May 1940)

Interior illustrations by **Trevor Erick Hawkins** (based on the work of **Ogden Whitney**)

Interior Design and Formatting: **Safari Heat Book Covers & More** safariheatbooktoursandauthorservices.com

Cover Colors by **Randyl Bishop & Pat Boyette**

Copy Editor: **Cookie Morris**

Table of Contents

DEDICATIONS

To **Gardner Fox**, **Ogden Whitney**, **Mart Bailey**, **Ray Krank**, and **Vincent Sullivan** for giving me many pleasant hours of research.

To **Ron Frantz** for his faith, good advice, and most of all, his friendship.

To **Cookie Morris**, **Trevor Erick Hawkins**, and **Sean Dulaney** for their advice, assistance and talking me off the ledge more than once.

To **Jennifer Merritt** and **Randyl Bishop** (**www.timebound.co**) for their vital help to Trevor.

To **Kim Lockman** (www.kimlockman.com) and **Vicki Rose** (http://platinumbookreviews.blogspot.com) for their encouragement and friendship.

To **Comic Book Plus** (comicbookplus.com) and **The Digital Comic Book Museum** (digitalcomicmuseum.com) for their invaluable aid in my research.

And this book is primarily dedicated to **Anne and Mel Mills** for adopting me. My life's been a blessing ever since.

A FOREWORD BY ROY THOMAS

Skyman was one of the great early super-heroes. Captain Midnight in a gaudier costume and with a faster plane ... a one-man Blackhawk squadron, keeping the air waves safe from Nazis and other nasties.

Gardner Fox, one of the greatest comic book writers ever, created him ... and now Brian K. Morris' book suggests that perhaps, after all, the proper mode for Skyman is straight-ahead, flat-out prose, spinning words across the ether like the trail of his amazing aircraft.

If pulp magazines ever make a comeback, Morris' Skyman may become the new Doc Savage!

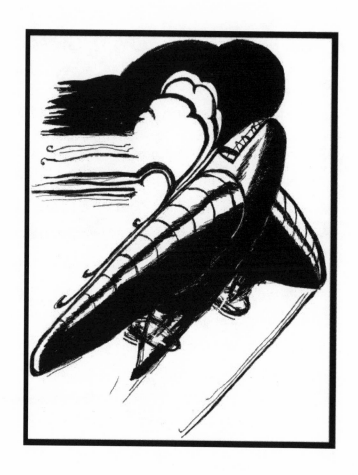

The Wing takes flight!

ONE – Taking Two For the Steam

Almost a year earlier, before the engineer

gave him the nightly cue, Tony Trent always whispered, "Never a dull moment, darn it," as his good luck phrase. Depending on the news of the day, that oath could be either a statement of fact or a complaint, but it always proved true.

From his vantage point behind the WBSC microphone, Tony glanced up at the engineer whose own good luck regimen consisted of lighting up a cigarette and giving the newsman's script one more glance before airtime. Unconsciously shifting his weight from one foot to the other, Tony watched the sweep hand of a clock on the far wall move towards the zenith of its eternal orbit.

The engineer held up both hands, all ten fingers extended.

Tony nodded in acknowledgment.

One finger moved towards the palm ... then a second, leaving eight ... seven ...

Tony cleared his throat.

A hand dropped to the control board, landing on top of the switch he'd turned five nights a week for the last two years. At the engineer's left hand, a diamond needle waited patiently inside the usual groove of a well-worn 78. Five ... four ...

"Never a dull moment," Tony whispered, "darn it."

Two ... one ... the engineer turned on the phonograph without having to look. A second later, Tony's headphones filled with the sound of an orchestra playing the show's theme, twenty seconds of dramatic horns backed by silken violins, all conveying the importance of the news of the day.

Another gesture and a quick nod from his engineer later, Tony took a deep breath. "Good evening, America. From The Statue of Liberty, through the Gateway Arch and deep into the Hollywood Hills, welcome to your nightly news. This is Tony Trent reporting from the studios of WBSC in New York City."

Tony allowed the first script page to slip through his fingers and float quietly to the floor. "Tonight's main story, another scientist has disappeared under mysterious circumstances. Professor Clyde Hemmer never showed up to his Aeronautic Engineering 101 class yesterday morning, the first day he'd missed in his sixteen years at Kent State University's hallowed halls of learning.

"The President of the college summoned the police to investigate the professor's absence. However, firefighters were already at the Professor's home, attempting to extinguish a three-alarm blaze that took almost eight hours to contain. Authorities revealed this afternoon that no bodies have been found in the ashes so far and have reason to believe the Professor may still be alive.

"This pattern of abduction and arson matches a *modus operendi* that's been seen in twelve other cities here in America as well as our Canadian neighbors to the north, Switzerland, and Great Britain since August of 1937, less than a year ago. The Federal Bureau of Investigation has agents in Ohio searching the remains for clues in the hopes of putting an end to this six-month long mystery. Now in other news ..."

Click!

Eight hundred miles to the west, in Urbana, Illinois, Dr. Kevin Carson leaned back, sinking into his favorite chair like settling into a mother's warm embrace. He stretched, locating the indentations in this threadbare ottoman that perfectly matched the back of his heels. As he listened to Tony Trent's description of the world's woes, he unconsciously stroked the tips of his silver mustache. After a day of theorizing and experimentation, it was good to listen to the radio and unwind, leaving the computations and test reports to the past … at least until Monday morning.

A cool breeze entered the upstairs window, causing Carson to smile appreciatively. A few years ago, he'd converted the attic into a den of sorts where he could look over the town and see his office in the Physical Sciences department of the University just on the edge of the horizon. It was close enough to barely see and far enough away to remind him that most of the department's problems would wait for him to arrive at the start of the next business day.

The springs in his chair creaked as they compressed, which was fitting for furniture he'd owned since he graduated from the U of I back before flappers were the rage. Sure, those dark, rusted coils drowned out the radio sometimes, but he felt about this heirloom chair-and-

4

footstool set like he felt about his women … if they felt good, he didn't mind if they made a little noise. Not that he sought out many of the ladies since the Hoover administration, not after Science stole his heart.

Carson's less public work took up too much of his time these days, sorry to say, for any thoughts of fooling around. But the end result might be worthwhile if he could complete his computations before his European counterparts could finish theirs.

Dr. Carson turned the pages of the local newspaper, the *Courier*. He scanned the length of each column, looking for more information coming out of Europe. But just because he didn't see anything unusual about the paperhanger and his army of thugs as they swept across Europe, it didn't mean that he'd report to work in three days with any less urgency. Lives depended on his research and he knew it.

The government's gentle inquiries about his progress never sounded as if there was any true urgency lurking behind the bland smiles and square-jawed faces. But Carson knew better. A terrible war on the Eurasian continent appeared to be as inevitable as the next sunrise to many people. America needed to be ready to strike and strike decisively.

The doctor contemplated his current research, wrestling down the obsession to work on the numbers inside his head instead of relaxing. However, he knew that should his team's findings prove true, he could change the face of warfare forever, perhaps even eliminate armed conflict between nations once and for all.

Assuming the planet survived the first test of the weapon.

"Cripes! Did someone reinstate Prohibition?"

Carson looked up to see Fawn Carroll entering the study, a good two fingers worth of expensive bourbon in each hand. A year earlier, while Dr. Carson labored to meet a deadline that threatened to be more "perish" than "publish," Fawn became his personal secretary, referred to him with the most impeccable of credentials from a certain agency that wouldn't take "No" for an answer.

At least twenty-five years younger than himself, Fawn maintained her youthful appearance, even at her tender age when most of her high school friends had already given up on college, married, and began filling their households with children. Her auburn hair cascaded onto her shoulders, tresses that framed a face that should have been on a movie screen. A good girl who never found a fella that met her moral standards or level of intelligence in her brief lifespan, Carson became more than just a mentor to the woman. He also became a friend.

Fawn seemed to enjoy the doctor's company in the way two buddies could listen to the radio and share a drink together at the end of the day before heading to their separate quarters. As he settled into middle age and a distinguished career as the head of the U of I Physical Sciences Department, Kevin found listening to a Dorsey Brother more satisfying than chasing skirts every evening.

Speaking of skirts, Fawn didn't exactly shop for clothing that concealed her figure. Dr. Carson, despite his almost paternal attitude towards his assistant, didn't mind the occasional glance at her and neither did she. The only curves potentially more dangerous than Fawn's were at a race track.

After handing the doctor his drink, Fawn settled into another chair, one that didn't hug her hips like a evening gown. "Anything interesting on the radio, Doc?"

"Just the usual from overseas." Carson took a stronger pull on his glass than he originally intended. He blinked rapidly as the fumes invaded his sinuses. She smiled softly as she sipped from her own glass with a teasing look that almost screamed, "Pantywaist."

The Zenith radio occupied the far corner of the living room. After a couple of human interest stories, the voice of reporter Tony Trent yielded to that of a staff announcer extolling the virtues of Serutan.

Suddenly, a sense of unfamiliarity filled the air, like a front door opening downstairs that had been locked; like the whisper of foreign voices as they deployed to different locations downstairs; like heavy footsteps sounding in an unsuccessful attempt to move stealthily.

Both Carson and Fawn put down their drinks quietly. The doctor reached for the volume dial on the radio but Fawn gestured firmly and shook her head. "Let them think we haven't heard them," she advised in a whisper. Carson nodded.

Fawn reached for the telephone. Carson originally

8

resisted the idea of having a link to the outside world inside his sanctuary, but he knew of no other way to summon the police in case of trouble. However, Fawn's frown and the silence from the earpiece confirmed his suspicions. Someone already cut the phone lines.

He turned to the window and opened a cedar box located just under the sill. Inside was a rope ladder that was firmly secured to the base of the box which in turn was bolted into the floor. Carson gathered the ladder into his arms. He took a swift glance behind him, but Fawn had already vanished down the stairway that led to the first floor of his house, locking the study door behind her.

Downstairs, all Marco Roove could hear was the pounding of his heart and the squeak of his worn leather shoes. When he was a numbers collection guy in Philly, he could afford a new pair of Florsheims every other week of the year. But now, he could buy a new custom-fitted suit every month and pay for it with what he carried in his wallet. All he had to trade for it was his conscience, such as it was.

A circle of cold steel pressed against the base of Roove's slicked-back, jet black hair and his bulk froze in place. His beefy hands rose slowly into the air out of habit.

"You move towards that bulge under your left armpit," Fawn whispered as she closed the door behind her, "and they'll find your brains in the neighbor's garden."

Before she could ask how many other intruders were in the house, a creak at the end of the hallway distracted her for the merest of moments. It was long enough that Roove could whip the back of his hand around to knock Fawn's gun arm to one side. Following up, he balled up his other fist and slammed it into her jaw. Fawn slid down the length of the wall into a sitting position, unconscious, with her .38 revolver resting in her open palm.

Roove surveyed the attractive woman, noticing how her skirt rode up her leg, exposing a holster that lay strapped to the inside of her shapely left thigh.

Back in Philly, a reluctant "client" landed a lucky blow that broke the enforcer's nose, leaving a permanently crooked reminder in the mirror to never let his guard down. One retaliatory punch and a couple of hours later, the other man woke up, tied to a radiator and forced to watch Roove crack his knuckles while casually strolling in a circle around the guy's wife. She sat in a chair, trembling inside the ropes that held her fast and silently pleaded for her husband's help.

"You wouldn't strike a woman!" the frightened husband declared.

Roove searched his feelings and smiled softly. "Wanna bet?" He then illustrated his point for the next hour, making certain that her husband would live with her eternally visible reminders of regret.

The man paid early from that day on.

Roove now found himself smiling as he surveyed his helpless victim-to-be and wondered who needed a lesson today.

Before he could move towards the unconscious woman, the creator of the distraction moved awkwardly to Roove's side. A bulky figure wrapped in an old Inverness cloak looked into his employee's eyes without blinking. In a heavily-accented voice, he said, "Take her to the vehicle and wait for me." With a casualness that spoke of inhuman strength, the man pulled Fawn's body out of the way effortlessly, opened the door, and ascended the stairway.

Roove feared no ordinary man's muscle, courage or

ferocity. However, he realized that standing almost shoulder-to-shoulder with his employer often left him unconsciously biting his lower lip. Without a moment's delay, Roove scooped Fawn's limp body into his arms and walked with purpose towards the black Studebaker waiting in the alleyway behind the house, contemplating no mischief with his prisoner.

Upstairs, Carson heard the brief scuffle. He and Fawn had discussed the possibility of this event several times and their plans were already in place, hence the rope ladder that Carson prepared to drop out the window.

But a glance towards the ground revealed a man in a slouch-brimmed hat and a cheap suit who nervously surveyed the street from one end to the other, his hand resting inside his jacket. Carson was trapped inside his own sanctuary.

At least Fawn locked my door on the way out, Carson reminded himself, sweat trickling down his temples. *She should be able to fend for herself.*

The door knob rattled once, twice.

Fawn would have allowed herself back in with her own

key without rattling the knob. Only two keys fit that particular deadbolt lock and the other rested in his pants pocket. Without delay, Carson thought to drop the ladder on top of the waiting gunsel below in the hopes of stunning him long to enough to effect an escape.

Carson's hasty plan died in his mind in the second that the oak door exploded inwards, propelled by a gloved hand. The last chunk of wood barely struck the hardwood floor when the figure walked into the room.

The man entered, stepping carefully as if he had to plan each and every heavy step. His stance hinted at some kind of extraordinary power in his compact frame. Steely eyes twinkled with amusement and anticipatory triumph, accompanied by a thin-lipped smile that verged on a smirk. He removed his hat and dropped it onto Carson's chair.

As the stranger approached, Carson hurled the bundled rope ladder at him. But with a sweep of an arm, the ladder flew to one side as the man strode forward with the confidence of a tank.

Carson backed up towards the window, contemplating a leap through it and chancing injury or worse. But for a heartbeat, he found himself distracted by the level trimming of the stranger's hair, leaving it as flat as a serving tray. In fact, all of the hair on the man's head was shock-white.

However, the intruder's face was heavily scarred as if he'd been scalded more than once. And his eyes burned, wide eyed and unblinking with a smile that was anything but warm.

Still several feet away, the man opened his coat. His torso was covered completely with gleaming silver tubing that ran along his body as if mimicking his own muscles. *Armor*, Carson thought.

Welded to the invader's pectoral area, a crest of stainless steel and copper tubing approximated the appearance of a dragon, rising proudly on its hind legs and ready to breathe heated death upon its enemies.

Distracted by the armor's accessories, Carson saw the man had a gun in his left hand. It was like no pistol he'd been shown by Fawn. It too seemed to be little more than tubing shaped into a parody of a firearm, like something in a W.C. Fields movie. What appeared most striking was instead of a trigger guard, the weapon – it could be nothing else – had a protective shield like the Navy sabers of the last century.

The man turned a dial on the back of the pistol before bringing it up and squeezing the trigger. Suddenly, the world went cloudy and Carson felt as if he was drowning and burning alive simultaneously. He couldn't breathe, he couldn't see, and every nerve ending felt like it had been lit by a match.

His senses overwhelmed, Carson surrendered to a cool darkness in his mind. His hands dropped limp to his sides and he fell to the floor, silently asking what he thought might be his final question: *Hissing?*

Graduation Day for Allan Turner

TWO – Raised From the Ashes

Not quite a year later, **Allan Turner could do**

just about anything well except be nineteen and not a little self-conscious of his accomplishments.

Sitting towards the back of a sea of students, just one more graduate in the 1939 class of Harnell University, Allan fought off the urge to take a nap as the school President began his speech, probably the same one he gave every year to every graduating class. But who would stay awake long enough to confirm this?

In his three years of college after graduating from high school at sixteen, Allan aced just about every class he took in engineering, aeronautics, chemistry, biology, and electronics. Allan might still be signing up for new classes, hungry to fill his mind with knowledge, if his uncle hadn't badgered him to escape academia and enter the real world for some genuine challenges.

If Allan squinted his blue eyes sufficiently, he could just about make out his uncle Peter up in the bleachers, placing that ever-present crutch at his feet. His mentor and guardian sat in the same space he occupied for every sporting event that Allan ever played during his college career. Touchdown after goal and miles of yellow ribbon breaking across his chest, Allan could rely on hearing the cheers from the man who raised him from the age of eleven to now.

Although he tried not to dwell on the memory too much, Allan could never forget watching his parents' airplane approach the field for what should have been a routine landing. His folks loved to fly and spent many hours in the air, showing their only son how to work the controls. But this one time, the couple decided to make a short business trip from upper New York State to Rochester to check on some of their business holdings.

As his youthful heart beat happily at the thought of being with his folks again, Allan recalled feeling as if paralyzed, unable to turn away, while the plane appeared to shake itself apart as it descended. Almost as if hurled from the aircraft, pieces of steel tore away in shreds and flew towards the ground.

Allan felt his Uncle Peter push him away just before a

knife-shaped chunk of shrapnel tore into the older man's right leg. Peter tumbled to the asphalt, but retained the presence of mind to cover Allan's body with his own. By the time the fuselage slammed into the runway and transformed into a ball of unapproachable flame, Allan already fell into a state of shock.

The grief-stricken young man didn't remember dressing himself for the funeral three days later, just kind of showing up and being surrounded by strangers in a large hall rented for the occasion. Numbed in his heart, Allan forced himself to accept the condolences of the many people his parents had touched with their philanthropy and the employment they provided with their various financial interests. That day, he became aware of how his parents received satisfaction from improving the lives of others and it was up to him to continue this legacy.

Once the services for the ashes of his parents ended, his uncle Peter remained after the last mourner left. Allan had always loved his uncle and the older man's zest for learning. The two spent hours talking about wild ideas for inventions that wouldn't have sounded out of place if one was, say, starring in one of those Sunday funnies in the newspaper.

Except where some writer made up words to justify how his creations could work, Uncle Peter tied real science to his theories to make the devices come to life in the Harnell campus laboratory where he also made his home. Between the numerous papers he wrote to impress the deans of Harnell where he taught, and the patents he sold on a regular basis, Peter was clearly an expert in just about everything he set his mind to. He could also convey his excitement in the act of discovery, an excitement that proved infectious.

Vaguely registering that he was being led towards the potluck left behind by the funeral guests – mostly because Allan hadn't eaten more than a plateful of food since witnessing the accident – the boy turned to his uncle. After a couple of half-hearted bites of some kind of salad, Allan worked up the nerve to state, "I wish I knew what happened to my parents' airplane."

Peter laid his left hand softly on his nephew's shoulder, the other tightly clutching the handle of the crutch that his doctor said he might need for the rest of his life. "I manged to … pry some information out of the investigators. You are an orphan due to faulty material in your father's airplane. It's no one's fault that those two died, except for the greedy rat who pocketed the money he saved in using those garbage parts." Peter's voice quavered with anger as he recalled reading the police report, his wallet twenty bucks lighter and his tears staining the paper in his shaking hand.

With a loud clearing of his throat, Peter said, "I've accepted the responsibility of your further upbringing, according to your parents' will." Allan responded with a grateful nod and the first real smile he'd worn in days.

With a sweep of his hands, as if urging Allan to behold the splendor that surrounded him, Peter continued, "Here at Harnell University, you will live with me."

Allan nodded. "I can sure live with that. That would be swell, Uncle Peter."

"I'll tell you what else is swell, Allan." Peter guided their path towards a specific building on the edge of the quad. "Your parents didn't exactly die penniless. When you turn of age, you're going to be a wealthy man."

Allan muttered, "You know that's not important to me."

Peter grinned in response. "And I'll see that it stays that

21

way, young man. I'll keep you involved in knowing everything I do in administering your inheritance because you'll have to take it over one day." His smile faded. "The world economy is in a shambles right now. We have the Great War to thank for that. Anyway, your parents left around eleven million dollars in a trust fund that you will receive upon your 18th birthday. I have a plan to ensure that you keep as much of it as possible."

Having sat too long today, Peter used his crutch to push himself to his feet. "You are very wealthy, Allan. But forget that. Live simply, I say. Go to prep school near here and later to Harnell."

Allan stood up and smiled at Peter. "Anything you say, Uncle. Anything."

"Good. Now let's go have some tea in my office and relax a while. This house stinks of funerals and tears right now. How about we let it air out?"

Allan listened to their steps echo in the massive main hallway. Suddenly, he stopped, his jaw meeting the knot in his necktie.

Trying to force his voice past the shock, Allan managed

to whisper, "How many million was that again?"

Sitting in the stands today, Peter Turner smiled at the memory of his ward as the boy matured and at the strides he made in his education. Allan became a knowledge sponge, absorbing any fact he could, able to turn that information into practical use. Even before he came into his fortune, while still in his teens, he'd already sold several patents that would ensure financial security for the rest of his life in addition to his inheritance.

The only tinge of regret Peter felt in raising the boy was the young man inherited his parents' love of flying. After the accident that took his brother's life, he would have been much happier if Allan showed more inclination to drive busses blindfolded or disarm explosives than to take to the air. But damned if the young man wasn't good at almost everything he set his mind to.

And still, the boy didn't care about money. He gave tons of it to worthy causes, backed other projects that needed an inspiring angel, and still lived like any other properly-bred, highly-intelligent, well-adjusted, smartly dressed, witty, handsome, physically perfect young man … objectively speaking, of course.

Then Allan's name was called by Harnell's President. Peter could almost see his nephew turning crimson with self-consciousness as he reluctantly made his way to the podium to accept his special commendation.

Peter's grin couldn't have been wider, nor could his pride and love been larger. He knew he wasn't just watching his only family accept the reins of adulthood. He suspected he was a witness to history.

However, had Peter Turner kept the presence of mind to be aware of his surroundings, he might have noticed the only pair of eyes in the entire auditorium who weren't focused on the reluctant valedictorian. Peter would have felt the appropriate spinal chills once he realized those eyes were aimed at him and no one else.

THREE – Here Today, Fawn Tomorrow

Keeping his eyes closed, Carson felt the drone

of powerful engines coursing through his body along with the odor of old engine lubricants and wished for a less unpleasant piece of evidence that he was still alive.

We're in the air, he realized. The thought gave him absolutely no comfort whatsoever.

"Wakey-wakey, Doc." Marco Roove cleared his throat. "The boss wants to talk to you."

Carson slowly opened his eyes, trying to see past the rainbow of explosions filling his field of vision. He looked up to see a thug with a broken nose sitting over him. Beside him sat the man who Carson last saw standing outside his window. The thug still glanced around nervously, his right hand never far from the left-hand side of his sports jacket.

Later, Carson would find out the other man was Stanislaus Lange, a former Army pilot, later a hit man for a New York mob gang with a penchant for cruelty and rock-solid loyalty as long as the money was good. Stan and Roove

25

shared a respect for each other's reputation and also knew the other would sell him out to the highest bidder in a heartbeat.

A further hasty survey of the interior of the aircraft – some kind of cargo plane, probably not American – revealed that he was in the hold with the two men who broke into his house. He tried to sit up, discovering that his wrists were handcuffed securely. Carson struggled to a sitting position and caught a glimpse of Fawn who sat in the very back of the dimly-lit bay. Her face was puffy, her lower lip was painfully swollen at one corner and her eyes blazed with hellfire. Without intending, Carson gasped with concern at the sight of his friend.

Fawn's gaze met Carson's. Her almond-shaped eyes stared back at him with an unusual hardness. She didn't appear to be frightened in the least, more like she was angry … perhaps at herself for not foiling their kidnappers, for letting them get the first telling blow in, or perhaps just at their captors because having been awake longer, she'd had time to contemplate their possible fate.

Stan made his way into the cockpit. A minute later, the armored stranger emerged, now wearing a cloak like some kind of villain from the serials. The bizarre white-haired man walked with deliberation towards where Carson sat. He smiled faintly and bowed at the waist.

"*Herr* Doctor. My name is Albrecht Bruhner. I am from Prussia – hence my accent – but I now call Germany my home. Welcome to my care, Dr. Carson. I look forward to many long, rewarding talks with you for I too am a scientist, albeit an engineer. I am certain we have much in common."

"I'd tell you to turn this plane around and release me," Doctor Kevin Carson stated, "but I doubt my words would have much influence."

Bruhner laughed and Roove joined in, albeit nervously. "And this, Herr Doctor, is proof of the vast intelligence that brought you to my attention, and to my employer's. What a bonus to possess such a splendid wit."

Carson forced a smile onto his face. "So just what do you think you're doing?"

"Oh?" Bruhner gestured around the cargo hold. "I believe your puritanical so-called 'justice' system would call it 'kidnapping'."

"And just what would *you* call it?" Fawn almost spat

each word as she strained against her own handcuffs.

Bruhner regarded the woman like a chef would regard a lump of mold on a slice of bread. "I would call it marshaling potential resources in the service to the German Empire."

"A Nazi." Fawn sneered with contempt at her captor. "Should have recognized that Brownshirt stench."

Ignoring Fawn, Bruhner knelt and lifted Dr. Carson's chin so their eyes could meet. "Doctor, we are both experts in our particular scientific disciplines. Here, your talents would be forced to merely serve the political ends of your pathetic government, which is such a waste." He smiled coldly. "Instead, you can be part of a movement that will create a better world, every man living under one flag. You read the newspapers, you hear the news on the radio. Soon, all of Europe will fly the colors of Germany." Bruhner smiled again. "Why squander your talents on the losing side of history?"

"Maybe because the good guys are going to tear through Berlin like Sherman through Atlanta," Fawn cried out with the ferocity of a mama bear.

Bruhner rose to his feet with a speed that belied his

heavy-footed gait. He stormed over to Fawn and pulled the woman by her hair to a standing position. "You will be quiet when your male betters are speaking, woman."

"Leave her alone!" Carson regretted his emotional outburst as soon as he saw the cruel smile spread across Bruhner's face. Fawn returned his disappointed expression, knowing he just handed the man the keys of control. Carson sighed. "All right … please let her go. Let's talk."

Fawn growled at Bruhner. "You drop your guard for a half second and I'll kick you so hard, your grandchildren will walk bow-legged."

At the mention of family, Bruhner scowled before twisting the fistful of auburn hair in his metal-covered hand. He ignored Fawn as he spoke. "Doctor, I am not a man who enjoys trifling matters. You are no doubt attempting to delay or prevent my injuring – or worse – of this female. You probably will even bring up the notion that if anything untoward happened to her, I would lose my … what do you call it? My bargaining chip?"

Despite her hands being cuffed behind her back, Fawn struggled to free herself, however much in vain. But Bruhner held her easily by her hair. "*Owwww*!!! Let go of the perm, goosestepper, or else."

Bruhner turned towards his captive. "I checked the identification in her purse during my visit, Dr. Carson. Were you aware that this woman worked for your Federal Bureau of Investigation?"

Carson swallowed hard.

"Yeah, Ratsi," Fawn said with her warmest smile and the coldest stare most men would dread receiving. "My college grades were so good – better than most men – that Washington decided to test the idea of female field agents for the first time in a decade."

Bruhner shook his head sadly. "Director Hoover never seems to learn from his failures, does he?" He pulled Fawn's face close to his, allowing her to smell his scalding breath. "Goodbye, little girl. You should have resigned yourself to making dinner and half-witted babies."

With no emotion on his face, Bruhner walked with purpose towards the nearest exit, pulling the still-struggling Fawn with him. With one hand, he easily turned the latch and pushed the door open. Immediately, the air pressure inside the cargo hold dropped and Carson found himself struggling to catch his breath.

Ignoring the winds whipping against the door, Bruhner kept it open with just one hand. Without hesitation, the man casually tossed Fawn through the portal with no more effort than it would take any normal man to toss a cigarette butt from the window of a moving car. Carson heard her cries briefly as the winds and gravity took her away from the plane.

Bruhner locked the exit door and moved towards Carson again. He looked down at his captive. "So confident am I in your future cooperation that I would kill someone close to you. Rather makes you wonder what I know about your situation that you don't, eh?"

With that, Bruhner turned back towards the cockpit where he closed the door upon his entry, allowing Carson just a glimpse of the other crook in the co-pilot's seat. The scientist looked over at the remaining thug who sat staring at the closed door, his expression pale and uncharacteristically fearful.

Carson slumped onto the floor of the cargo hold, his

heart breaking. *Oh, Fawn …*

* * *

Fawn Carroll could barely pull in a full breath as she tumbled in the skies over … well, she really had no idea where she might be. Her view of the world changed rapidly from spinning relief map of the Earth to whirling clouds and brief glimpses of the Moon then back again. Wash, rinse, repeat.

Without thinking, the F.B.I. agent pulled her legs up tight against her chest as she forced her wrists towards her feet. Fawn felt her back or shoulders might crack soon but with a desperate movement and a grunt, she forced her cuffed hands past her hips and then her feet until her hands were now in front of her.

Immediately, Fawn thrust her palms straight ahead and forced her feet apart. The wind made a pocket in her wool skirt, slowing her descent ever so slightly. She took in the view – it would have been a thrilling nighttime image for the ages if only she was still inside an airplane.

Moonlight provided its teasing illumination of the ground below. Actually, Fawn could just make out a winding road that bisected a small grove of trees. To her right, she could see the Moon reflected in a small lake. *At my velocity,* she thought, *I could aim myself towards the water and end it quickly. It would be like diving into a concrete pool from the top of the Chrysler Building.* She bit her lip furiously. *But if I have even one chance in a million of living, I'm going to repay that Nazi pig tenfold for this.*

Fawn moved her shoulders ever so slightly and the cool night winds that numbed her flesh now pushed her subtly away from the lake. However, the trees came up faster than she could have imagined. With a fearful swallow and a girlish moan, Fawn closed her eyes and willed herself to go completely limp. Before she could say goodbye to her Creator, she struck the upper branches of the largest tree in the grove.

Sliding down a major limb of the majestic oak, Fawn felt every branch strike her like a cat-o-nine-tails, tearing away at the clothing, digging into her flesh. She was vaguely aware of being battered again and again, turned around and around, the smell of leaves filling her nostrils, along with her blood. Fawn tried to bring her arms up to protect her face and eyes when she slammed hip-first into the main trunk of the tree, bringing her downward momentum to a halt.

After a moment, Fawn passed out completely. Her body went limp and she resumed her plummet through the mighty branches until she finally slammed against the leaf-covered ground, landing flat on her back and striking her head violently in the process. Fawn lay on the ground, unmoving, unconscious.

* * *

Abner Penwright never let a day off from the Texaco go by without at least an hour at the local lake. After five solid days of pumping gas, washing windshields, and trying to keep the local kids from stealing all his boss' candy and smokes when he wasn't looking, Abner loved the serenity – that's a word his mom taught him when praying – of the lake and the taste of the fresh fish for lunch. And a beautiful sunny morning like this would even make coming home empty-handed a pleasure.

While walking his bicycle through the grove, Abner looked down to see what appeared to be a pool of blood by a huge oak tree. While trying to puzzle out what could have left such a mess, he noticed some more crimson a little further down the trail and then another measure of the same smeared against a tree past that. Abner leaned his bike against the oak and cautiously moved forward towards the lake, hoping he didn't find a skinned pig or something worse.

Emerging into the clearing, Abner saw a figure sitting in the water near the ramp that he and his friends used as a diving board when they were still in grade school. As he slowly approached, Abner saw ... well, he was hard-pressed to say what or who it was, only that it was either lucky to be alive or determined to remain that way.

Fawn looked up from the cooling water and pulled another small tree branch from an open wound. She winced and tossed the branch into the pinkish water. She smoothed her matted hair from her eyes and asked hoarsely, "Hey ... fella ... give ... a girl ... a ride ... to town?" just before she passed out.

Abner looked at the girl, then into the water. So much for getting some fishing in today.

The Original Skyman Battles the Master of Steam

Fawn Carroll

Brian K. Morris

FOUR – Demonstrative Results

"Let's hope," Allan Turner said sincerely,

"that I'm never forced to dress funny again unless it's Halloween. I'm so glad the big tah-dah is over and done with."

With the graduation festivities concluded at last and the sun crawling to the edge of the sky, the Turners strolled leisurely towards the far end of the quad. Allan listened to the sounds that surrounded them ... the rubber tip of his uncle's crutch, the squeak of his leather shoes, the rustling of the trees and leaves in their wake.

Peter laughed and clapped his nephew on his well-muscled shoulder. "My boy, you're graduating from one of the most prestigious learning institutions in all the Fruited Plains at the age of nineteen. Believe me, you've got a lifetime of indignities to endure by the time you get to my age."

Allan grinned. "True. If wearing a robe and funny hat is the strangest thing I ever do, I'll be fortunate." He sighed. "I

37

guess I'm supposed to talk to some of your peers tomorrow?"

"Yes, my boy. I put in a word to the head of my department to see if they'd like to check out some of your research, maybe offer you a teaching position here."

The pathway turned towards Peter's on-campus home. "Well, I'll talk to them, Uncle Peter. But I think I have my life already planned."

Peter grinned. "I'm not surprised. When they realized you were graduating, they set up this meeting to see your latest project. I'd say just give them a listen, let them think they're important, then you say you'll consider it and then don't commit to anything." He fumbled in his trousers for the keys. "You'd think I'd have learned to keep the keys in my other pocket, out of the way of my crutch."

Allan quickly pulled his own keyring out and opened the front door. He waited for his uncle to go inside and then whirled around.

A figure darted behind a tree, but not before Allan made out its silhouette. He smiled grimly as he closed and locked the door for the night.

Early the next day, in his uncle's laboratory, Allan pulled

a protective cloth free of the device resting on his workbench. He added a bit of showman's flourish to the act as three men walked in, led by Peter. Allan finished his set-up by placing a wire cage beside the device. Inside the enclosure, a couple of white lab rats moved freely. One raced desperately inside a metal wheel leading to nowhere while the other dived through a seeming ocean of brown wood shavings.

Peter quickly made the introductions between Allan and his own colleagues. Their apparent supervisor, Dr. Tom Dodot, a man with more hair under his nose than atop his own head, gave Allan a look that absolutely screamed *Kids today!* "So what have we here?"

Allan rested a hand on the device. To the uninitiated, it appeared to be something from a Buster Crabbe serial, all lenses, shiny metal, cooling vents, buttons that blinked in all the colors of the rainbow, and strange, inexplicable noises coming from within. As Allan carefully nudged several of the dials, a humming seemed to fill the room from floor to ceiling.

Allan smiled as he addressed his uncle's peers. "Good

morning, gentlemen. I am honored to show off my newest invention to you, the Stasimatic Ray Emitter."

Elvin Maywear, an electrical engineer with close-cropped dark hair smiled benignly. "And just what does this Stasimatic Ray Emitter do?"

"Obviously, it emits Stasimatic Rays." Allen waited for the chuckling that never came. His uncle Peter gnawed his lower lip self-consciously. "Seriously, gentlemen, I feel this could be a leap forward in medical science, particularly in anesthesia."

"How so?" asked the third man, George Theele, a man with dark brown hair and a pair of glasses so thick, Allan had no idea how the man could see anything in front of him. Of the three, only Theele wasn't introduced earlier by his particular scientific discipline.

"Imagine," Allan continued, "if you will, that a person could be rendered unconscious for a controlled period of time. When they woke up, they wouldn't have to worry about the side effects of ether or any other chemical as it coursed through their blood stream. They'd waken as if from a brief nap."

"This might create less stress on the body," added Peter, "allow the recipient to spend less time in Recovery, possibly heal faster as it were. It could also be used to induce a safe medical coma in the case of more severe injuries."

"Very good," Allan complimented his uncle. He'd left the man in the dark to gauge his reaction. Leave it to the smartest man in just about any room to not only figure out the device's purpose, but to add a level to the expectations of what it could do in the right hands.

Gripping a switch on the back of the Ray, Allan nudged the machine's main lens in alignment with the mice who exercised, oblivious to the humans that surrounded them. "If you'll watch the cage ..."

FLASH! A burst of yellowish light later, the wheel stopped to become a hammock for its operator while the other rodent disappeared under the wood shavings.

The man with the close-cropped hair nudged one of the mice with a pencil through the bars of their prison. "They're still breathing," he observed. Without even looking at Allan, he asked, "What did you do?"

"The Stasimatic Ray disrupts the electrical signals in the

human body," Allan explained, "along with certain gas exchanges and chemical reactions, but only for a fraction of a second. Just long enough for the recipient to pass out painlessly."

"And the effects last how long?" The man with the pencil continued to poke at the mice almost fearfully.

"Usually, a couple of hours. The time can be adjusted for shorter or greater periods, but I feel it's too early in my research to call a longer-range time frame a certainty." Allan worked to power down his device.

Rubbing his hands together in anticipatory glee, Dr. Dodot smiled broadly at Peter, all differences in their ages forgotten for the moment. "Congratulations, Turner," he said, looking at Peter rather than Allan, "Your ray successfully and safely paralyzes living tissue. The mind boggles at the applications."

"What a boon to science," the man with the soda-bottle bottom glasses agreed. "It'll turn quite a pretty penny for the University."

"Excuse me?" Allan looked to his uncle, who also appeared surprised.

"This isn't a fire sale. The invention is Allan's completely," Peter explained to his peers. "I didn't even know what it did until you learned yourselves. My nephew is certainly fond of surprises." He glanced at Allan with a quick wink. "But I think you'll agree that the boy might make a terrific addition to our faculty."

"Oh, yes he would," Dr. Dodot agreed too quickly for Allan's comfort, his eyes never leaving the Stasimatic Ray.

"You see," the man with the crewcut explained, "part of what keeps Harnell financially solvent involves selling patents from the faculty to various industrial and governmental concerns."

Allan nodded and spoke slowly. "I see."

"Allan Turner?"

The teenager turned around to see the most beautiful woman he'd ever seen. He gave a quick glance from the hat that framed her auburn hair, down her trench coat to the tops of her high heeled shoes. In college, he'd been on the receiving end of more passes from Harnell's cheerleaders and would-be actresses than he ever did on the gridiron. In this one moment, Allan forgot about all of them.

"Well, hel-lo!" he stated, feeling a flush growing under his collar.

A flick of the wrist later, a badge appeared in the woman's hand. "I'm F.B.I. Agent Carroll and I'm here to escort you and your documents to Washington." She smiled sweetly. "You can call me Fawn."

"I'm FBI Agent Carroll..."

FIVE – Reluctant Goodbyes

Allan Turner leaned towards his uncle and whispered, "Is it always this exciting around here?"

Rolling his eyes, Peter replied, "Fortunately, no."

"I'm claiming this in the name of the Federal Bureau of Investigation," Fawn announced. "The university will be paid a generous finder's fee, of course."

"Finder's –" Dodot sputtered for several seconds before he felt it safe to continue. "This was created on Harnell property and as such, it belongs to Harnell."

"Actually," Allan interjected, "I brought it in just this morning. I worked on it in another location entirely."

Dr. Turner noted the strained expressions on the F.B.I. Agent's face as well as his department chairman's. "Let's remember to remain civil, shall we? Okay, begin arguing … now!"

During the next twenty minutes, Dr. Dodot and F.B.I. Agent Carroll discussed the ownership of the Stasimatic Ray device in conversational tones frequently delivered through gritted teeth.

Pulling on the corners of his mustache, Dodot declared, "Harnell has affiliations with several major medical hospitals that would pay a great deal of money for this machine. And since we are planning to offer Mr. Turner a position here at Harnell –"

"That would allow me," interrupted Fawn, "to exercise the government's option to declare ownership of any discovery that could be put to use by the military or the law-enforcement arms of the United States government, which I happen to represent."

"Government?" Allan rose to his feet and clutched the device protectively. To Dr. Dodot, he stated, "This machine is in the early stages of development and not yet ready for human testing." To Fawn, he took a milder tone of voice. "As for the government, I would like to know what your intentions would be."

Fawn's eyes turned hard, unblinking. "Imagine our Army with a ray that could render enemy combatants unconscious immediately. Think of the lives that would save."

Allan nodded as he loosened his grip on the machine. "Go on."

The agent took a deep breath. "Imagine a hostage situation. The F.B.I. could sweep a building with this ray and pull out the bad guys almost at their leisure. No shots fired, no blood spilled, no stand-offs, no one has to die." The last five words issued forth with a slight quaver in Fawn's voice.

"I'm sorry," Allan said softly, "but the device is too new to be put up for sale to anyone. There's a lot more research and development to do."

"Do you need money?" Dodot pushed past Peter to Allan's side. "I can give you your own budget. We might even get around the teaching obligations if you're of a mind, get someone to ghost write your papers for you."

Fawn placed a slender hand on Allan's forearm. "No one has deeper pockets or greater gratitude than Uncle Sam."

Allan turned to his uncle. The older scientist stroked his Van Dyke thoughtfully and smiled with bemusement in anticipation of Allan's response.

Never one to disappoint, Allan smiled gently. "Doctor Dodot, Agent Carroll, I sold patents that have made me wealthy before I left high school. This is in addition to the eleven million dollars I inherited from my late parents last year on my eighteenth birthday. I appreciate your concern for my financial well-being, but I think I'll muddle through."

"But Mister Turner," Dodot pleaded, "you need a job. Everyone needs a job." He smiled. "Don't they?"

Fawn snapped her fingers and smiled. "That works! Take a job here at Harnell and if you create more items that the F.B.I. can use, we'll reimburse the college for your salary and –"

"But," Dodot interrupted, "the medical industry is poised to ..."

The rest of the high-volume conversation between Dodot and Fawn rose in pitch and intensity. Allan walked over to his uncle. "Thank you for the best laugh I could have all day. See you later." Without any further notice, Allan took his jacket and exited the building.

The sun shone warmly on Allan's face. His step was brisk as he took to the quad. He envisioned a good long walk to a newsstand and then some effort to get back to the apartment and work towards his true calling.

As Allan crossed the well-manicured lawn, another set of footsteps labored to keep pace. Allan heard the sound and smiled.

* * *

"MEN!"

Fawn slammed her purse on her desk with enough force that either the stitching should have given way or the sturdy furniture collapsed. She was mildly disappointed that neither occurred.

A secretary stood in the doorway of Fawn's office and cleared her voice softly. "Um, Miss Carroll. Miles would like a word with you."

Sighing, Fawn strode to her supervisor's office, feeling like a schoolgirl who got caught passing notes. She knew this conversation would be one-sided and probably unpleasant.

Miles Rockwell puffed on his pipe with the regularity of a steam engine taking a steep uphill grade, just as he always did when he was uneasy. The torrent of Virginia tobacco-scented smoke ended when he heard the knock on his door. "Enter." Miles placed the pipe into its usual slot in the ashtray.

49

Fawn entered the room and closed the door quickly behind her. She sat down in the usual chair in front of the desk. "Okay," she sighed, "what did I do now?"

Miles cracked his knuckles as he framed his next words. "Oh, Fawn, you know I hate this as much as you do."

"And I'm trying to make it as easy as I can on you. I really am. I know all you've done for me."

The two never kept score about who owed who the most. Miles recruited Fawn as she graduated from Wesleyan just a couple of years ago. Her grades put her in the top 1% of the top one percent of her college which brought her to the attention of a local recruiter for the Federal Bureau of Investigation.

Most female agents assisted the males assigned to any particular case, mostly those involving possible violations of the Mann Act. However, Miles saw Fawn's potential and quietly gave her the assignment to bodyguard Dr. Kevin Carson. Unfortunately, what was supposed to be a babysitting job, pretty much, ended up with her subject being kidnapped almost a year before without a trace and her barely surviving the confrontation with the kidnappers.

"Fawn," Miles said evenly, "why were you talking to Dr. Peter Turner today?"

The woman leaned forward in the chair. "Actually, it's his nephew I wanted to see. The guy's been a regular Edison since his voice changed. I wanted to see his newest gadget before the university sold it to build another library for a major donor."

"And the device does what?"

Fawn described the effect on the lab mice that she observed just as she entered the Turner laboratory. "Imagine aiming that thing at Capone's gang. Or stopping a bank robbery in progress where the bad guys just fold up and take a nap."

Miles nodded slowly. "Did you procure the device and the blueprints?"

"Turner won't cooperate, Miles."

"Do you think his loyalties lie ... elsewhere?"

Without hesitation, Fawn stated, "No, he's as red, white and blue as anyone." *No one that cute could be a Nazi dupe*, she reasoned silently.

"So what made you attend that meeting?" Miles leaned

back in his chair, glancing at his pipe.

Fawn sighed. "You know why."

Miles closed his eyes and inhaled deeply. "Fawn, Dr. Carson's probably in Berlin by now, designing a new aircraft fuel for Hitler."

"No," Fawn declared forcefully. "I have a feeling that Bruhner is still here and if you call it 'women's intuition', I'll throw something heavy."

"Well, it doesn't matter. Word from D.C. says you're to give up looking for Carson. You've stepped on a few too many toes and somebody called in some favors with someone higher up than me."

"Markley!" Fawn spoke the agent's name with the same distaste one might feel in calling up a demon. "Reg Markley, what a kiss-up. That's not a scar on his nose, it's a –"

"Fawn!" Miles sat forward again. He dropped his voice to a whisper, "He's the agent in charge on the Harnell watch because he gets the job done. He claims he saw you following Turner more than once which could have compromised his team's efforts."

"What efforts?" Fawn laughed and shook her head.

"He's tailed Turner how long and what has he uncovered?" The woman turned serious. "Look, Miles. This is personal. I want – no, I need to know what happened with Carson. I blew that assignment –"

"No, you didn't," Miles interrupted. "The Bureau's lost several agents on this kidnapping escapade. You are the only person who survived one of Bruhner's attacks."

"Barely! My joints still hurt so bad, I can tell you when it's going to rain a week out." Fawn grimaced at the memory of waking up in the hospital the first time and blacking out from the pain. She was fortunate that whoever found her – not that she could remember it now – didn't leave her for dead, but carried her fifteen miles on a bicycle into the nearest town with a doctor. "I wanted that ray-thing so I could take Bruhner alive to stand trial."

I want him to stand trial and spend the rest of his existence in solitary, feeling himself rust a little more hour by hour. And I'll visit him every day to make sure he's dying by inches ... and to spit in that slab of scars he calls a face.

"Fawn, I have no choice." Miles opened a drawer in his desk and withdrew a single sheet of paper. Without looking at it, he turned it to face Fawn. "You have two choices, Agent Carroll. You may accept a new position with the Bureau in a secretarial pool, the location of which will be determined by the Regional Supervisor within three working days."

Fawn felt her bones creak upon hearing that news. She wasn't as full of herself as a lot of her pretty friends from college, but she knew her worth. Putting her talents for investigation and fitting the puzzle pieces of any mystery together – to say nothing of her dogged determination – and demoting her to being just a secretary would be like putting Charles Lindbergh in charge of an amusement park merry-go-round: a total waste of time, energy, and talent.

She glanced at the top of the paper. LETTER OF RESIGNATION. Fawn looked up at her supervisor, her heart breaking.

"Yes, Agent Carroll. This is the only other option available to you." Before she could reply, Miles stated, "Once you affix your signature, I will formally co-sign the document and send it via courier to F.B.I. Headquarters in our nation's capital."

Despite her desire to show no weakness, tears welled at

the corners of Fawn's eyes.

Miles continued, "Your remaining pay will be calculated and a check for that amount cut to you sent via Special Delivery to your home." He raised a finger to cut off Fawn's potential reply. "Furthermore, you will be asked to turn in directly to me your firearm, your Bureau identification, along with any items that belong to this organization."

Miles leaned forward, his eyes locking with Fawn's. "And finally, you will be asked to immediately clear out your desk, taking all personal belongings ... which will include, I'm sure, a stack of files concerning Albrecht Bruhner, his alleged operations, and dossiers on all kidnap victims as well as Peter Turner and several other potential candidates that I took the liberty of copying and placing on your desk blotter."

Fawn barely kept her smile hidden behind her hands. Miles felt a grin spreading across his own face.

"You must also take the folder that contains a slip of paper that will contain my direct office line as well as my home phone number that you are to call at any hour of the day or night when you catch a lead."

Miles stood up and walked to his office door. "Young

lady, I trust you will think long and hard about the consequences of not having to deal with government rules and inter-office politics."

Fawn rose slowly from her chair. "I have thought about it in the last few seconds very carefully, sir." Suddenly, a huge grin covered her face as she launched herself at her supervisor to give him the warmest, tightest hug he'd ever gotten.

"Thank you," she whispered into his ear, fighting back tears. "I won't let you down."

Miles smiled. He felt certain he'd never hear any truer words today.

* * *

Later that night, Reg Markley lit another Lucky Strike with the remnants of the previous cigarette. He ground the old butt under his heel before resuming his circuit around the Turner house. Sticking to the shadows of the trees, he saw the laboratory windows remained dark, as did all but a couple of panels in what had to be the living room.

Taking a huge draw from the freshly-lit cigarette, Markley didn't hear the figure moving behind him, almost stepping in the exact same spots on the grass. The stranger then halted, wrapped his cloak tightly around his body, and remained perfectly still until Markley disappeared around the corner of the building.

With a quick glance to ensure no one else would see him, the figure moved swiftly to the rear door of the building. Without a second's hesitation, he turned his attention to the lock and within a second, the reinforced door moved swiftly and quietly inwards. A heartbeat later, the figure closed the door without re-locking it.

Confidently walking through the building, the stranger walked into the laboratory. Moonlight poured through the windows, framing the Stasimatic Ray emission device in a pale glow.

The device weighed enough that two of the people who witnessed its operation earlier in the day might have been able to carry the machine between them. Tossing the cloak back over his shoulder, the mysterious figure threw a covering over the device and hefted it easily under his left arm. Even with the added weight, the stranger's footsteps were as silent as a breeze.

A minute later, after ensuring the coast was clear, the figure re-locked the door and sprinted to a waiting automobile a block distant. The figure swiftly dropped the Stasimatic device into the trunk before slipping into a trench coat to conceal his uniform. Then he slid in behind the steering wheel and after starting the vehicle, drove off calmly into the night.

Once certain that no one followed him, the stranger unhooked his mask and lifted his visor. Unable to restrain his grin, he thought, *Not bad at all for the first night out.*

The car moved away from the Harnell University grounds towards downtown. Driving through the nearly-deserted streets of the business district, the driver looked forward to locking up this car and changing into some normal clothing before making his way to bed.

And even when he slipped into the world of dreams, the stranger continued to grin triumphantly.

SIX – Pain From the Past

Albrecht Bruhner silently assessed the progress he'd made in the last eighteen months and saw that it was good. He sat in a reinforced metal chair just inside his private office, mentally running through an agenda he'd memorized before leaving Berlin almost two years before. After entering the country via Canada and then recruiting Roove and Lange, Bruhner reached out to a pair of known sympathizers to the Aryan cause. Within a month of arriving, Bruhner had a cargo plane and a "gang."

Bruhner tapped the metal plate that covered his chest. The armored man smiled as he listened to the *hissssssssss* of the escaping steam from the pipes that circuited the room. He felt the need to once again have the wondrous vapors fill his suit, caress his ravaged flesh, and clean away any traces of his previously-finite human life.

But first, he needed to check on his "guests."

Lumbering from his living quarters through the building into a dormitory of sorts, Bruhner stood on the upper walkway, looking down on a set of two dozen beds, most of which were occupied. Some men lay down, either staring at the slow-moving fans overhead or face down, their arms around their ears, attempting to block out the reality of their incarceration.

Others who were taken more recently, such as Professor Hemmer or Dr. Carson, looked up at the walkway, their fury evident in their gaze. However, upon seeing the armored man, the ones who still clung to a little bit of their backbone sat up on the edges of their cots as if preparing to flee like rabbits from a wolf.

The demonstrations of obvious fear amused Bruhner. Let them tremble, he reasoned, and the resistance of the others, such as it was, wouldn't last much longer.

Bruhner descended cautiously down a flight of metal steps. Once on the ground level, he confidently walked down the gap between the two long rows of cots to Carson's space. The scientist's eyes burned with loathing.

"Dr. Carson," Bruhner said with a nod, "how are you today? Are you prepared to begin working for us on this secret project of yours?"

Chuckling, Carson stated, "No more than I was when you first kidnapped me and murdered my friend."

Bruhner placed his hands behind his back with a *clang* and stared down at Carson. "Apparently, some of the rooms were classrooms back when your government owned this building. A number of your peers have seen reason and have been working on their individual projects."

Shaking his head, Carson whispered, "They'll have to answer to their own consciences."

Bruhner smiled. "They will take pride in being a part of the great German sweep across Europe and then the world. One world, one government, one planet finally at peace."

Carson gave no reaction. "Honestly, I'd rather talk about your armor and that gun of yours."

Bruhner smiled. "And here I thought you were going to interrogate me about my life's history."

The doctor smiled back. "That did cross my mind. So what is the story behind your armor? You're also a scientist, you like to brag about your accomplishments I bet."

Bruhner allowed himself another smile as he sat down on the corner of Carson's bed. The wooden slats groaned in protest.

"I left my family to join the Prussian Army during the Great War. My wife and daughters, two of them, were so proud that I offered my life and my engineering skills to preserving our way of life.

"Of course, my officers welcomed my talent for understanding and repairing machinery. They also were delighted when I presented my blueprints for a device that would revolutionize chemical warfare forever."

"You mean mustard gas?" Carson recoiled at the thought of so-called civilized nations using such a harmful weapon. "Hopefully, it was a device that could neutralize it."

Bruhner shook his head. "No, Doctor. Imagine a whirlwind, a spinning column of air, that I could solidify, aim and then plant the base of it anywhere I chose within a couple hundred yards. Then imagine that tunnel of air filled with the chemical agent of my choice. Believe me, there are chemicals that are far more dangerous than mere mustard gas."

"That's difficult to conceive."

"Be that as it may, we were set to test my machine one

night in the trenches. After much effort to transport this device, I prepared the machine to guide its deadly payload directly into the British trenches in what came to be known as 'No Man's Land.'

"However, something went wrong."

For a moment, Bruhner found himself back in that muddy trench, pelted by the icy, unforgiving rains from the dark clouds overhead as Allied bullets whizzed past him and his men. He risked a glance upwards at the machine, seeing the dents deepen as each bullet slammed into the casing to bounce away in random directions.

Unable to wait any longer, Bruhner pulled the lever to activate the device. However, instead of summoning and concentrating the air into a pipeline of death, the machine shook and made a sound like a demon's claws raking across a steel floor. Before Bruhner could kill the battery power, mustard gas emanated from his creation, surrounding the device in a yellow-brown cloud of death. Bruhner closed his eyes and held his breath, which might have been all that saved his life.

Groping blindly, feeling his flesh burn and blister,

Bruhner somehow managed to turn off the device. The storms quickly washed away any trace of the gas, leaving Bruhner unconscious, near death.

Immediately hospitalized, a semi-comatose Bruhner barely managed to be aware of the passing of time. He saw the beds in his hospital ward empty out then a blink later, his wife would be there, tears rolling down her face as his children forced themselves to smile and somehow look past the chemical blisters on his face. Another blink, the girls were taller and finally, his wife left a tear-stained note saying she could no longer bring herself to visit.

However, as he slept, as he planned for a life in a sterile ward, barely able to feed himself, he sketched in his mind both day and night. His body might now be frail, but Bruhner's mind, his intellect, his creativity, were all as vital as ever.

Then one day, several men entered the ward. Dressed in long black coats, they commanded their brown-shirted subordinates to search the room from the floor to the rafters. The soldiers performed their task efficiently in grim silence before leaving the room.

A minute later, a dark-haired man entered. He was of average height, average build. The only things that Bruhner thought were striking about the man were his blazing eyes that didn't seem to blink and the thick mustache that rested just under his nose.

One of the long-coated men swiftly pulled up a chair and placed it beside the bed before leading his comrades from the hospital room. The special visitor waited for the men to leave before sitting down. He locked his eyes to Bruhner's and a gentle smile covered his lips.

"Herr Bruhner," the man said softly, "I am Adolf Hitler, the *Vorsitzender* of the Republic of Germany, your Chancellor. Being in this hospital as long as you have, I'm not sure if you know who I am."

"I do," Bruhner replied, awestruck, "mein Fuhrer. The nurses have read the newspapers to me. But why have you come to see me?"

"You are a hero of the people. I am honored to be in your presence." The visitor stared into Bruhner's eyes. "Let me get to the point quickly. I am assembling motivated men of destiny. I have a vision to rebuild Germany into a world power once again, *the* world power. My men tell me of your engineering genius."

Bruhner described the designs developed and stored in his mind, machines built upon the impossible foundation of imagination and powered by clean, plentiful steam. Hitler listened intently, as if his impassioned stare could see every facet of the designs carved into the ether.

After listening intently for several minutes, the Fuhrer's voice rose in volume as he replied, "I am no engineer. I am a former soldier, just like you. I too have felt the horrors of mustard gas." Hitler placed his hand upon Bruhner's. "But I can see that you are the man to be *mein Dampf Ritter* ... my Steam Knight! A Master of Steam!"

Hitler found a piece of paper by Bruhner's bedside. "I once thought of making my living as an artist. Please allow me an indulgence."

Pulling a pencil from his pocket, the Chancellor sketched a set of armor that made the engineer's eyes go wide. It was precisely as he saw the design in his mind, a steam-powered exoskeleton, one that would become his new home, his conveyance, his chance for something resembling a real life.

Then Hitler sketched a crest upon the chest plate of the armor. A steel dragon, its jaws open, ready to vomit hellfire on its foes. Bruhner could barely contain his excitement.

"I want this one built first, Herr Bruhner. I will give you workers and every resource at my disposal to make this a reality for I have a scheme that only you could execute. All I ask in return for all this is for your unceasing loyalty to my cause."

The man's magnetic voice grew louder as he continued to speak, "You shall not be in this hospital one more day than you need to be, I so vow this. No, you shall stand beside me as we march across Europe and then Great Britain before crushing America in our steely grasp. Are you with me, Herr Bruhner?"

Bruhner felt his lower lip tremble as he nodded enthusiastically.

"Bruhner?"

The Nazi blinked in confusion. He turned his head to see Carson looking at him with puzzlement and no small amount of concern. All of the other scientists stared at him now in wide-eyed terror.

Bruhner enjoyed a tingle that moved along his spine as he once again realized his power over these so-called men of learning. He cleared his throat softly and inhaled slowly, an act that sounded like the hiss that might come from a loose radiator pipe.

"Pardon me, Doctor. I was lost in thought for a moment. Anyway, my Fuhrer gave me permission to gather the greatest scientific minds for delivery to the Fatherland. You should feel complimented, Dr. Carson."

Carson frowned. Apparently the honor of his situation was lost on the man.

Bruhner rose to his metal-clad feet. "The foundation for the Third Reich's rule grows more secure with every new day. It must be so because the weight of history shall rest heavy upon it"

"There are men," Carson warned, "who will fight. You won't have an easy time of it."

Ignoring Carson's warning, Bruhner said with a smile, "You'll be happy to know that one more scientist is in our crosshairs. Once we have him in our protective custody, we shall return to Berlin and not long afterwards, Germany shall rule the skies."

Dr. Carson sank back onto his cot, feeling helpless and completely overwhelmed by Bruhner's conviction.

Dr. Peter Turner

SEVEN – A Pair of Invitations

"**You look far too pleased with yourself**, young man. Just where have you been hiding?"

Allan Turner grinned as he stirred his coffee. A quick look around the restaurant confirmed that this particular late lunch hour wasn't a busy one. This would allow them to speak as openly as one could in a public place.

"Guilty as charged, Uncle. I've been busy, but it's paying off." His expression turned serious. "I do hope I didn't embarrass you in front of your colleagues yesterday. If so, I'm sorry."

Chuckling, Peter Turner unfolded his napkin and laid it across his lap. "I was actually going to apologize to *you* for their behavior." His expression turned dark, thoughtful. "I can't put my finger on anything concrete, but I'm getting hints and whispers that we are headed towards war. Certain members of the faculty seem quite interested in a closer relationship with the government, the military in particular."

"For what advantage?"

Peter played with his mustache as he pondered the question. "It usually boils down to either money or favors. I know we have military recruiters on campus as well as – well, it doesn't matter. I believe it's just a matter of time before some fool forces America to enter the European war, just like fifteen years ago." Suddenly, Peter grinned at his nephew. "Listen to me prattle on. So what have you been doing since that debacle yesterday?"

"Well, I've been thinking and as much as I enjoy living with you, I thought it was time I started finding my own place. I spent most of the afternoon with a realtor who's been quite helpful, if unsuccessful, in helping me look. But then I have some specific requirements for my new digs."

Peter nodded. "I figured you'd want to leave the nest sometime. Can't say I'm disappointed. Maybe I'll start hosting some orgies to make up for lost time once you're out from under foot." They shared a laugh before Peter asked, "So what's on this real estate shopping list of yours?"

"I'm looking for a place where I can perform my experiments in private, especially where my Stasimatic Ray is concerned. I have high hopes for that one."

Peter smoothed the napkin across his thigh. "Oh, about that. I popped into the lab this morning and it seems your –"

Allan leaned forward and grinned. "Also, I'd like a hangar, lots of living room, and scads of privacy. You see, Uncle, I want to fulfill a promise to you and to my parents' memory, to make the skies safer for everyone."

"Are you planning on finding the man who built your parents' airplane?"

Allan leaned back in his chair and pondered his uncle's question seriously. "I'll never say never. On the other hand, a lot of time has passed and he's not my immediate priority." He smiled again and spoke excitedly, "I had this idea of a freelance aerial investigator, but in a way that ensured my personal privacy … and the possible safety of those I care about."

"My boy, you sound like you want to become one of those mystery men I hear about on the radio."

Allan grinned. "Well, maybe I did take a little inspiration from them." He leaned forward and whispered, "Sure, I could take my millions and lobby the government to change aircraft construction standards. However, I have no desire to line some politician's pockets in exchange for favors that someone else could undo by spending more. No, I figured being a freelance social engineer would be quicker to bring about some needed changes and perhaps a little more fun."

Peter gave a mock frown. "Have you been reading too many issues of those *Big Shot Comics* I keep confiscating from my students?"

Allan allowed himself a smile. "No, I don't have time to read funnybooks. Anyway, I thought about what I'd call myself and –"

"As I live and breathe! If it isn't Doctor Peter Turner!"

Both of the Turners spun in their seats to see a man approaching them. Tall, slender, and carrying himself with an air of elegance, he grabbed a chair from a neighboring table and sat between both men without waiting for an invitation. Truthfully, his bearing hinted that he rarely waited for anything, least of all permission.

Peter smiled politely. "You do, you do, and I am, which you most certainly know after all these years." He turned to his nephew. "Allan, this is my next door neighbor, after a fashion, Braden Kendall. I guess my attempts to keep you from the less-than-modest side of the tracks finally failed."

Kendall gripped the young man's extended hand and delivered a surprisingly firm grip that Allan returned. The older man nodded once and smiled. "So young Mr. Turner is now a college graduate. How does it feel to be among the nine-to-fivers of the world?"

"I'm still easing my way into the workforce, Mr. Kendall. I figure there's plenty of time to settle down, should I decide to, one of these decades."

Peter's eyebrows almost touched his hairline. Instead of his usual confident voice, Allan affected a slightly aloof tone, almost fey. In fact, Allan's posture changed from its usual coiled spring state of readiness to a state of fluid relaxation. Peter tried to catch Allan's eye, but the young man gave Kendall his full attention.

"I'm sure we've never spoken before, Allan. I confess that I don't enjoy dealing with unimportant people which includes most people under the age of majority," Kendall confessed. "I don't believe I spoke to my own daughter until she graduated from high school. Anyway, given your uncle's brilliance, I should have realized some of it would have trickled down the family tree."

Allan smiled. "Let me think, I believe you have something to do with metallurgy, right?"

Kendall ran a perfectly-manicured finger along the seam of his left shirt cuff. Allan guessed that every single stitch was done by hand and Kendall wouldn't know how to find his way through a department store without a map, a sherpa and a trail of bread crumbs.

"No, but I like that word." Kendall's chuckle was dryer than the Gobi Desert at high noon. "I'm known as 'The Scrap Metal King' on both coasts and all points in between. I know how to buy metal in large quantities, reform it, and give it new purpose. I also know how to make money both when I take delivery and again when my clients pick it up."

"Absolutely riveting," Allan stated while suppressing a yawn.

"You'd be surprised how interesting it can be." Kendall picked up a spare napkin and gently buffed the crystal on his wristwatch. "I got into the field just before the Depression and I've managed to fill my address book with politicians,

Hollywood directors, and some rather infamous people as a profitable result."

"We met at a faculty party," Peter explained to his nephew. "Braden heard what an up-and-comer I was and we've been pals ever since." Allan noticed the slight roll of his uncle's eyes during his last statement.

Kendall folded the napkin neatly and placed it back on the table. "Anyway, I've spent a couple of hours hoping to 'accidentally' run into you gentlemen. I'm throwing a party just for the heck of it and I'd like to invite you both. Call it a post-graduation party if you must, but I insist you both attend." He leaned towards Allan. "Besides, there's someone I would love for you to meet."

"It's got to go more smoothly than the last meeting I attended," Allan stated blandly.

Kendall grinned as he rose to his feet. "Then it's settled. Seven p.m. to start and it's casual dress."

"Which means 'no tuxedo' but a suit and tie will do," Peter explained, something he constantly felt the need to do whenever Kendall entered the vicinity.

"What a coincidence. That's casual for me too." Allan

extended his hand. "I will see you Friday night."

Kendall shook Allan's hand enthusiastically. "I am absolutely giddy with anticipation. Have a splendid day, my friends."

Allan and Peter watched Kendall leave the restaurant as quickly as he breezed in. Once the door closed, Peter shook his head. "I believe it was Oscar Wilde who said, 'An excellent man – he has no enemies; and none of his friends like him.'" Peter gripped his crutch and leaned forward. "And what was that about?"

"That?" Allan shrugged.

"That! You went from Clark Gable to Stan Laurel and back in less time that it took for Dorothy Gale to go from sepia to Technicolor. So spill!"

Allan's eyes darted around the nearly-deserted restaurant and he covered his smile with his hand. "As I said earlier, I'm laying the foundation for something I think will do the world some good." He glanced at his wristwatch, then wiped his mouth quickly with his napkin. "I promise I'll give you the full story when everything's set up. In fact, I have an appointment with my realtor in just about five minutes less time than it will take me to drive over to see him so I'm late already."

Allan snatched the bill and grabbed his hat. "I'll catch you at home sometime. Have a good afternoon, Uncle." With that, Allan went to the register to pay as his uncle grinned – except when the older man rose painfully to his feet, supported by his crutch.

Once Peter exited the eatery, another man gestured for the waiter to bring his bill. Five minutes later, that man sat inside a phone booth. He glanced through the fingerprint-festooned glass to make sure no one stood close enough to overhear him. The man dropped a nickel into the pay phone, dialed a local number, and waited for the usual terse greeting on the other end of the line, "Yes?"

"Hey, boss. It's Cooper. Yeah, I've got a report." He shot a look outside the booth before declaring, "The contact's been made."

"I'm going to enjoy my money. You know I'm wealthy,

don't you?"

EIGHT – No Fun At the Party

"Allan, I know you think this will be slightly

less fun than pulling out your own teeth," Peter Turner said with no small amount of exasperation, "and you're probably correct. When we get home later, I'll rustle us each up a couple of beers, a pair of pliers, and we'll top off the evening the right way. How does that sound?"

Peter turned the car into the street. If they walked, the trip would take about five minutes, cutting across the back yard of the Kendall estate that just happened to be across the street from the university's lab/housing for their favorite scientific genius.

However, that might be considered gauche so the Turners elected to travel ten extra minutes just to have an automobile handy for a quicker escape from the party, at least in theory.

Laughing, Allan asked, "Okay, tell me again which circle of Hell I'm entering tonight?"

"Kendall has these parties every couple of months,"

Peter explained as he navigated the streets along the edge of the campus. "He invites me – most of the time, I find a decent reason not to attend – and just about every politician and celebrity, local or otherwise, to the party. By the time the last car pulls out of his circle drive, chances are Braden Kendall will have doubled his already considerable wealth."

"Why you, Uncle Peter? I've never known you to have a thing for scrap metal."

"I think I'm there to amuse some of his guests with my charm and great big brains." Peter's expression became serious. "Speaking of amusement, are you going to continue the foppish masquerade?"

Smiling and waving broadly, Allan asked, "Like this, Uncle dearest?" In a heartbeat, Allan resumed his normal tone of voice. "Call it intuition, but I think the sooner I convince these people that Allan Turner is some kind of dandy, the better it'll be for my new enterprise."

"The one you won't tell me about."

"Not yet, Uncle. Earlier today convinced me that timing is everything so let's do this after we escape this party. Is this the house?"

The building looked like a three-story tall slab of the whitest sandstone he'd ever seen. Windows covered all sides of the building and an uninterrupted line of elderly oak trees ringed the property. A trellis carried a weave of solid vines along one wall from the foundation to the top floor. Every window in the building emitted light and Allan wished for a moment that he could see Kendall's electricity bill just out of morbid curiosity.

The last time Allan saw this many Kleig lights in one place was during a Movietone News that covered a recent Hollywood film premiere. In fact, Allan could have sworn he saw some of Filmland's best and brightest emerging from their limousines before entering the mansion.

A wall of blood-red brick surrounded the edifice except for the wrought iron gates that allowed entry and exit from the marble-inset driveway. A procession of large automobiles clogged the entrance.

"Look at that," Peter complained. "The line to get in stretches beyond the horizon."

Allan pointed to an empty parking spot at the end of the block. "Let's park on the street. That way, we can leave just that much sooner without having to wait on the valet to find our car. We'll sprint out the front door and dive in through the side windows, just like in the movies."

"I think my sprinting days are far behind me," Peter offered as he swung the car onto the edge of the street, just barely missing a scrape against the curbing. "I admit I always feel uncomfortable, swimming in so much blue blood."

"I'm only looking forward to this like a dentist's appointment," Allan admitted. "I know it's important that I be here, but I'd rather be someplace else. I guess we should get this done with."

Nodding with agreement, Peter engaged the parking brake and straightened his necktie one more time before emerging from his car. A few seconds later, he and Allan strolled across the street, past the gates, and made their way to the front door.

Allan wanted to maintain his aloof persona this evening, but that would be a challenge in this setting. The main ballroom appeared to have seized the front room and a couple of dining rooms to create one giant receiving area for guests. Embedded in the impossibly high ceilings overhead were several chandeliers, each one holding a dozen large electric lamps that poured illumination into each of the genuine crystals that surrounded each bulb. The effect was like pure sunlight at high noon filling every corner of the room, dispelling any attempts at creating a shadow.

Glancing around, Allan saw several local politicians, including the Mayor. To one side, a well-known physician held an animated conversation with a State Senator and a male contract player for MGM. In another corner, the wife of a Indianapolis 500 driver held a martini in one hand as her other arm stretched over the shoulders of a popular novelist who was known to spend his leisure time in the bars surrounding Wrigley Field in Chicago. No wonder his uncle – knowing he felt the same way around people of quickly-accumulated wealth and prominence – appeared to be as uncomfortable as Allan.

Over the melodies of a major swing orchestra off playing in a corner of the massive room, Peter said to his nephew, "Let's get a couple of drinks to nurse until we can blow this joint."

Allan nodded his agreement. A highly-popular stage

actress disengaged her arm from her director-husband upon seeing the young man and began to move towards him. Allan halted, unsure of what to do. He looked to his side for some advice, but his uncle already found a place to lean at the nearest bar.

As the actress opened her mouth to speak, a resonant voice called out, "Sheath your talons, dear heart. I've got plans for this boy."

Braden Kendall clamped a hand on Allan's shoulder and turned the young man to face him. The industrialist grinned as if he'd caught Allan with his hand inside a wall safe, clutching an orphanage's funding.

"Good evening, Mr. Kendall," Allan said lightly. "Pleasant little soiree you have here."

Kendall gripped Allan's hand firmly, almost as if testing the young man's strength. "Glad you like it. I fully expect you and your uncle to feel at home. There are no strangers here. That's why you need to start calling me 'Braden' like your uncle does." The industrialist grinned again. "That's a strong grip you have there. Left over from the gridiron days?"

Upon seeing the handshake, the actress gave an audible *harumph*! before turning on her heel and striding back to her husband who didn't seem to notice her absence.

"Say I want to have a nice house like this," Allan gestured broadly, "how does one imitate you to get one?"

Kendall laughed heartily. "Nicely said, Allan. The trick is to read the newspapers and know what your customers will want before they know it."

"So you're saying my intense study of *Dick Tracy* and The *Katzenjammer Kids* will pay off someday?"

"More the latter than the former, trust me." Kendall put his arm around Allan's shoulders and guided him towards the rear of the ballroom. "There's people in Europe who wish they had a huge supply of scrap metal waiting to be turned from plowshares into swords. But that idiot at Pennsylvania Avenue wants to keep America's head in the proverbial sand. New Deal? More like No Deal Whatsoever!" The creases in Kendall's face turned slightly reddish.

Allan dismissed the thought with a wave of his hand. "I'm tending towards apolitical anyway. A war would just spoil my plans, don't you know?"

Kendall leaned in closer to Allan and whispered conspiratorially, "Don't discount politics as a source of income. I've invested in a few lawmakers and if America winds up fighting Hitler, I'm working to get a deal going with Great Britain to sell them some scrap and there's some major industrial performers who are pledging to get in on the action through me."

"You make scrap metal sound a lot more fun than laboratory work," Allan lied. He glanced to the far side of the room where the actress appeared to have cornered Peter Turner. He leaned on his crutch and smiled nervously as she rested her slender hand upon his arm, which seemed to make the older scientist more nervous than the prospect of working with explosive chemicals.

"Listen." Kendall slapped Allan on the shoulder, a solid blow from a man who seemingly should find exercise only in lifting the phone with one hand and his coffee cup with the other. "I want to talk with you more later, but I've got to mingle and seal some deals." He glanced at the actress across the room. "She's cute, boy, but I've got someone I'd really like you to meet later. Don't go far."

"Does walking to the other side of the room qualify as 'far'?" Allan muttered. Feeling slightly claustrophobic in the press of people and a thickening haze of cigarette smoke, he moved towards the nearest open door that led outside.

Emerging to what appeared to be a marble veranda, Allan took in a lungful of the sweet air. From all the lights pouring from every window in the house, to say nothing of the numerous lights that surrounded the mansion, Allan could barely make out the last rays of sunset. The thought made him slightly unhappy.

"Penny for your thoughts?"

Allan whirled around to see his Uncle Peter moving towards him and grinned. "I see you escaped your legion of admirer."

"Yes, I managed. But all she could talk about was you. My fragile male ego took quite a beating in there, I'll have you know."

Allan tilted his head back and laughed. Peter shot him a brief look of mock hatred by way of reply, then said, "Don't let all this go to your head, young man." His expression softened. "I know I'm being overly curious, but about this plan of yours, Allan … I –"

"Now's as good a time as any," Allan interrupted. "Uncle, I'm fitted now for my task. I've studied and worked to develop my body. The sports were just a way to bring myself to near-Olympic levels of physical readiness."

Peter nodded. "Go on."

"I'm pretty much an aviation expert after majoring in the Air School here. I've also absorbed as much of the physical sciences as I could from my classes and from you. I can apply this in my new identity as a special kind of investigator, one who has an air of mystery about him and who can't be coerced by, say, threatening those I love."

Allan's eyes unconsciously darted to Peter's crutch for a moment.

"So that's why I'm outwardly a loafer, the wealthy good-for-nothing, Allan Tur –!"

A quick noise drew Allan's attention. He spun around, his left fist up and ready for action.

And that's when he saw the person who'd trailed him from the other night.

* * *

At the University of Buffalo, Professor Ivor Perkins chaired the Mechanical Engineering department. Noted for his penchant for hand-crafted clothing to fit his generous frame, his articles in his field of expertise were syndicated across the country and picked up in such highly-regarded magazines as *Time* and *The Saturday Evening Post.*

However, after almost a year and a half of captivity and intimidation, Perkins' clothing hung from his body, just as his flesh did from his skeleton. Eyes that once contained the focus of a Russian chess master now darted from side to side, almost as if expecting an attack from the shadows. He clutched at the outside seam of his trousers, pulling his numbed right leg along the concrete floor as he shuffled towards Albrecht Bruhner's steam-filled room.

Bruhner watched the professor limp towards him. His eyes twinkled as he refused to acknowledge the man. Rather, he waited until Perkins entered the ever-shifting curtain of steam that filled the opening of the chamber before giving the man his full attention. Perkins came to a halt three feet from the Steam Warrior's chair and bowed his head before the Prussian said, "Yes?"

"Sir," Perkins said in a low, quavering voice, "I have a message from the radio room. The agent is moving into place and the target will be captured within the hour."

"*Gut*. You may leave now, *danke*."

Perkins spun around on his good leg and made his way back to wait for the next transmission.

Bruhner smiled. One more task after tonight and then he would leave this barbarous nation for the civilization of Germany. *Once I leave these shores*, he mused, *I vow to not return until the Swastika flies over every home.*

For now, however, Bruhner luxuriated in the scalding embrace of his beloved steam and waited for his cue to enter the fray. Tonight's blitzkrieg would signal the downfall of Democracy and the inevitable victory of the Nazi ideal.

NINE – Grabbing the Turners

Slipping a delicate foot back into a less than

sensible shoe, Fawn Carroll smoothed down her dress and calmly walked away from the wall she'd just scaled. She approached the Turners with her brightest smile, acting as if she'd just done nothing out of the ordinary. "Hello, boys. Nice night, huh?"

Peter began to speak when he noticed Allan walking towards the woman. Whatever the elder scientist was about to say probably would go unheard so he chuckled. "Ah, youth calls to youth." Peter vacated the veranda, leaving the two young people their opportunity to be alone.

Back amidst the drone of conversations struggling to be heard above the live swing music, Dr. Turner navigated a route towards the rear of the house. However, his attempt to escape attention didn't go unnoticed.

"Peter, my friend!" Braden Kendall left a gathering of state senators, looking every bit like a canary that just taught the cat how to reach the fishbowl. "Lord, this is exhausting. Can I steer you to the kitchen so I can actually speak to someone who doesn't want to take my money?"

Noticing that the ice in his drink had melted, Peter said, "Sure, why not?" With a glance back, he wasn't sure that Allan would even know he left the veranda, a thought that gave him a smile.

In college, Allan had his share of dating adventures. Rather than using some pick-up line, he always found the direct approach useful. "Hello. What's your name?" He noticed the red and white print dress and the way the blouse was free of her perfectly-shaped shoulders and the sweep of her long, auburn hair and the way her perfume floated upon the night breezes and –

"Fawn Carroll. We met the other day at your uncle's laboratory." She leaned against the stone wall that fenced off Kendall's house from the vast back yard. Because of the brilliant lights surrounding the estate, however, she couldn't see the majestic trees, nor the sweeping carpet of expertly-trimmed green grass.

"Ah, yes." Allan grinned. "You were the G-girl. But that's all I know about you, really."

"Woman," Fawn corrected gently. "And I'm not with the Bureau any more."

"See? I didn't know that. Now I'm smarter." Allan flashed his most disarming smile at her.

And it worked, but Fawn would rather take another tumble from an airplane before revealing that information. "Mr. Turner, you see, I know all about you, how marvelous you are." She looked up into his perfect blue eyes. "What are you going to be? President?"

"What? And take a cut in pay?" Allan deliberately laughed a little too loudly. "Oh dear, no! I'm going to enjoy my money. You do know I'm wealthy, don't you?"

Allan silently congratulated himself on his portrayal until he saw the hurt in her eyes, like a fire being doused. "Well," she said flatly, "so it was all a pose."

"How'd you like to help me spend it? Night clubs and such, you know."

"And I –" Fawn seemed to choke on her next words. "I thought you were such a swell guy. No thanks. I don't care to associate with you. I'm a working girl at heart."

"Good!" Allan grinned, finding himself respecting this

woman. The fire in her eyes and the flush in her soft cheeks returned and he couldn't help but admire that. "I like working girls, you know. They're so – so adventurous." He took her elbow and moved her away from the brick wall.

Fawn grinned, realizing that Allan was leading her into the heart of the party. "In spite of yourself, I can't help liking you," she admitted. "There must be something beneath that attitude."

"Not much," Allan lied with a grin. "So why aren't you trying to steal my inventions for the government any more? Or is that classified information?"

Fawn's expression turned dark for a moment, reliving the first moment when she felt herself in free fall. "There was an incident. I wound up getting hurt very badly. It may be indelicate, but I have scars that will probably make some poor sap start screaming when he sees them on our wedding night."

I can't imagine that! Allan thought. He thought about guiding her to an area where several couples were dancing to the band. However, better to move slowly than to risk scaring her off. "So how did you get an invitation?"

She grinned. "You think I'd have crept across a couple miles of back yard and scaled a wall if I had an invitation? No, someone's in this country who shouldn't be and while he's free, your uncle could be in jeopardy."

"How so?"

"His name is Albrecht Bruhner, but he calls himself the Master of Steam. No ego, huh? He's a twisted genius who wears a steam-driven power suit and likes to kidnap scientists. I also owe him a rather substantial amount of pain."

Allan fought to keep his voice light. "So what does he want with my uncle?"

"He's collecting the brightest minds in Great Britain and North America. These are guys who know chemistry, ballistics, engineering, metallurgy, biology, you name it. If they can talk over your head, Bruhner puts the snatch on them."

"But Uncle Peter –"

"Nobody knows more about manned flight than your uncle. That's why my former co-workers have been watching him – and you – around the clock. What if the Nazis are making some kind of uber-weapon? They'd need a delivery system." Fawn looked around quickly. "So where is your uncle?"

"Good question," Allan replied. He found himself straightening up, pulling his shoulders back, instinctively getting himself ready for some kind of action.

"I know where he is."

Fawn and Allan turned around to see a girl in her late teens. Her floor-length sequined gown, her bouffant hairdo, her luxuriously matching scarlet nails and lips, everything about her spoke of money and lots of it to burn.

She held out her hand for Allan to kiss. "I was waiting for Daddy to introduce us, but apparently it wasn't convenient yet. I'm Ellyn Kendall, your host's only daughter."

"A pleasure to meet you, Miss Kendall." Allan struggled to sound sincere as he shook Ellyn's hand. He glanced over at Fawn who seemed to be assessing the blonde as she would a gangland informant on a hospital gurney. "I'm Allan Turner."

Ellyn flashed a smile that almost outshone the spotlights

outside. "Yes, the second generation genius. I think smart men are very desirable. Now, I'm no genius myself –"

"Imagine that," Fawn said dryly. Allan thought for a moment that if she was a man, he'd have to elbow her in the ribs. But if Fawn was a man, chances were she'd be just as intrigued by this woman as he found himself to be.

Ellyn surveyed Fawn from shoe to hairdo and dismissed her with a sneer and a brief, gentle laugh. Returning her attention to Allan, she said, "I saw the two of them duck back into the kitchen. That's where Daddy goes when he needs a breather from the deal-making. Let me show you."

With that, Ellyn wrapped her arm around Allan's and escorted him through the crowds with Fawn close behind. He caught a glimpse of the actress from earlier, her eyes wide with surprise, no doubt from his accumulation of female admirers. He smiled and shrugged as if to say, *What can I tell you?*

As the trio pressed their way through the crowd of partyers, in the entrance to the kitchen, Braden Kendall filled two brandy snifters from a bottle that the scrap magnate kept inside a locked cabinet. After securing the bottle again,

Kendall offered one of the glasses to Peter Turner. "I don't know if you're a drinking man, but you'll find this stuff so smooth, Sonja Henie could skate on it."

Peter filled his nostrils with the aroma rising from the rich brown liquid. He swirled the brandy around the glass, mostly because he saw someone else do it at a faculty party. Following his host's example, Peter then took a small sip, then another.

Kendall smiled. "I'm glad you approve, Peter. And thank you for attending. It's good to see you and meet your nephew. You must be proud of the boy."

"I am," Peter confessed sincerely. "I think he's going to be a great scientist and will succeed in whatever he puts his mind to, whatever that is."

Nodding, Kendall took another drink. "I plan to introduce him to my daughter tonight. I think he'd like her and she could certainly stand dating someone with a few more I.Q. points than most of the skirt chasers she loiters around."

"Allan just graduated from college," Peter said with a grin. "Let's wait at least a month before we marry him off, okay?"

But Peter's smile faded as he watched Kendall try to lower his snifter onto a nearby counter top ... and miss ... and miss again ... and again ... the businessman began to weave from side to side.

Peter rose to his feet to try to help, but his crutch slipped from under his arm to fall onto the tiled floor. The scientist looked at the glass in his other hand ... *DRUGGED*!

He looked up at Kendall who slowly sank to his knees ... the man's glass struck the floor with a sound like a gunshot ... Peter found himself collapsing as well, just as the back door swung inward.

Two men entered quickly and quietly. Both men were dressed in business suits and didn't appear to be surprised at what, or who they found. Then Peter closed his eyes and reasoned no more ...

... but as if eavesdropping from the end of a long, dark tunnel, Peter heard one of the men grunt and the fabric of Kendall's expensive suit folding and unfolding as he was lifted off the floor, then unceremoniously allowed to fall again.

"Grab the one we came for, will ya?" one of them asked in a low growl. "And make sure you pick up his crutch."

TEN – Fingered By Fawn

After a while, Ellyn Kendall's incessant chatter became part of the ambient noise in Allan Turner's ears. Occasionally, he glanced back at Fawn. The woman refused to look him in the eye, instead carrying an expression one might wear on the way to a funeral parlor.

"The kitchen is back here," Ellyn volunteered. "I tried cooking once. Horrible idea. Never going to do that again."

Fawn moved close enough to whisper in Allan's ear, "It's hard to tell when something's done until you hear the fire trucks pull up." Allan turned to see a mischievous gleam in Fawn's eyes and a wicked smile on her lips. Allan found himself winking in response and wished he could return to the veranda with the brunette.

Ellyn pushed the kitchen door open just in time to see Braden Kendall lying unconscious on the floor and two men dragging Peter Turner through the back door. "Daddy!" Ellyn shouted.

However, Allan pushed past the heiress with Fawn

almost on his heels. "Go see about your uncle," Fawn volunteered, "I'll check Kendall."

With a curt nod, Allan leaped over the prone figure and raced towards the exit. He grabbed the door before it could close. "Going somewhere, guys?"

One of the men, a slender, dark-haired fellow with cruel eyes carrying Peter's crutch, stopped and turned towards Allan. "Get him to the car," he commanded his compatriot who redoubled his efforts to pull his captive's limp body to a waiting sedan. "This is none of your business. Go back to your party and forget you saw me."

"And this *is* my business," stated Allan firmly, "because that's my uncle. So you tell me what's going on or –"

Suddenly Fawn called out, "Hey! What the hell are you doing, Cooper?"

"You know this clown?" Allan realized he'd dropped his act, but this was no time to try to recover.

"She knows me," the man said without an ounce of pleasure. "We used to work together." He fished inside his jacket and pulled out a black leather wallet. With a practiced flip, he revealed a badge and government identification that said Foster Bruce Cooper, Field Agent, Federal Bureau of Investigation.

"Your dad's just doped up," Fawn told Ellyn sympathetically. "I think the old man will be fine once he sleeps off whatever was in his drink." She rose to her feet and angrily shortened the distance between her and the Fed. "Allan, this is Foster Cooper, one of the team following you and your uncle. I bet Moe and Shemp are in the car."

"Can it, sister. Since you turned in your badge, I don't have to be nice to you." Turning back to Allan, Cooper returned his I.D. to its home pocket and stated firmly, "Your uncle is in good hands. He's entering protective custody and we'll contact you when it's safe to talk to him again."

Fawn readied a retort, but Allan turned to face her with a finger to his lips. Returning to the agent, his voice was light again. "Well, gosh, who am I to argue with J. Edgar Hoover's finest?"

Cooper gave a brief smirk to Fawn. "We sure are now, unlike some people I could name." Allan could almost feel the waves of hatred emanating from the woman behind him. The agent continued his warning, "Don't try to follow us.

You don't want any trouble from D.C., any of you." With a mock salute, Cooper pulled the outer door closed behind him.

Allan whirled around, "Ellyn, is your father okay?"

The young woman's eyes were wide, fearful, and almost ready to erupt with tears, but her voice was surprisingly strong. "Yeah, I think he's coming around."

"Great." Allan turned to Fawn. "Stay with her." Before the brunette could ask what Allan intended to do, he opened the kitchen door and raced through it into the night.

Once outside, Allan saw a car slowly accelerating through the lane that allowed food deliveries to the kitchen. Without hesitation, the young man sprinted in the direction of the automobile. While at Harnell, Allan set track and field speed records that would stand for generations. *Time to demonstrate some practical application of those skills*, he thought.

Without losing a step, Allan Turner loosened the knot on his necktie and took off after the dark sedan at a speed that threatened the three-minute mile. As the car wound around the access driveway cautiously, Allan applied his geometry lessons about the shortest distance between two points and ran a straight line from the kitchen door to the vehicle. Effortlessly, he leaped over a garden hose and two marble birdbaths before racing around a replica of Michaelangelo's statue of David, identical save for this one's loin cloth.

Suddenly, the front passenger's window rolled down. For all the lights that ringed the grounds, Allan couldn't see the man's face.

But whoever it was, the person extended an arm from the window. In his hand was the peculiar gun, the same one that Bruhner used to shoot Dr. Carson. The trigger finger tensed, but no familiar *cah-rack* like gunfire resulted.

Instead, Allan felt a white-hot stream of moisture fly a mere inch away from his head. Losing his rhythm, Allan stumbled as his feet left the lawn and touched the cobblestone drive. He didn't fall, but he cursed himself for losing even a second's momentum.

By the time Allan reached the main street that ran alongside this portion of the Kendall Estate, the vehicle had already picked up speed and rounded a nearby corner, effectively vanishing from view.

The Original Skyman Battles the Master of Steam

I'll find you, Uncle Peter! I vow this! Allan grimaced as he began the walk back to the kitchen, re-buttoning his shirt before anyone could view what was underneath.

Allowing himself back inside, Allan saw Mr. Kendall sitting in a chair, holding his head in his hands. Fawn carefully helped him take small sips from a glass of water.

Ellyn saw Allan and flung herself at him. Instinctively, he wrapped his arms around the girl. If Fawn noticed, she gave no outward sign.

"Oh, Allan. Someone got into Daddy's private stock. They tried to poison him. Who could do such a terrible thing?" She shook in Allan's arms as she clutched his jacket like a life preserver.

Fawn picked up the decanter and brought it to Allan. "I think I want to test the rest of his private stash, see what they gave him. The only problem is I don't have a lot of friends back at the Bureau labs."

Allan bit his tongue, keeping his *I could see that* to himself.

"I might be able to find a private chemist, but –"

"But nothing," Allan said softly. "Gather up the bottles

and I'll test them in Uncle Peter's lab." He smiled softly. "I know a little about chemistry too."

Fawn nodded and smiled slyly. She was familiar with chemistry also, but one of an entirely different nature. "Give me a call when you find out something, okay?" She handed Allan one of her last business cards from the Bureau with her hotel room phone number penciled on the back.

Disengaging Ellyn from his shirtfront, Allan told the girl, "You take care of your dad and see about calling an early end to the party. Tell them he –"

"No!" The businessman rose slowly to his feet. "There are deals to make." He looked at Allan with what appeared to be genuine concern. "Whatever I can do to find your uncle, boy, you ask me before anyone else. Got that?"

"We sure can't go to the cops," Fawn theorized aloud. "With a kidnapping beef, they'll go straight to the Bureau. But rivalries being what they are, along with my rep, they'll make certain that we won't have an easy time with the local field office. Besides, we have to wait at least 24 hours before phoning it in."

"This is all over my head," Allan said lightly. But in his

109

thoughts, he added, *But I think it's time to call in my secret helper a little before his time.*

* * *

"Okay, I gave him a little more of the juice," Cooper told the driver. "You sure he's going to be okay?"

"Just like the others, G-man. Stop worrying.

Cooper looked around, sweat trickling into his collar. "That Carroll dame fingered me. If something goes south, she's got a name and a face to pin it on."

The passenger stuck a Lucky Strike in the corner of his mouth but didn't light it. "By the time they get themselves organized, we'll be on the lam. So just quit worrying and stick to the plan, just like the Boss said."

Cooper sat back in his seat, grumbling under his breath.

"Yeah, everything's gonna be smooth sailing from here on in," Marco Roove stated with authority as he handed his lighter to the man to his right.

Stan Lange waved the lighter away and enjoyed the feel of the cool night air on his pallid face.

Agent Cooper looked out the window and wished he'd left the kitchen just a little bit faster.

*"I couldn't help a program that would have killed
thousands of people..."*

"I don't have many friends at the Bureau..."

ELEVEN – Enter ... THE SKYMAN!

Fawn never got a lot of men to call back after

the first date. *Probably can't handle an assertive woman,* she reasoned. So she didn't expect her telephone to ring around eleven that night, nor did she expect the caller to be Allan Turner.

"Hope I didn't wake you," Allan said with a tinge of the tone he used just before chasing Agent Cooper's vehicle, the one that made her smile inside. "I'm usually up this time anyway, I think. I should probably look at my watch more often."

"It's okay." She turned down the radio and stretched out on her bed. "So to what do I owe the honor, Mr. President?"

From the other end of the line, Allan chuckled. "Laugh it up, Fawn. I may call you that, I trust? Anyway, the Mickey Finn was only in the one bottle, the one that Kendall and my uncle drank from."

"All that tells me is Kendall was a creature of habit," Fawn offered. "He knew where his own hooch was."

"Hmm, no doubt." Allan pondered for a moment. "But who else knew about his private stock and where he kept it?"

"Good question." Fawn ran through a list of potential suspects. "Little Miss Bottle Blondie would know where he kept his good stuff and what he liked to share, I'd wager. But where's her motive?" Fawn couldn't keep the grin from her voice. "Maybe if you investigate her more deeply? Go undercover, as it were."

If Allan noticed the innuendo, he gave no sign. "What's interesting is that most of these magic potions are pretty much like recipes. There's not a lot of difference between them for the desired effect, just the brand name changes. However, this one was a special formulation with a couple of ingredients that are available primarily in Germany."

Fawn sat up. "Not surprised if Bruhner is involved. This explains who put the snatch on your uncle." Fawn then explained what she knew about Albrecht Bruhner.

"Some kind of steam-worshipper, huh? Oh, I almost got hit by what felt like concentrated, super-heated gas. Anything in his files about that?"

Fawn sighed unhappily, recalling the chemical gas

114

delivery system whose malfunction left the Prussian engineer scarred. After describing the device to Allan, as well as the events from twenty years before, Fawn added, "Sounds like he's been working on a more compact fluid delivery system. Not surprised, but I'm glad he hasn't worked on the sights on those things. You sure you're okay?"

"Yes, I am. Thank you, Fawn." Allan sounded genuinely pleased at her sincere concern. "Listen, I have to take care of a couple of things before I turn in. I'll talk to you soon, okay? Good night and pleasant dreams."

"Yeah, you too." Fawn hung up the telephone and rolled onto her stomach. *Butterflies in the stomach*, she noted, *pulse racing, feeling like a schoolgirl, I do believe I've fallen for the lug – the loafer. But I – I'll reform him.*

Fawn grinned at the fantasy, her arm entwined with his forevermore. She hadn't been on many dates since high school. Focusing on her studies and then her career in the F.B.I. left her little time or inclination to find a steady guy.

Maybe I'm making up for lost time? Fawn smiled at the image of the take-charge Allan Turner, but couldn't ignore the moments when the unmanly side of his personality surfaced. She cringed at the very thought of such a smart and handsome man squandering his life with idle pleasures.

That's what I'll do. Reform him.

* * *

Marco Roove pulled into the garage. He was surprised to see Albrecht Bruhner waiting for him just inside the doorway.

The Master of Steam held up a hand and Roove brought the sedan to a halt, rather than move to in its usual parking space.

Bruhner smiled as he inspected his newest guest. "Any problems in procuring our friend?"

Agent Cooper stepped out of the car and walked quickly to Bruhner's side. "The grab went by the numbers, Herr Bruhner. However, someone who used to work in the Bureau identified me."

Bruhner frowned, but Roove came to Cooper's defense. "Our man here made it look like the F.B.I. was grabbing Turner for their own purposes. I bet she bought it."

"*She*? The Carroll woman you've mentioned?" Nodding, Bruhner rubbed his hands together. "Well played, Agent

116

Cooper."

Lange wrestled Turner's limp body from the back seat of the automobile. "He'll be out at least another hour," the thug guessed.

"Splendid." Bruhner grinned broadly, a pathway of yellowing teeth appearing amidst the scar tissue on his face. "Roove, Cooper, you have one more errand to run tonight." The Prussian thrust his hand into a metal gauntlet. "While the Bureau's forces are divided, now is the time to collect a bonus for our efforts."

* * *

Back in his uncle's lab, Allan removed his lab coat and hung it back on its usual peg, next to where his uncle's spare set of car keys hung. He would have saved some time if he could have started his uncle's car. Fortunately, Allan's time on the Harnell cross country team served him well. He simply ran across the back of the Kendall estate to his uncle's laboratory so he could get immediately to work. With his analysis completed and chronicled, Allan considered trying to get some sleep, if he could work past the worry.

Then he heard the noise again from outside.

Allan moved across the room and took a peek through the curtains. He saw a familiar sedan parked behind the building, one he'd seen just a couple of hours before.

Someone – Allan couldn't quite make out who it was because of the slouch brim hat that concealed the stranger's features – got out from behind the driver's seat and opened the trunk. Alarms began going off inside Allan's brain as he began to remove his shirt with urgency, exposing another set of clothing that no other man had ever seen.

Outside, the figure opened the automobile's trunk and rummaged around for a moment before pulling out a pair of cylinders that he plunged inside his jacket, followed by what appeared to be a brass key. Looking around, certain no one was around to see him, the man confidently strolled up to the back door of the house and let himself inside.

Cautiously, the man moved through the house, making his way directly to the laboratory. Ignoring the racks of chemicals, as well as the remains of Allan's diagnosis of Braden Kendall's liquor, the figure moved towards a large safe that rested in one corner. It sat in that spot because once the two strong moving men set the steel block into place six years earlier, nothing short of an earthquake was going to relocate it.

Pushing his hat back with his thumb, the man grunted at the combination lock. *Why didn't anyone use keys except on doors anymore?* But his frustration passed in a heartbeat as he recalled that he brought a cure for a stubborn lock. Two of them, in fact.

After a minute's work, the man was startled to hear a voice behind him.

"Mind telling me what you're up to?"

Marco Roove whirled around to see someone standing in the doorway. However, it was no one he expected to see.

This man wore black riding boots and white leggings that stretched up to his sternum, bisected by a blue belt around his waist. A red tunic with what appeared to be a black and yellow steering wheel of sorts upon his chest was framed by a long flowing blue cloak and matching head mask. A flat white visor of non-reflective material covered the man's eyes. In fact, the only exposed flesh was at the man's hands and lower face ... and he wasn't smiling.

"Who –?" the wide-eyed invader managed to say.

A grim smile now came to the costumed man's lips. In a voice that was not quite his own, Allan Turner stated, "You can call me the SKYMAN. Now don't make me ask you twice."

"Get outta here," Roove said urgently and barreled towards the costumed man.

The intruder usually relied on his strength and momentum to move his opponents. However, Allan Turner was noted for never allowing the most powerful of football linemen past him. The Skyman planted his feet, braced himself, and blocked Roove's escape cold, knocking the thug a couple of feet backwards.

While Roove contemplated his failure, the Skyman caught a glimpse of why the guy seemed intent on a quick exit.

Two sticks of TNT were taped around the lock of the massive safe and the fuse on each explosive had burned down sufficiently that running clear of the building was no longer an option.

"So you know Allan Turner, do you?"

Enter the Skyman!

TWELVE – To Escape the Blaze

The Skyman looked into Marco Roove's eyes

which were now wide and filled with mortal terror. It probably didn't help the other man's composure that not only did the powerful Skyman prevent his safe exit from the room, the guy could see his own fear reflected in the hero's white visor.

"You idiot!" the Skyman growled. "There are dangerous chemicals in here! They could –"

To punctuate the Skyman's point, the dynamite erupted in a tsunami of sudden heat and percussive energy. Roove's body pushed into the Skyman with inhuman force, almost as if shoved forward violently by a godly finger. The costumed man felt himself slammed into a wall just as the ceiling of the laboratory fell on the rest of the room. Then came another small explosion and still another as certain chemicals ignited, opening fissures in the stone walls outside.

The Skyman struggled to get Roove off of him, but the body was now dead weight in every sense of the term. Then another violent explosion occurred and suddenly, the world went dark.

He had no idea how long he was out, but the sting of the flames surrounding him pierced the Skyman's cocoon of unconsciousness. From a million miles away, he could hear the scream of sirens approaching.

With all the strength at his command, the Skyman pushed Roove's corpse off and to one side, the ex-mobster landing on his stomach, along with a layer of bricks that covered the man like a winter blanket of snow. Smoke rose through the holes where the roof used to be and numerous fires illuminated the immediate area. In fact, one such set of flames touched Roove's pants leg and quickly devoured the fabric, moving rapidly upwards along the man's body. A wedge torn from the corner of one of the wooden lab tables rested deep inside the base of Roove's spine.

Nothing I can do for the rat right now, the Skyman thought. *I'll be lucky to do something for myself.* He ached as he pushed himself to his feet, shedding debris as he moved. While the heat of the conflagration pressed against the Skyman's exposed flesh painfully, the special construction of his costume kept the worst of the flames at bay at least for a little while. The Skyman stumbled over the piles of what used to be the ceiling and around the areas where the flames were the worst.

The back door was barely connected to its frame now. Through the gaps, the Skyman could see that the dark sedan had already fled the scene, only to be replaced by a couple of fire engines and at least three police cars. Water poured from the fire hoses, massaging the building in its cooling touch and preventing the fire from igniting the trees or any nearby buildings.

Not wanting to answer too many questions right now, mostly those concerning his attire, the Skyman moved towards the front of the house and hoped the fire proved entertaining enough that all possible attention would be drawn there.

As he passed the laboratory one last time, the Skyman noticed the door of the safe lay flat on the floor in front of the rest of the metal box to which it had once been attached. His instincts compelled him to give the safe one last look before the flames could claim the contents, to see if anything was worth salvaging. He forced himself into the heart of the fires for one quick look.

The Skyman's heart sank when he saw the contents of the safe now thoroughly afire. He thought of his own notes as well as those of his uncle's, all that work and precious time spent together on what might advance the world's standard of living. Now it would be ashes, all because of someone's avarice.

All because of a careless man who died in his arms.

His heart filled with disappointment and fury, the Skyman turned to leave the room when something caught his eye. A chunk of the ceiling had crashed down upon one of the lab tables, one in a corner that he and his uncle rarely utilized. And a corner of that table appeared to have an extra drawer that The Skyman was unaware of. Ignoring the blaze around him, he stepped over to the drawer and saw some papers inside, each one covered with drawings, diagrams, and typewritten text, all in a shade of dark blue that implied they were carbon copies.

Without a second's hesitation, The Skyman pulled all the papers – probably a hundred pages in all – and jammed them into his insulated tunic for protection. He could sort them out once he left the blazing building.

By now, the fire spread through the rest of the house, despite the firefighters' best efforts. The Skyman tried not to think about his belongings, as well as those of his uncle's, shriveling and lost to the touch of the blaze. With his insulated cloak wrapped around his body tightly, the Skyman knew the flames would soon consume the entire building. He certainly didn't want to be around when that happened.

Upon finding an island of relative safety inside the foyer from the fire that approached from the rear of the house, the Skyman distinctly remembered locking the front door upon coming home. However, for security's sake, the deadbolt lock required a key not only to enter the domicile, but to exit it as well. So just as Allan Turner once left the blocks for one of his many sprint races, the Skyman knelt down, lifted his backside, then raced towards the door as quickly as he could.

Pulling his cloak up to his face for a moment, the Skyman felt the flames caress his body and superheat the very air around him. Less than a heartbeat later, he rammed into the wood with all his might. If he didn't shatter the door on the first try, there wouldn't be an opportunity for a second attempt.

Fortunately, the door cracked down the center and the hinges gave way. The Skyman stumbled at the top of the landing, crashed onto the broken door, and tumbled across the front step onto the front lawn.

Coughing furiously and grateful to still be able to do so, the Skyman pushed himself towards a standing position, hoping to leave before the police could arrive.

"Freeze, mister!"

The Skyman turned to see a pair of shapely ankles and his heart sank a little. His gaze moved upwards, following the curves of Fawn Carroll's form, up to the .38 revolver aimed directly between his eyes.

THIRTEEN – Questions and Lies

"**O**kay, **Mr.** **Halloween**," **Fawn** **said** authoritatively, "put your hands behind your head, lace your fingers, and don't move until I tell you."

"Please listen, Miss Carroll," the Skyman said as he painfully rose to his knees, "I can't be found by the authorities, not yet."

Fawn's grip on the pistol tightened visibly. "Aside from the fact that you know my name, why shouldn't I turn you over to whatever passes for an arson investigator in this burg?"

The Skyman pulled his hands from behind his head to indicate his red, white and blue uniform. "Take a look, would you? They'd lock me up before I could solve the –"

Fawn motioned with her handgun for the Skyman to place his hands behind his skull once again, which he promptly did. She leaned forward and squinted at his face. "Just who the heck are you?"

Taking a deep breath, he said, "I am ... the SKYMAN!"

Fawn pondered this for a moment, her eyes surveying

every pore on her captive's face. "Oh-kay, so you're the Skyman. So what were you doing inside the Turner home?"

The Skyman's eyes were invisible to Fawn behind his visor, but after a few seconds of studying her expression, he realized, *She doesn't recognize me*!

"Listen to me," he said urgently, "I know Allan Turner and I know what happened to his uncle tonight. We are on the same side, honest!"

Fawn wrestled with this new information and the circumstances of meeting the costumed man. She bit her lower lip hard enough that the Skyman feared another shade of red would be matching her lipstick.

At that moment, the familiar black sedan slowly wheeled into view. *It probably made its exit just as the firetrucks pulled up*, the Skyman reasoned.

Then a hand extended from the passenger's side window, aiming the same gun from earlier this evening.

"Fawn!" The Skyman rolled towards the woman, knocking her off her feet just as a stream of compressed steam flew into the spot where she'd just stood. Another column of water vapor dug into the dirt where the Skyman lay a moment before. Fawn and the costumed man rolled towards a thick oak tree to gain some cover. This gave the sedan the opportunity to make its escape, the driver leaving a stream of shouted obscenities in the vehicle's wake.

"So you know Allan Turner, do you?" Fawn's tone, although a little breathless from her exertions, was less accusatory than before, now just inquisitive.

The Skyman realized his hands rested familiarly on her shoulders as he pressed up against her. He cleared his throat, released the girl, and leaped to his feet to take a quick step backwards. He wiped the soot from his visor at the moment she glanced backwards with the faintest of smiles.

"I do. I was inside the Turner home as a part of my investigating the doctor's abduction. Also, I was there earlier as Allan analyzed the brandy from Braden Kendall's house." *Well*, he rationalized, *I'm not telling any lies. Not large ones, at least.*

"So you've got the gun." The Skyman reached down, took Fawn's hand in one of his as she lowered the pistol. "I think we need to regroup, share information, and check our next plans."

131

"I disagree," Fawn said as she plunged the revolver into the waistband of her dress. "I want to talk to the authorities on the scene and pick their brains first." She smiled sweetly. "And before you ask, I got a good look at the plates this time. Someone plastered some mud on them. I probably couldn't read the numbers if I pressed my nose against them." She motioned for the Skyman to move to her waiting car. "Let's get going. When we get there, you sit in the car while I turn on the charm."

The Skyman grinned. "You're the one with the firearm." He walked casually towards Fawn's car, making a quick bolt to the driver's door before she could react. He smiled and opened it for her.

Unable to resist grinning, Fawn slipped in behind the wheel as the Skyman closed her door. She watched him walk with purpose towards the front of the car, halfway expecting him to make a bolt for freedom. However, he then calmly moved to the passenger side and let himself in.

As they drove to the rear of the Turner house, the Skyman said, "You didn't seem very surprised by that steam pistol."

"I've seen it before," Fawn stated flatly through gritted teeth. "You didn't seem terribly startled either, Skyman."

Rather than risk revealing his dual identity, the Skyman smiled softly and kept his silence. In turn, Fawn pondered why he didn't ask any further questions of her, a train of thought that remained uninterrupted until they turned the corner, driving to the back of the Turner house.

Light from the fire cast a brilliance over the crime scene that rivaled the artificial illumination last seen at the Kendall party. A pair of fire engines seemed to almost vanish inside the crimson glow coming from the building. Two fire hoses relentlessly poured water into the building and only now seemed to be making any headway against the blaze.

Fawn aimed her Buick towards the touring car that sat behind one of the fire engines. She pointed at a man standing beside one of the fire fighters, wearing the standard black suit-white shirt-red tie that seemed to scream "government service."

"That's Steve Kraddock," Fawn explained to the Skyman. "He's Chico to the other two Marx Brothers."

Skyman grinned. "I detect a certain level of contempt

133

for your former associates."

"Brother, you don't know the half of it. Those clowns, like too many in Mr. Hoover's employ, seem to think wearing a skirt denotes incompetence."

"Talk about a new level of wrongness," the Skyman commented casually.

Fawn looked over at the Skyman, but his gaze appeared to be locked on the fire. The tone of his voice, however, reassured her that his comment was sincere. "Anyway," she said, "I need you to stay here and be inconspicuous." She eyed his body-hugging uniform. "I have just the thing to keep you from attracting attention."

Reaching into the back seat, Fawn pulled out a blue wide-brimmed hat. A pale ribbon served as a hatband and trailed another foot or so past the edge of the headgear which was lined with small crocheted flowers of yellow and white.

"I don't think so." The Skyman crossed his arms as if that would end the discussion.

By way of reply, Fawn jammed the hat over the Skyman's helmet. "Sorry, but the fashion consultant, the driver, and the girl holding the firearm voted and you are out of luck. Now just sit there and look pretty." Before the Skyman could voice an objection, Fawn already slammed the door shut and had closed half of the distance between the car and the suited man.

"Gosh, look who finally decided Markley and Cooper did too much of the work. Steve Kraddock, right? I have trouble remembering names when their owners leave the heavy lifting to someone else." Fawn stopped and briefly flashed her sweetest smile.

The agent turned towards Fawn with an expression reserved for things to be scraped from one's shoes. "A kidnapping, an arson, now you. I think the plague of locusts are next." He pulled a handkerchief from a back pocket to dab at the sweat under his receding hairline.

"Where's your cohorts in crime fighting?" Fawn asked. "It's not your style to be at the scene when something's happening."

Kraddock ran a hand over his perpetual five o'clock shadow and then removed his wire-rimmed glasses just long enough to rub his weary eyes. "Lady, the other two might sprain something in an effort to be nice to you. I have no such inclination. Scoot!"

Fawn sighed. "Look, I apologize for being such a wise-acre. I saw a kidnapping tonight and –"

"Ex-agent Carroll, I know nothing about any kidnapping. But it wouldn't surprise me in the least." Kraddock sneered. "People around you tend to disappear, don't they?"

Fawn's jaw dropped. Kraddock couldn't have hurt her any more effectively if he'd slugged her in the face.

"Furthermore," he continued, "I am not compelled in any way to answer your questions. In fact, I'll inform you that anything you do to interfere with this investigation, or if you flash your gams anywhere near this or any other crime scene, I'll have you held on suspicion of everything I can think of. Now get lost."

With that statement, Kraddock turned his back on Fawn. But she'd already swung around to keep him from seeing the tears welling in her eyes. He was right … losing one person was careless and losing two was inexcusable. Wounded as deeply as any cut could go, she made her way back to her automobile.

Then her jaw dropped again as she looked inside to see her spring hat resting where the Skyman sat not two minutes ago.

* * *

Perkins hobbled quickly into Albrecht Bruhner's steam chamber. Without waiting for permission, he called out, "There's a fire at the Turner home. A couple of fire engines have been dispatched and –"

But the chamber was empty, save for the heated vapors that emanated from the walls.

* * *

Drumming his fingers on his knee from the sanctuary of the car, Skyman watched Fawn approach Agent Kraddock. Then a sudden movement in the corner of his eye caught his attention.

Agent Cooper peered from around the corner of the burning house, concealed by what was left of a rose bush. The rogue agent watched as Fawn spoke with his colleague for a moment before turning to sneak towards the front of the former laboratory and living quarters.

There's someone I need to speak to, the Skyman thought.

He quietly opened his car door and slipped into the night, leaving Fawn's less-than-heroic hat behind.

Running beyond the glare of the burning building, Skyman moved towards the front of the edifice. He could see the dark sedan a safe distance from the scene, but still within sprinting distance. A couple of recently-arrived firemen sprayed water on the flames from a tanker engine, but no one else was there.

Then the Skyman noticed a bedroom window was broken. The earlier explosions and heat blew out many of the windows, but this one aroused his curiosity and required verification. He moved closer, grateful that the firemen were distracted by their jobs.

Sure enough, unlike the ground beneath the other windows, the soil under this one was clean. A peek through the frame showed all the glass lying on the carpet inside.

Looking around, the Skyman couldn't see Cooper. The Fed might have doubled back once whoever broke the window got inside. Or perhaps he needed to get inside without being seen. But the Skyman decided that he couldn't worry about that now.

In one smooth motion, the Skyman leaped onto the window sill and dove into the room.

Meanwhile, on the other side of the building, Steve Kraddock glanced back at Fawn Carroll. The girl seemed to be pacing in a tight circle beside her vehicle as if deciding her next move, pausing occasionally to kick at the grass under her feet in some kind of frustration. Kraddock grinned. *When Hoover starts wearing a skirt, then maybe we should have gals in the field. But not one day sooner.*

One of the firemen approached Kraddock. A mask of fatigue, sweat and soot covered the man's face, but his gaze was strong, determined, like a warrior on the verge of vanquishing a deadly foe. Kraddock respected that. "Agent Kraddock? We've got the fire out, pretty much. I'm sending all but one engine back to the firehouse, if that's okay."

"Sounds fine to me," Kraddock pulled a pair of canvas work gloves from a back pocket. "Good work. Is it safe to go in?"

"As safe as a freshly-burned building ever is. I think there's a basement and the fire may have compromised the ground floor so just be careful when you get whatever it is you're looking for. I'll go in with you, just for safety's sake."

Kraddock shook the fireman's hand, unmindful of the grime and sweat coating it. "I appreciate your letting me in. I'll be in and out so I won't be interfering with your own investigation too much." With that, he walked towards the back door of the former Turner home.

"Hey, partner."

Agent Cooper jogged to Kraddock's side as a fire engine pulled away from the curb. "Nothing's happening at the Kendall party. I thought I'd come be another pair of eyes for you."

Kraddock shook his head. "Thanks, but the building's pretty burned up. How about you stay here and arrest the building if it drops me into the basement?" Both men chuckled as they noticed the fireman walking towards the house. Kraddock moved to catch up.

Ash and water collected upon every flat black surface still existing inside the building. Both men carried a flashlight, creating circles of white dancing amidst the wreckage of what used to be the Turners' home.

Walking by what once was the laboratory, Kraddock

peered inside through the doorway, pointing at the remains of the former safe. "I think I found where the blaze started."

The fireman whistled at the extent of the damage inside this room as he made his way around the debris with Kraddock close behind. Their flashlight beams moved around slowly inside the main body of the safe. "Whatever was in here," the agent declared, "is nothing but ash now. Hope nobody –" The agent moved in closer to look at one pile of ashes, then another, a space, then more ashes ...

"I think we're missing some papers," Kraddock announced.

The fireman knelt by the safe door, studying the area where the TNT twisted the metal. After a couple of moments, he noticed an odd sound that shouldn't have been there. He thought he'd turned off the water to the building so it shouldn't have been the radiators emptying their contents.

The beam swept over a figure standing in the farthest corner of the laboratory. Slowly, the character drew his cloak back over his shoulders, revealing a metallic emblem on its chest, a dragon built from steel and copper. The fireman's gaze tilted upwards until he stared into the unblinking eyes of Death itself.

Revealing a similar gun to the one that kept Allan Turner from catching the sedan back at Braden Kendall's party, Albrecht Bruhner aimed the pistol at the fireman's chest.

A pencil-thin tube of compressed steam erupted from the barrel of the gun. It touched the fireman's chest and kept on going through, just like a straw penetrating a tree during a tornado. The heat from the tunnel of steam was so great, it cauterized the wound as it penetrated cloth, rubber, canvas, bone, and human flesh.

The fireman stared at the hole in his jacket and felt a moist warmth spreading across his shirtfront, knowing it wasn't his blood, but water. A few seconds later, all strength left his legs and he fell to the wet, soot-covered floor, dead.

Kraddock whirled around, his service revolver drawn. He called for his backup, "Cooper!"

However, the other agent was down on one knee, having turned Marco Roove's corpse on its side. He expertly searched the man's pockets until he pulled out an envelope. It was made of no material Cooper had ever seen or felt before and a quick look inside told the agent that the contents

142

were safe from fire, flood, or blood. Cooper brushed off his pants leg as he stood up and handed the envelope to the cloaked man.

Albrecht Bruhner said, "*Danke*, Agent Cooper."

"I'll handle everything else," Cooper said. It took Kraddock a second before he realized that his colleague wasn't speaking to him, but to the mysterious intruder. However, before he could ask his partner what in the heck was going on, Kraddock felt a white-hot finger of pure steam penetrate his skull, a moment of searing pain and then he felt nothing more.

Six feet from the rear door, Cooper mussed up his hair and began stumbling from the building. A pair of firemen and three policemen rushed forward to steady him. He went limp and allowed them to drag him to the running board of the one remaining fire engine.

From the corner of his eye, Cooper could see a man scribbling in a notebook, no doubt someone from the local press. The agent almost smiled at how easily this came together.

"One of Turner's inventions survived the fire," Cooper

143

lied breathlessly. "We got into the lab and it went off. My partner, Steven Kraddock, and the fireman who accompanied us, died immediately from it."

The reporter scribbled frantically, trying to capture Cooper's every word. Then Cooper looked directly at the reporter and said slowly, "In addition, I made a positive I.D. of a third body in the room. I regret to say that it was the charred remains of –"

* * *

Albrecht Bruhner made his way towards the window through which he'd entered earlier. He examined the papers inside the envelope and his eyes went wide. *What genius! Once these plans are in the hands of the Fuhrer …*

Bruhner replaced the papers inside the envelope, concealing the package inside a slot built into the side of his power-armor.

He didn't realize he was smiling until someone else in the room commented, "I believe those papers belong to someone else. I'll accept them as well as your surrender."

Stopping in his tracks, Bruhner stared hatefully at the grim visage of the man who stood between him and his exit, the Skyman.

Bruhner's free hand folded itself into a fist, an act that brought the cruel smile back to the steam warrior's face.

The Original Skyman Battles the Master of Steam

"Freeze, Mister!"

FOURTEEN – In Combat With the Steam Master

Bruhner threw a punch with the speed of a

steam-fueled cobra, one that would have transformed any man's head into a fine red mist. But the Skyman's Olympic-level reflexes saved him from a swift and certain death as he dodged the lethal blow.

While Bruhner pulled his arm back to strike again, the Skyman attempted a savate kick to his enemy's face, hoping to dislodge the steel helmet. However, the blow's energy was absorbed by the metal and padding that protected his foe's skull.

Before both of the Skyman's feet could touch the floor again, Bruhner lashed out with his other hand. The flat-palmed blow connected squarely with the emblem on The Skyman's chest, sending the caped man flying into the far wall.

As he caught his breath, the Skyman saw Bruhner launch himself from the far side of the room, accelerating like a railroad engine leaving the station. The lumbering gait rapidly turned into a smooth thundering sprint with the inevitable damaging force of an earthquake. A small jet of steam propelled the Prussian's bulk forward like something out of the Sunday funnies.

Instead of dodging, the Skyman got to his feet and raced forward. He leaped into the air, placed his hands on Bruhner's helmet, and pushed himself upwards to pass above the charging engineer. Just shy of striking the ceiling, the Skyman executed a perfect flip to kill his momentum before landing on his feet like a cat.

On the other hand, the force of the acrobatic maneuver pushed Bruhner's helmet down onto his face. Blinded, the self-styled Master of Steam crashed headlong into the outer wall. A rain of bricks and other debris fell on top of him and a larger amount came down when he pulled himself free, a flesh and metal Excalibur.

The Skyman reached down to pick up a couple of bricks. He hurled one and then the other in rapid succession at his foe.

Bruhner slid his helmet back into place, just in time to expose his lower face and feel a brick smash into his mouth.

Before he could taste his own blood, Bruhner caught the second hurled brick in his steel-jacketed hand. Locking his eyes with Skyman's, the Prussian slowly crushed the dried clay and allowed the pieces to fall to the floor.

The Skyman judged the distance between himself and the doorway into the main hallway of the house and his odds of crossing the space without getting nabbed. But during that split-second of calculation, Bruhner jetted himself again towards the American. However this time, the Prussian spread his arms wide as if ready to catch his foe should he try to leap out of the way.

Instead of vaulting over his enemy again, the Skyman dropped to his knees and rolled towards Bruhner's feet, striking one just as the Prussian was lifting it. Off-balance, the armor kept pumping its legs while fighting to stay upright as the Skyman rolled past and out of the way of danger.

The upcoming wall was not quite so fortunate. Bruhner struck it face-first, moving through it like a wrecking ball. More of the ceiling began to pour down upon the room.

However, the Skyman executed a perfect tip-up and dove through the open window. One flip later, his booted feet touched the ground while the sounds of destruction erupted from inside the house. *Sounds like Bruhner needs to install some brakes in that armor of his*, he observed with a grin.

Moving towards the front of the house, the Skyman saw Bruhner crash through the remains of the front door as if they weren't there, which they barely were to begin with. The Prussian almost looked comical, covered in pieces of the Turner house as he raced to the black sedan. He dove through an open door into the back seat before the automobile roared into the night.

Suddenly, a high-pitched whistle filled the air. The Skyman looked to his right to see Fawn pull up to the curb, tires screeching in protest. She opened the door behind the driver's seat and gestured wildly for the Skyman to approach, which he did at a full sprint.

Fawn suppressed a grin at the mystery man's athleticism. *He could give that Allan Turner a run for his money, no pun intended.*

Slamming the door shut upon his entry, the Skyman felt himself being pushed into the cushions of the back seat as Fawn slammed the accelerator hard against the floorboards.

He forced himself up to a sitting position and looked behind at what used to be his home. A couple of figures ran to the edge of the property, one of them being Agent Cooper.

"Thanks for the save, Fawn," the Skyman said slowly. Fatigue began to gnaw at his body as despair washed over his spirit. In one night, he'd lost his creations, his uncle and his home. All of a sudden, he felt eleven years old again.

"No problem, masked man." Fawn expertly navigated her vehicle through the back streets of the city until she was certain no one tailed her. Fortunately, she'd also smeared a handful of dirt on her license plates. Two could play that particular game. "So what did you find?"

The Skyman's jaw tightened. "Two men died because I was too slow to arrive, that's what. One of them was a fireman." He paused. "The other was the man you were talking to behind the house."

Fawn gasped. "That was Kraddock. I didn't like him, he didn't like me, but he didn't deserve to die on the job." She sniffled once, then asked, "Did you see who –"

"Bruhner." The Skyman said the name as if it described a particularly malignant form of cancer. "He used that gun, that solid steam gadget." He placed a hand on Fawn's shoulder. "I swear to you, by all that's holy, I will find him and make him pay in the eyes of the law."

Then you better find him before I do, thought Fawn. "So what's our next move, Skyman?"

For once, the Skyman didn't have an answer.

* * *

In the other car, heading towards the far side of the city, Perkins gripped the steering wheel like it was a lifeline. His haunted eyes scanned the rear view mirror for pursuit, but it never arrived. Feeling the silence digging into his brain, the professor asked, "Did it go well?"

In the back seat, Albrecht Bruhner pulled out the envelope from the storage area of his armor. From all the exertion tonight, he was eager to return to his special room and recharge his armor. But for all of his pain, for all the warmth being leeched from his core into the tubing that enveloped his body, all his woes vanished as he scanned the papers.

"It seems to have gone very well, indeed." An evil grin almost glowed amidst the scar tissue. "Hurry back to the base. It seems there's work to be done."

* * *

"It's been five minutes," Fawn announced. "I don't want to criticize you, of course, but I'd think a costumed adventurer like something out of the comics would have a plan ready."

"I don't yet," the Skyman confessed. He added with a grin, "However, if you have a handkerchief, I might be able to take you to my secret lair."

The Original Skyman Battles the Master of Steam

"You can call me The Skyman!"

FIFTEEN – The Skyman's ... Secret Lair?

"**S**ecret cesspool is more like it. Put the **hankie** back on, would you?"

"Kindly remind me to explain the direct relationship between beggars and choosers." The Skyman folded Fawn's hankie neatly and handed it back to her. After blindfolding the woman and commandeering her automobile, he drove her to the only place he could call a base, namely the apartment in the aptly-named Downtown Hotel that Allan Turner rented to put the final touches on his Skyman disguise.

No kind of trial quite like a fire, the Skyman thought with a smirk.

After a couple of minutes to ensure that no clue to Allan Turner could be seen, the Skyman unveiled his "secret lair" to Fawn Carroll, who couldn't bother to conceal her disdain for the hotel's decorations, or lack thereof. "Anyway," the Skyman said, "I am relying on you to not poke your nose through the blinds to figure out where you are. It's not exactly the high-rent district." *All the better to hide Allan's projects. And Uncle Peter wanted me to have an empathy for those whose prosperity didn't match my own.*

"If I do look outside, it's only to plot my escape route." Fawn moved to a chair in the corner and sat down with a sigh.

The Skyman turned on the radio. "Would you like a little entertainment?"

"That's sweet," Fawn said softly, "please."

A click later, the strains of Bing Crosby's *Deep Purple* filled the air.

"Where are they?" Fawn's eyes narrowed. "The cars, the general hubbub of people outside. I can't hear them. Surely, we can't be downtown."

Looking through a slat in the blinds, the Skyman noticed a general lack of activity, the very thing that attracted him to this neighborhood in the first place. Fewer prying eyes and all that. But looking outside, just as Fawn said, there should have been more cars moving down the thoroughfare, more people strolling along the sidewalk, more patrons walking into and stumbling out of the bars.

But there weren't, a fact that made the Skyman wrinkle his brow under his mask.

"And most of the ones who are present," the Skyman observed, "are dressed much better than the usual ne'er-do-well that inhabits the more economically depressed parts of town." He allowed the slat to drop back into its usual place. "Perhaps we should solve the current mystery before tackling another." He turned to face Fawn again.

However, Fawn simply stared straight ahead, her thoughts apparently a universe away. The Skyman pulled up another chair and sat beside her.

"Kevin and I, we used to listen to the radio in the evening," Fawn volunteered. "Just like this." She smiled softly.

"You were ..."

Fawn added quickly, "We were friends. Nothing more." Then her smile vanished. "He was my first field assignment and I messed it up. He has no family, but I feel I owe the guy to find out what happened to him. Does that make sense?"

The Skyman nodded. "I am operating from the basis that

every one of those scientists are still alive. And Bruhner will answer for every death he and his steam-gun have caused in getting them. I promise you that."

"If you need someone to pull the switch on him," Fawn said with a grim smile, "give me a call." The music filled the empty spaces of the conversation, leaving an awkwardness that hung in the air like stale cigarette smoke.

Leaning back in his chair, the Skyman felt something crinkle and bend uneasily under his tunic. Remembering his accidental find at the laboratory, he pulled out the fistful of papers he rescued from the building and began examining them. He became keenly aware of Fawn looking over his shoulder as he read.

"Sure wish Allan was here to interpret these." Fawn rested her hands on the Skyman's shoulders.

"It's okay. I can make them out." At a glance, The Skyman recalled his uncle's genius, evident in every line on every sheet. He saw some of his own designs shuffled into the pile, but most of what he saw belonged to his Uncle Peter. A fresh wave of pain washed over the Skyman's heart.

"Okay," Fawn said, "what are we looking at here?"

"Copies of technical drawings made by the Turners." One by one, The Skyman flipped through the illustrations until he found one for his early model of the Stasimatic Ray Projector. He smiled briefly and continued to study each sheet nostalgically.

Fawn left the living room to investigate the kitchenette. She soon located some tea and enough fixings for two sandwiches. As she prepared the only food they'd had in hours, Fawn asked, "So did you find anything in those papers worth killing for?"

The Skyman looked up. "Most definitely. Most of these designs could be used for evil purposes if built by the wrong people." He returned his gaze to the sheet in his hands.

Bringing over their dinner, Fawn looked at the plans in the Skyman's hands. "What's that? A child's toy?"

"No, it's not. It's a plan for an aircraft that has the most unique propulsion system the world has ever seen. Fortunately, it would take more manpower and time to construct here than I suspect Bruhner has."

Fawn *hmmed*. "Well, we know it's him and that rat Cooper. Who else?"

159

"Wish I knew." The Skyman looked up towards Fawn to see her studying the lines in his face, what little of it she could see. He smiled and returned his attention to the schematic, tilting his head slightly to make any resemblance to Allan Turner a little less easy to discern.

At that moment, an announcer filled the silence of the room. "That was a request from a member of our loyal listening audience. We'll return to the latest music at the top of the next hour. But now, we present the news of the nation with Tony Trent." A second later, majestic orchestral music heralded the arrival of the popular newsman.

Fawn sat down again, batting back tears and unbidden memories.

"Good evening, America. From The Statue of Liberty, through the Gateway Arch and deep into the Hollywood Hills, welcome to your nightly news. This is Tony Trent reporting from the studios of WBSC in New York City."

Fawn sobbed involuntarily, drawing the Skyman's attention. Before he could even think, he moved to her side and wrapped his arms around her. She did her best not to bawl, but rested her face on the Skyman's smoke and soot-covered costume, grateful for his powerful embrace.

The pair remained still, holding each other tight as comfort against the perils of the last few hours. Fawn contemplated asking the man to remove his mask while the Skyman wondered silently what harm there might be to reveal his true identity to the woman.

Before the Skyman could reach under his chin to undo the secret latching system that held his helmet in place, Tony Trent reported, "– upstate where the noted metal magnate Braden Kendall talks to the F.B.I. at this late hour, concerning the kidnapping of scientist and lecturer Dr. Peter Turner."

The Skyman flinched at the hearing of his uncle's name. If Fawn noticed, she said nothing. *Perhaps she's already figured it out.*

"And this just in – thanks, Babs," Trent stated in even tones, "three bodies have been discovered in what's left of the house where Doctor Turner made his home. Names are being withheld, pending notification of their next of kin. However, our sources inform us that one was an agent of the Federal Bureau of Investigation, Foster Cooper."

Tony Trent's next news item left both the Skyman and Fawn Carroll slack-jawed with amazement.

"The other body found in the blaze has been identified as Dr. Turner's nephew, Allan."

SIXTEEN – Dr. Turner Gets the News

"**Got it!**" **Stan Lange announced triumphantly** as he switched the wire recorder off.

Albrecht Bruhner chuckled mirthlessly. "If engineering has taught me anything, Stanislaus, it's that the tiniest bit of support can hold aloft the mightiest of creations. Are you ready to be my main support?"

"I'll be honest with you." Stan leaned back in his chair and stretched. "I hooked up with the Mobs because I saw they had money and a pull that the legit world couldn't get. While I'm not nuts about a lot of what's in *Mein Kampf*, I kinda enjoy the idea of working for someone who wants to put the whole world in order, as long as I get my own line to push around. Count me in."

Bruhner nodded and smiled sincerely. "Good. I trust you'll be more careful than Mr. Roove?"

Stan chuckled. "He blew himself up because he didn't know what he was doing, but wanted to play big man for you. If I know how to do something, I'll tell you. If I don't,

163

I'll either learn or find an expert." Leaning over, Stan pulled the machine's plug from the wall socket and wound the power cord into a knot that resembled a hangman's noose.

"That seems like a fair arrangement, Stanislaus. Come, let us visit Dr. Turner and give him the news. It's time to tear his foundations down so we can rebuild him properly."

With that, Stan picked up the wire recorder and followed Bruhner into the main dormitory.

* * *

Fawn slept quietly on the sofa, a blanket covering her from foot to shoulder. Meanwhile, in the bathroom, Allan Turner sat on the rim of the bathtub with his Skyman uniform across his lap, a sewing needle in one hand and a length of thread in the other.

While the costume contained enough padding in the right places to be comfortable, it was still a relief to take it off for a little while. Allan inspected his stitching around the periphery of his blue cloak. Adding some boning to the cape gave it a little more strength, the reason for which he hoped to never test.

But the way things had gone so badly in the last few

hours, Allan shook his head to dislodge any stray negative thoughts. He then picked up his helmet to examine the interior earpieces. *I believe*, he thought, *we could miniaturize a radio transceiver, perhaps run the microphone and wiring just under the lining. Uncle Peter could help* –

Allan's shoulders slumped, the weight of potential failure lying oppressively upon him.

* * *

Outside, a patrol cop strolled down the sidewalk beside the Downtown Motel. For the last decade, the old business district was considered at the Police Station to be the beat one got when one was a rookie without any connections or those cronies failed to keep you out of trouble with the brass.

However, during the last year, the less savory elements of the neighborhood seemed to have vanished. Officer Roger Belzer couldn't have been happier about his job becoming easier and less hazardous. With no fights to break up, no thieves to chase down, no drunks to pull from the bars, the Beat From Hell became Belzer's Heaven On Earth.

Officer Belzer glanced down the alley that ran behind the motel. The employees parked near the garbage cans stationed beside the rear exit of the building to leave the street parking for their guests. After walking this exact same route five days a week for several months, he knew all the employee's makes and models by heart.

Tonight, one vehicle seemed to protrude from the midst of the scene like a stalk of corn rising from a rose garden. Belzer strolled closer to the parked cars, pulling a small notebook and a stub of a pencil from his jacket pocket.

Kneeling down behind the car, Belzer carefully wrote down the license plate number. After double-checking the numbers, the policeman strolled towards the sidewalk, intending to resume his circuit until he could get to a police call box. But until then, Officer Belzer intended to enjoy the night's quiet.

* * *

A gentle chorus of snoring filled the dormitory, but Peter Turner's was not among them. He stared upwards at the ceiling, trying to figure out the time.

Poor Allan must be out of his mind with worry. It felt like days had gone by since he passed out in Braden Kendall's kitchen and awoke in this stone prison.

166

Peter tried to identify the noises drifting in from the great hall next door. Since he woke up on this bunk earlier in the day, he could hear an almost industrial type of ambient noise, like many hands moving machinery, operating various power tools, perhaps a foreman – whether it was one of the thugs or one of the more cowed of the scientists – barking commands and urging the labor force to greater levels of productivity.

Something was going on next door. Dr. Turner was almost certain that any attempt to sate his curiosity would end badly for him. So he sighed ... and tried to close his eyes ...

* * *

"Check it again," the desk sergeant commanded.

"I already checked it three times," the officer responded.

"Then check it again dammit! I've dealt with the Feds enough to know to – oh, forget it! I'll call them myself!"

After dialing ever so carefully, the receiver on the other end of the line picked up on the second ring.

"Hello, Agent ... which one am I talking to? Oh, Agent Markley? This is the night desk sergeant. One of our foot patrolmen believes he's located Allan Turner's car."

* * *

Fawn Carroll grinned at the sight of the Skyman dozing in the bathtub, his cloak folded up under his head like a azure pillow. *Does he always sleep in his costume? Does he ever take off that helmet?*

She softly closed the bathroom door. Perhaps the aroma of a home-cooked breakfast would provide a gentle greeting to a new, and hopefully better, day.

* * *

"Good morning, Doctor Turner. How pleasant of you to join me for breakfast."

Stan nodded to the doctor, indicating he should sit down on the opposite side of the table from Albrecht Bruhner where a plate, fork, and coffee cup – but no cutlery, unsurprisingly – waited for his use.

Professor Perkins emerged from the steam chamber, pushing a steel cart. On top rested a silver-plated dome that covered a matching serving tray. Peter noticed the handle at the apex of the dome featured a crest that matched the one on his host's chestplate.

The Professor lifted the curved lid and swiftly distributed several sausages, grilled potatoes, and a couple of poached eggs to each plate before hurriedly exiting the room. Peter noticed his fellow scientist took pains to not even glance at Bruhner or himself. He wondered what it might take for him to reach that state of emotional emptiness ... and how soon he might reach that same zombie-like existence himself under these conditions.

"Please help yourself, Doctor Turner." Bruhner motioned for Peter to begin his breakfast. "Your colleague should return in a few minutes with some fresh coffee. I admit I've developed a taste for that brew during my time here. I may have to take a percolator with me when we return to Germany."

Peter noticed the emphasis on the word "we." He tried to keep a casual tone to his voice. "I believe I've got an extra pot at home. If you'll have your thug take me back there, I could pick it up for you."

Bruhner laughed. "What an extremely generous offer, Doctor Turner. However, I'm not sure it's an offer you can fulfill." The Prussian reached under the napkin spread across his armored lap and revealed the blueprints stolen from the Turner laboratory.

Recognizing the papers, Turner gasped involuntarily.

"But as you can see, Doctor, I already have everything I want from your former home. Yes, I'm afraid it's no longer standing so you no longer have a place to return to. I also fear the worst for your coffee maker." Bruhner glanced at page after page with an appreciative smile. "Fascinating work, Dr. Turner. My compliments to your genius."

"H-how did you get those?" Turner started to rise, to seize the blueprints, but a stern glance from Bruhner warned the doctor against making any sudden aggressive moves across the breakfast table. "My nephew would have given his life before he let you –"

Bruhner interrupted his guest with a chuckle. "Funny you should mention that."

With that, the Steam Master pulled the wire recorder from the floor onto a corner of the table. A push of a button and adjustment of the volume control later, the voice of Tony Trent repeated his report from the night before:

"– upstate where the noted metal magnate Braden

Kendall talks to the F.B.I. at this late hour. Concerning the kidnapping of scientist and lecturer Dr. Peter Turner – and this just in, three bodies have been discovered in what's left of the house where Doctor Turner made his home. Names are being withheld, pending notification of their next of kin. However, our sources inform us that one was an agent of the Federal Bureau of Investigation, Foster Cooper."

Stunned, Turner looked up at Bruhner. The engineer sliced his sausages calmly, glancing up with a soft smile before returning to his culinary surgery.

Trent's recorded voice continued, "The other body found in the blaze has been identified as Dr. Turner's nephew, Allan."

Peter Turner's numbed expression brought a grin to Bruhner's face. The Master of Steam attacked his breakfast with gusto and successfully resisted the urge to make a joke about the meat also being over-done.

Allan Turner

SEVENTEEN – Calling On the Kendalls

As sunlight painted the Harnell University

campus in early summer colors, the Skyman pulled his own car up to the curb a block away from the woman's hotel. "I probably should have brought you here last night instead of sullying your reputation from spending the night with me. We'll get your car later when things quiet down."

"You'll have to work harder to sully my rep, flyboy. I've worked pretty hard to ruin it at the Bureau, according to Markley and his drones."

Skyman grinned under the slouch-brimmed hat that covered his helmet. "Listen, I'll call you later this afternoon."

Fawn opened the door and looked both ways to make sure no one observed them before exiting. "And you're going to do what again? And with Allan Turner's car, no less."

Checking the buttons on his costume-concealing

overcoat for the third time since stopping, the Skyman reminded his companion, "I'm going to return to the scene of the crime."

"Which one?" Fawn smirked. "We've got plenty to choose from."

"I'm thinking I'll check the mansion where Peter Turner was abducted."

"Good idea," Fawn declared as she slid back into the passenger's seat again.

The Skyman stared straight ahead. "I thought we were going to go our separate ways, Fawn. Cover more ground as it were."

"I changed our mind," Fawn declared. "I'll talk to that faux-blonde tramp, maybe sweet-talk her old man if he's around. Start the car."

Starting the car again, just as he was told, the Skyman pulled away from the curb. "And just what suicide mission are you sending me on?"

"You check the rest of the house. I'll provide enough distraction for you to snoop around without any interruption."

Of that, I have no doubt. "And I'm looking for what, specifically?"

Fawn smiled sweetly at her driver. "You're a reasonably smart boy. I'm sure you'll know it when you see it."

About six blocks from the Kendall mansion, the Skyman turned the car over to Fawn. As she drove away, he thought, *I hope she doesn't think to look at the registration*, then, *Why am I working so hard to keep my identity a secret from her? She probably doesn't need another shock in her life.*

Sure ... that's as good a reason as any.

* * *

"Back so soon?" Ellyn Kendall stood in the doorway of her home like Cerberus at the banks of the River Styx. However, it would take more than a couple of coins to persuade her to allow Fawn Carroll entry.

"Good morning, dear," Fawn replied with a brilliant smile and an edge in her voice that could slice steel like bread. "I was wondering if your father –" *Or any responsible adult*, she injected mentally – "was home."

"Sorry, but he had some business in the city. Wealth waits for no man." Ellyn's eyes narrowed slightly. "And why are you asking questions? After you were here – with no invitation, I'll bet – that F.B.I. Agent Markely said you were drummed out of the Bureau."

"Former agent, yes." Fawn's eyes lit up with inspiration. "But I'm now a … private investigator." She dropped her voice to a whisper. "Listen, I wasn't thinking a hundred percent clearly last night in all the excitement. I'd like to take a look around, see what's shows up in the cold light of day." She smiled. "I'll pull in my claws if you do the same with yours. I think we both just want to help find Peter Turner."

Ellyn visibly relaxed and a smile briefly wafted across her features. "I'll try, but I can't promise anything about the claws." She motioned for Fawn to enter and then led her into the grand ballroom.

Before she crossed the doorway, Fawn thought she caught a glimpse of a blue cape flapping around the corner of the house.

Now empty of partyers, the clacking of the two women's heels echoed like gunfire. Ellyn led Fawn to the nearest of the standing bars and took the bartender's position. "My daddy recommends drinking before you burn too much sunlight. Care to join me?"

176

"Not yet, but go ahead." *Get liquored up and maybe your tongue will wag a little more freely.* "Learn anything new since last night?"

Ellyn mixed herself a vodka and tonic, more the former than the latter. "Afraid not. Once that Markley left, I haven't seen hide nor hair of him or his crew."

"Chances are you won't." Fawn resisted the urge to reveal that one of them might be a rogue agent who tossed the rule book away. "They're very good at what they do."

"I hope so." Ellyn took a hard pull from the glass before setting it down on the counter. "And Daddy told me what happened to Allan." Her eyes turned towards the floor. "I thought he was kinda cute."

"Yeah, he was," Fawn agreed. *And even if he wasn't so cute, I'd go after him just to keep* your *talons off him.*

From a nearby doorway, someone cleared their throat. In response, Ellyn sat up straight. "Excuse me," the heiress said as she rose to her feet as if shot out of a cannon. "The servants summon me." Fawn watched her move towards that specific doorway with purpose.

And I'd love to know what that purpose is.

The Original Skyman Battles the Master of Steam

* * *

Outside, a couple of minutes earlier, the Skyman moved quickly, but with the silence of a summer breeze, from the car to the side of the mansion. As Allan Turner, he'd patented a new kind of rubber sole that absorbed impact and sound, making the soles of his boots both more comfortable and also very stealthy.

Finding a trellis, the Skyman carefully climbed the vine-covered woodwork to the second-story. He slowly pushed at the top of the window, lifting it quietly. A moment later, he pulled himself inside as quietly as a phantom.

However, from behind one of the majestic oaks that ringed the estate, agent Ray Markley witnessed the costumed adventurer's every movement. Once the Skyman disappeared into the mansion, Markley pulled his service revolver from the holster under his left armpit. "Tell the heiress what we're doing," he commanded. "I'll make that call."

"Will do," Agent Cooper said with a grin. He sprinted from his hiding place to the side entrance of the mansion. Within a minute, he stood just outside the gigantic ballroom, listening to the two women talking about the night before. Keeping himself out of Fawn's sight, he cleared his throat, a signal he and Markley arranged with the Kendall dame on the previous night.

Rushing away from the bar, Ellyn joined Cooper. Before she could ask why he was inside, the agent said, "He's here. Like we planned."

Ellyn swallowed hard, accepted a gift from Cooper's coat pocket, then moved to her appointed position.

Cooper looked out to where Ellyn entertained her company a minute earlier. However, no one stood at the bar or anywhere inside the room. Cooper clenched his teeth and bolted towards the back of the mansion.

Upstairs, the Skyman silently moved from room to room, opening one door after another, until he found what appeared to be an office. Slipping inside silently, he glanced at the top of the majestic desk that dominated the room. The desktop was empty, save for a blotter and a telephone. He tentatively tugged at one of the desk drawers, but it refused to move. In fact, all the drawers proved to be locked. The Skyman made a mental note to incorporate some lock

179

picking tools into his uniform first chance he got.

A quick sweep of the room revealed no key, no way to gain entry to the desk. *A lock means there's something you don't want someone to see. And when I see a lock, I want to see what it's protecting.* But without a way to open the drawers, the Skyman promised himself that he'd return with the proper equipment.

Moving silently into the upstairs hallway, The Skyman heard footsteps moving up the stairway. Time to leave. He moved towards the window by which he entered and looked outside to make certain his exit would be as silent as his entry.

However, a ring of men in black suits stood outside, their hands filled with rifles, each one aimed at the window where the Skyman stood. The only man without a firearm held a megaphone.

"This is the Federal Bureau of Investigation. You are under arrest," Agent Markley said dramatically. "The house is surrounded. Come out with your hands above your head."

Skyman jumped back from the window and turned to flee down the hallway. However, he was brought up short as he saw the snub-nosed revolver in Ellyn Kendall's steady hands.

"Going somewhere?" she asked with a sneer.

"So, did you find anything in those papers worth killing for?"

EIGHTEEN – Flight From Arrest

The Skyman slowly brought his hands up over his head. "I really would advise you to put that gun down, young lady." He wrestled with the idea of unmasking. But if he couldn't bring himself to do so for Fawn ...

Before the Skyman needed to make a decision about his secret identity, a vase came down with unnecessary force against the back of Ellyn's skull. The heiress' body slumped to the floor, revealing her attacker to be Fawn Carroll. Fawn's triumphant grin matched the Skyman's perfectly.

A crash came from downstairs, followed by another. "They just broke down the front door with backup coming through the kitchen," Fawn explained. "You must be pretty important."

"One would think. So you have a plan? You've been doing so well so far."

Fawn looked at the Skyman incredulously. "*You* are the costumed hero here. *You* come up with a plan!"

Glancing outside at J. Edgar Hoover's finest, the

183

Skyman said, "Well, if you wouldn't mind making a nuisance of yourself … just this once, of course."

* * *

Outside, Agent Cooper rushed up to Markley. "They're inside, securing the exits."

"Good," Markley said. "I want that broad in cuffs. And I don't even know what to do with that guy in the Halloween suit."

Cooper nodded. "Well, my guys scoured the vicinity. They just now found the vehicle he must have stolen from Allan Turner. And I don't want to draw any conclusions – I'll leave that to a jury. By the same token, no one's seen Carroll's wheels, but I'm sure she's around. What do you want to bet this clown and the broad came in the same car?"

Markley nodded. "Makes sense. Find anything else?"

With a grin, Cooper resisted the urge to rub his hands together triumphantly. "Well, I just happened to … 'accidentally' jimmy open the trunk on the car and …"

"And you … 'just happened' to find what?"

"Funny you should ask that …"

* * *

Two F.B.I. agents ran up the stairs to the second floor, guns drawn and aimed towards the steps.

"Hey, boys! How goes the day?"

Fawn Carroll stood at the top of the steps, her arms extended to cover the width of the stairwell. She smiled sweetly at the oncoming agents.

However, her charm was totally lost on the men. They slammed into her with enough force to almost knock her off her feet. All that kept her from landing on her backside was one of the agents seizing her by one arm and twisting it behind her back. By the time she gave an involuntary gasp of pain, both of her hands were forced behind her back and a pair of handcuffs clicked into place painfully around her wrists.

The agent growled in Fawn's ear, "Cooper says you can come downstairs quietly with me or if you give me any grief, I have permission to toss you out a window. Got a preference?"

Fawn flinched at the agent's name and the feel of the cuffs around her wrists filled her with overwhelming dread. For a heartbeat, she envisioned herself flying through the window towards a grove of trees that reached up with their sharp branches and the moon shining too brightly and tumbling towards that pond and the –

Recovering quickly, she saw another agent race up the steps. Moving past her, he turned at the top of the flight and sprinted up the stairway that led to the third floor.

I tried, Skyman, Fawn thought regretfully. *I really tried.*

Upstairs, the Skyman surveyed the third floor hallway. He thought of hiding in one of the rooms, but that would only be a delaying tactic. He could hear Fawn struggling with someone on the floor below and the sound of footsteps growing louder as they joined him upstairs.

Setting his jaw firmly, the Skyman ran into the nearest room and glanced outside. A volley of gunfire from the lawmen on the lawn greeted him and he pulled back, luckily uninjured. He ran into another room across the hallway and looked outside to see a couple of Feds, their rifles already aimed directly at him. A heartbeat later, bullets tore into the ceiling, but the Skyman was already on the run.

Waiting for the adventurer outside in the hallway was a G-man who braced himself to tackle the Skyman. However, the Skyman barreled into the Fed, lifting him off his feet and slamming him into the nearest wall. The man slid downward to the floor, dazed as his attacker sprinted into another room at the end of the hallway.

Taking stock of the guest bedroom furniture, the Skyman lifted a wooden chair with one hand and hurled it full force through the window. In reply, several bullets demolished the window frame. But by then, the Skyman had already vacated the room.

Stepping over the half-conscious agent in the hallway, the Skyman gritted his teeth and seized the sides of his cloak. Darting into another room, he accelerated towards the window and dove through it head-first.

Amidst an explosion of glass and wood, the Skyman opened his eyes and spread his arms wide. Feeling the early morning air fill the ribs of his cloak, the Skyman almost allowed himself a smile as he glided over the line of trees that rimmed the estate, to say nothing of the F.B.I. agents who watched incredulously, momentarily too surprised to use the man for skeet practice.

His momentum nearly spent, the Skyman drifted

beyond the estate wall, landing in the middle of the street gracefully. However, before he could make his escape, the Skyman found himself pursued by the G-men and the local police, each one to a man with their guns out and ready to open fire.

Before he could weigh his options, rapidly diminishing in number as they were, the fatigued Skyman found himself surrounded. Not far behind them, Markley ran towards the would-be fugitive.

Recognizing the odds against him, the Skyman dropped his grip on the cloak and quickly thrust his hands into the air. "I surrender," he called out.

Markley produced a pair of handcuffs from his jacket pocket and immediately immobilized the Skyman's wrists. "You are under arrest," the agent announced formally.

"And for what?" The Skyman didn't resist the two agents who each grabbed one of his arms. "What are the charges?"

"Possible conspiracy to commit the kidnapping of Dr. Peter Turner, possible conspiracy in the Second Degree Murder of Allan Turner –"

The Skyman wanted to vigorously refute the charges, but kept his silence. It wouldn't do to give any clues to his dual identity quite yet. "I'm innocent, but go on if you have more."

"Do I ever!" Markley took at step closer, but just beyond the potential reach of the Skyman's possible kick. "I'll bet your fingerprints are all over the steering wheel of a vehicle registered to Allan Turner that we just located. And then there's that thing in the trunk."

Swallowing hard, the Skyman realized the Stasimatic Ray device – the one he stole the night after his graduation to keep it out of unsympathetic hands – was housed in the rear of his car until he could bring it into the rented room for further development. However, events conspired against him before he cold relocate his invention.

"So, do you have anything to say for yourself? And just who the hell are you, anyway?" The agent tugged on the helmet, but it held itself steady against its wearer's head thanks to Allan's design skills. In fact, Markley couldn't even find the latch to the strap that kept the helmet firm against his face. Growling with frustration, the agent walked behind the costumed stranger.

Now instinctively struggling against his captors, however much in vain, the adventurer said, "I'm ... the Skyman ... I'll want a lawyer, but I promise I'll go with you quietly."

"You got that right, sky-boy." To punctuate his statement, Markley pulled out his service revolver and slammed the butt of it into the base of the Skyman's skull. Only the helmet's padding prevented the agent's attack from being a lethal one. Just the same, the Skyman sank to his knees, then fell onto his face.

Markley looked down at the unconscious man. "I said I wanted him alive. I didn't say a thing about wanting him awake."

NINETEEN – Inside the Room of Hell

Peter Turner couldn't eat a bite of his breakfast after hearing the wire recording two hours ago. He lay on his bunk, replaying the horrific events of the last day over and over again in his mind. To lose his freedom, to discover one of his unwanted bodyguards was a double agent for the Nazis, to have his work stolen and in enemy hands, to know his home was burned to the ground, and then learning of the demise of his only living relative in so short a time, the doctor felt his world blurring around the edges, becoming more unreal.

Just yesterday, Peter Turner couldn't imagine anything that could shake his confidence so thoroughly that he might lose all hope and will to live. Now, his fellow scientists walked alongside his sleeping space as they moved into the next large room, each man looking down at Turner with pity. Their hollow expressions almost seemed to whisper *Now you are one of us*.

Ignoring the rattling in his stomach, Peter barely heard

Albrecht Bruhner scream out, "*Gott in Himmel*! Stanislaus, to me now! And get Perkins! I've deciphered Turner's notes!"

Rising from his bed with the use of his cane, Turner moved towards the steam chamber. Many of the other kidnappees congregated in the hallway outside, most of them in some form of collective shock. Turner pushed his way through them to reach Bruhner who greeted his newest captive from on top of the walkway with a triumphant grin.

"Doctor Turner! You are the greatest genius of them all. I finally see the promise in your aircraft concept. What a deceptively simple design for such a complex device. But you spelled it all out down to the last rivet and wire. Absolutely amazing!"

"Which one?" Turner growled. "I come up with so much brilliance that it's difficult to keep track of all my ideas."

Bruhner laughed. "The Wing, my dear doctor."

In response, Turner's eyes went wide with fear. "No! You can't build that. It's never been tested."

"It doesn't need to be! Although my discipline is engineering, your schematics for the electronics makes perfect sense. And they are amazing!" Bruhner turned to

Stan and Perkins. "Mobilize the workers. I want three shifts, let the work be done around the clock."

Stan nodded. Professor Perkins looked fearfully at Bruhner and then at Turner, unable to decide whose expression was more frightening to behold.

Turner moved forward towards the stairs that led to the walkway. He knew he couldn't take the papers back, but perhaps he could shred the most valuable part of the schematics, the unique engine. However, in his excitement to foil Bruhner's plans, he momentarily overlooked the limitations of his infirmity. A younger man with no limp might have made it onto the steps easily in a short time. However, Turner hadn't been that man since the fiery death of his brother more than a decade before.

For his efforts, Turner made it to the bottom step only to meet a jet of concentrated steam. Blinded, unable to breathe, and his face and hands feeling as if they were afire, Turner dropped to the floor. By the time Turner could recover his senses, Stan had the scientist's arms pulled up hard behind his back painfully.

Perkins trembled with awe as he glanced over Bruhner's

shoulder at the blueprints. So concise, so matter-of-fact, the plans were almost a step-by-step tutorial on the machine's construction. "So when do you want construction to begin on this?"

"Tonight." He smiled cruelly down on Peter Turner. "And I want the doctor to watch his device come to life. No … *wait*!"

Bruhner took a lumbering step forward. "I want him to witness the birth of *two* of his amazing aircraft."

* * *

Peter Turner hadn't wept since the day his brother died. However, now that Allan seemed lost to him, he allowed the hot tears of regret to flow down his face without restraint once again.

The other prisoners now gave Turner a wide berth. When he could focus his gaze between bouts of depression, Turner saw their eyes reflect their acceptance of his new grief and of him. He nodded at them and they returned his gaze with a knowing look.

"We've all experienced this too."

Turner looked up to see a man sitting on the edge of the

next bunk. His beard was long with just the merest traces of what used to be a Van Dyke trim and his dark eyes hinted at his emotional exhaustion. "I've been here almost a year. The name's Carson, by the way. Doctor Kevin Carson. Turner, right?"

Nodding as he sat up, Turner shook Carson's hand.

"Bruhner's got a steam-boiler for a heart. He killed my friend right in front of my eyes. I think I died with her."

"She wasn't –?"

Carson chuckled, "Oh, no. She was a Fed assigned to keep me safe. I guess the good news was she didn't have to face her boss the next morning." He sighed. "So you and your nephew were the Edisons of the New Deal, huh?"

"That's what the yellow journalists called us. So Carson, what field of study landed you in here?"

Carson appeared to shrink visibly. "I can't tell you." His eyes grew fearful. "I'm part of a team of scientists that have found – well, we think we have a doomsday weapon."

"That's a pretty ambitious tool of destruction, Carson."

"You don't understand, Turner. This weapon is fueled by the energy that bonds all matter together. We might unleash

195

the most hellish explosion imaginable ... or we might crack the planet in half ... or set the atmosphere aflame. And unfortunately, the only way to know is to test it."

Turner sat up and gripped Carson's shoulder. The latter man calmed down visibly, but his voice still shook when he whispered, "We're miles away from construction of a prototype ... but I'm bound and determined to slow down the Nazis by dragging my heels as long as I can. I'll probably die in Berlin, but they'll never tear the secrets of my research from me." He sighed. "At least that's what I'm telling myself."

Turner allowed himself a cynical smile. "Seems like you're the last one to have any fight left in them."

Shaking his head, Carson said, "Almost all of us have scars from our mental torture ... starvings, noise, intimidation, physical abuse ... we've endured it all. Most of them are like Perkins ... zombies who don't know they've died inside. I heard he was one of the first nabbed." He looked around cautiously. "Be cautious. There's a room here. A steam room that you don't want to be taken to."

"I've gotten a couple of tastes of the guy's steam fetish

already," Turner said. "I can only imagine –"

"No, you can't! It's where he refuels that damned armor." Carson's eyes were wide with memories of his time inside Bruhner's private area. "He had it built just for him. He goes in and becomes more powerful ... we go in and we get a taste of Hell itself." The scientist gripped his own pants leg in a way that had it been his own flesh, he'd have screamed in agony.

"Oh, now you went and ruined the surprise."

Both scientists swung around to see Stan Lange standing at the doorway with his pistol in his hand. "Come on, Turner. The big man wants to have a talk with you."

Turner glanced at Carson who shook his head violently, as if anyone had a choice. Before Turner could move of his own volition, Stan grabbed him by the back of his shirt collar and pulled him to his feet and towards the steam chamber.

Barely able to keep pace with Stan and barely capable of walking unassisted, Turner stumbled, almost falling several times before they reached Bruhner's private quarters. Once there, Stan shoved Turner inside and slammed the vault door shut. A sadistic leer crept across his lips as he recalled his employer's instructions.

Stan switched on the wire recorder with a full-out grin and gently placed his thumb on the volume wheel of the wire recorder.

Pulling himself into a metal chair painfully, Peter Turner felt the oppressive lack of space inside this – what had to have once been a bank vault. From several apertures in the walls and ceiling, fresh steam wafted into the chamber. Already, he began loosening his collar, feeling the heat of the situation even before the temperature rose enough to be a concern.

On the other side of the chamber, Albrecht Bruhner sat in a sturdy maple chair that had obviously been shellacked so many times that the steam would have no way to reach the wood underneath. A series of hoses ran along a wall upon which Turner could see a series of gauges, each one containing an arrow that tickled the edge of a red-tinged wedge at the far end of a printed scale.

Similar tubing emerged from numerous apertures in the wall of gauges and found a home in similar openings along Bruhner's torso and shoulders. The conduits pulsed and jumped as the needles caressed the danger zone readings. Each surge of power turned the corners of the Prussian's lips upwards and his eyes rolled as if in the aftermath of ecstasy.

Turner could see another man in the farthest corner of the room. He was dressed from head to toe in what appeared to be a white rubber-coated suit that resembled a deep sea diving outfit. The only exception appeared to be that the headpiece was more form fitting than a standard diving helmet. Unable to identify the person inside, Turner noticed the man held one of the dreaded solid steam pistols in his steady hands.

Super-heated water issued from underneath the collar of Bruhner's suit. But instead of burning the wearer, the Prussian almost seemed to be comforted by the scalding vapors. He gave what Turner would have called the first sincere smile he'd seen on the madman's face.

"Please forgive the terseness of my invitation," Bruhner said in a tone that reminded the scientist of opium fiends. "But I've just received an opportunity to end my time in this barbaric country of yours and to fulfill my sacred mission."

"Sacred?" Turner could no longer restrain himself. "The

Nazi doctrine is filled with lunacy and hatred. I could do nothing to assist a program that kills thousands of people."

Bruhner grinned. "No, my dear Dr. Turner. It kills *millions*. And it will remove millions more undesirables from the face of the Earth before the flag of the Third Reich flies over every nation on the planet."

"I won't help you." Turner found renewed courage. "I have no loyalties to divide between my profession, my family, and my country. You've taken away everything I hold dear. I have nothing more to lose and nothing else to give."

The suited man turned several dials in sequence. The armor filled with steam, almost glowing yellowish-red from the heat coursing through it. "As for your assistance, I no longer care about that, thanks to your thorough blueprints."

At that moment, Turner's attention turned towards the gramophone speakers in the upper corners of the room. Now that he and Bruhner no longer exchanged words, the scientist heard the accursed broadcast of Tony Trent's where he and the nation learned of Allan's death. Then the broadcast was replayed again in a cruel Moebius Strip that grew slightly louder with every circuit through the wire recorder, accompanied by an added volume of steam that issued into the room.

Bruhner fixed his frigid gaze upon his captive. "Imagine laying in a hospital bed for fifteen years, trapped in a body that bled every time you moved, a body that couldn't take in a full breath without searing agony ... watching your family regard you like a cancer until all they could do was walk away ... compared to me, you have lost so very little, Doctor."

Before Turner could refute his jailer's statement, a blast of steam hit him in the face, stealing his next breath. He dropped to his knees and tried to cover his face, but the steam was too pervasive. Trying to take a breath in this room was like trying to breathe at the bottom of a pool filled with boiling water.

"Is the embrace of steam not glorious, Dr. Turner?" Bruhner said evenly. "Steam is clean and cleansing. It is part of the cycle of nature, from the skies to the ground to the rivers, to us, to steam, to the skies again. It doesn't stink like petroleum. It shall be the power of the future, despite what Carson seems to think of his mystery project." Bruhner closed his eyes, almost enraptured. "The pressure of the sacred steam fuels my motions and keeps me alive. And when my exertions expend its power, I have but to make more."

At the mention of Carson, his new ally, Turner pushed himself to his knees. He could now barely see Bruhner through the veil of heated water, but he hoped the steam engineer could see his defiant smile.

"Give up, Turner," Bruhner taunted. "Your home is gone, your nephew is dead, and your plans will ensure a Nazi ownership of the very skies themselves. You have no resources left to inspire your resistance."

With that, Turner inhaled sharply. For a moment, Bruhner watched in confusion before he realized what the scientist was doing. Despite the furious pain, Turner filled his lungs with the scalding vapors again and again.

"Stop!" Whether Bruhner meant Turner or his mysterious accomplice, it didn't matter. The oddly-garbed man rapidly gripped a series of large steel flywheels and spun them with all his might. Immediately, cool air from outside dispelled the thick clouds of steam, revealing Peter

Turner lying unconscious on the metal floor.

Bruhner scowled as the fresh air rolled over his face.

The figure began to unhook Bruhner from his recharging device. Muffled by his thick hood, the man said, "I told you he'd be stubborn. Thank goodness his nephew is such a milquetoast or we'd have some real problems." Unlike Bruhner, his voice was unaffected by any accent but his own American one.

Nodding, Bruhner stated, "I agree. I hope hearing the reports of his own death, as well as any form of good sense, will keep young Mr. Turner from doing something adventurous until we are ready to return to Berlin." He smiled up at the hooded man. "And I'd like to remind you that you will find yourself more than adequately compensated for your loyalty when we reach Berlin. Once we conquer North America, you shall be given control of this country to manage for the Third Reich."

"I look forward to it." The figure then crossed the room to unlock the chamber door. No sooner had the massive door swung open completely, Stan entered to drag Turner back to his cot.

Moving back to make certain the vents on Bruhner's armor were sealed, the figure pulled off his hood to take a fresh lungful of air. "You'll find my allegiance is as good as gold, specifically yours."

Bruhner stood up, reveling in the power of his armor. He watched his accomplice remove the protective suit and wondered if he now knew a man who gave up more of a claim to his own soul. *What would it take for a man to sell his reputation, his family, and his soul for the Fuhrer's gold? Some days, I can't tell which one of us in our bargain has truly made a deal with the Devil.*

* * *

Half an hour later, to no one's surprise, Peter Turner was still unconscious.

Kevin Carson found a spare handkerchief and used it as a cold compress atop Turner's forehead. Poor Peter's flesh was scarlet from the scalding, but Carson was certain there would be no lingering external effects, nothing more than first degree burns. He trickled cool water into Turner's open mouth, hoping to replace what his new friend had sweated away.

After an hour, Turner's eyes flickered open. He looked around and saw some of the scientists being herded into the next area by that thug Stan. Turner tried to rise, but his muscles failed him.

He glanced up at Carson. Stan called Carson's name and the man robotically rose to his feet without protest. His eyes mirrored how totally lost and forlorn the man felt inside ...

But Turner had no way of knowing the same expression now found a home in his own eyes.

* * *

A couple of weeks later, in Miles Rockwell's office, the regional supervisor reported to his superior in Washington, D.C. The phone sat heavy in his hand as he updated the main office on the progress in the Bruhner case.

"No, sir. Agent Markley reports that this 'Skyman' refuses to talk about the kidnapping or Allan Turner's disappearance. Yes, sir, Markley's tried everything short of horse-whipping the suspect to get him to confess. Yes, sir, we've allowed the man every convenience, within reason. No, sir, we would never descend to the level of our enemies, as tempting as that might be."

Miles listened to his connection in the nation's capital, nodding as he puffed on his pipe. "No, sir, we also have former agent Carroll in protective custody as well. But sir, we are honestly no closer to learning what happened to Dr. Turner than we were when we captured them." Miles placed the pipe in his ashtray.

"Sir, this Skyman not only denies any involvement in the Turner case, he has been almost pleading with Agent Markley for the Bureau's assistance to bring Bruhner to justice." He paused to weigh his next words. "I think he might be telling the truth, sir. Aside from the costume, he doesn't seem insane. Plus, there's something earnest, something quite believable about him.

"I may be risking my career by admitting this, but I honestly think he's telling the truth. Miss Carroll believes his tale and despite her record with the Bureau, I trust her judgment."

Miles listened to the static on the long distance line for what had to be the longest ten seconds of his life. Then the man on the other end said, "This drain on the nation's sciences is important enough that the Director himself has been taking an interest in this case, as have other parties here in D.C." The man's voice took on a darker tone. "And it's essential in the case of Dr. Kevin Carson that he is brought back alive ... or his demise confirmed beyond any doubt. Is that understood?"

"Not really," Miles admitted, "but yes, sir. If nothing else, considering the reports of other 'mystery men' in places like New York and overseas, I think it's worth considering that we have one who doesn't seek an adversarial relationship with law enforcement. We can always use someone who isn't hamstrung by rules and regs who'll fight the good fight."

"Good point, although you didn't hear me say that." After another pause, "Miles, keep the suspects on ice for another 24 hours. Someone will be by to interrogate this Skyman personally."

"May I ask who?"

After a chuckle, "You may ask, Mr. Rockwell, but let's just say it's someone with a higher security clearance than even J. Edgar himself. Put out the good china because you're having company tomorrow."

Miles blinked as he realized who that company probably would be. All he could think of to say was, "Yes, sir!"

TWENTY – "I Am Allan Turner!"

"**I** know for a fact that I didn't murder Allan Turner."

The Skyman sat in the same chair he'd sat in for several hours a day for ... how long had it been now? Since his arrest, time lost all meaning for him. *At least I paid for the hotel room until the end of the month*, he thought with a mirthless smile.

Every morning, or as close as the Skyman could figure it was, someone came into the cell to shackle his wrists and ankles together while he sat in a metal chair. As he waited for the usual interrogation, the Skyman took inventory of the techniques Agent Markley used to break his resolve and force a confession from him. Sleep deprivation, hunger, thirst, intimidation, threats, rewards ... *The only technique left might be removing my boots and tickling me with an ostrich feather until I confess.*

All attempts to learn the Skyman's civilian identity met with frustration on Markley's part. Even trying to catch the adventurer with the helmet off while he cleaned up in his cell resulted in consistently dismal results. Repeated searches couldn't reveal the location of the secret buckle that held the helmet tight against the Skyman's head. Markley, almost as weary and annoyed as his prisoner, threatened to slice off the mask at the throat more than once in the last couple of days.

However, the disguise remained securely on its wearer, even down to the reflective visor. The Skyman was sure this was a victory of sorts, but he wasn't certain how long he could continue to hold out. And yesterday, he reacted to the F.B.I. agent dropping Fawn's name, unwittingly giving the man a lever against him. The Skyman regretted letting his guard down, even for a moment, because he just handed Markley an advantage over him … and over Fawn too.

Speaking of advantages, Agent Cooper – the dirty rat fink – delivered a tray of food or some water once or twice a day. But since Allan saw him steal his uncle away, the Skyman didn't touch the offerings for fear of some kind of poison.

The lack of sleep, the lack of exercise – except for when he was alone in his ten-by-ten cell – the lack of decent food and water, the worry about Fawn, this all wore down the Skyman's physical and mental reserves.

Today, Markley entered the cell, locking himself inside with the prisoner. Dark circles framed his eyes and he'd given up on changing his shirt, shaving and combing his hair. He carried an apple in one hand ... a bright red, juicy, delicious apple, probably picked fresh this morning, or so the Skyman fantasized. A grumble from under his tunic reminded the Skyman that someone forgot breakfast today ... again.

Markley preformed the same motions as he'd done every day since the Skyman became a prisoner of the Bureau. The agent turned the other metal chair around to face his prisoner. Then he opened his sports jacket just before straddling the seat and lowering himself. Following that, Markley folded his arms, resting them on the back of the chair before dropping his chin onto his forearm and staring at his suspect.

"Well, here we are again." The Skyman forced himself to smile. "Tongues will wag if we keep seeing each other like this."

The agent smiled painfully as if trying to show any form

of pleasure was now as agonizing for him as it was for the Skyman. "The only tongue that needs to wag is yours, Skyguy." He took in a deep breath. "I don't ask for me. Just tell us about your role in Peter Turner's kidnapping, why you stole Allan Turner's device, why you killed him in the fire, what you were doing at the laboratory, and why you were driving Turner's car. Then we can all call it a day and go out for beers."

The Skyman sighed. He gave up correcting Markley's nickname for him two days before. At least he thought it was two days ago. Without any windows or regular schedule, he really had no way of knowing how fast time was passing in the outside world.

"Okay, in order – none, I didn't, I didn't, looking for Dr. Turner, and – oh, bother. Why am I holding out?"

Markley stood up. "What are you trying to say?"

The Skyman cleared his throat. "If I come clean, will you …?" His voice trailed off into a raspy whisper.

"I promise," Markley took a step towards the Skyman. "She'll be freed. You'll have to answer for your actions, but I promise we'll let her go and I'll personally ask the judge to take your cooperation into account." The agent spoke in almost kindly tones. "Now what is it you want to say?"

"This isn't easy ..." He looked up at Markley. "I can answer most of your questions ... because I ... I am Allan Turner."

Markley narrowed his eyes. "You are saying that you are Allan Turner?"

The Skyman dropped his head and whispered in defeat, "Yes, I am Peter Turner's nephew."

Markley rose to his full height. "Bull."

"Huh?" The Skyman looked up.

"What kind of idiot do you take me for?" Markley kicked the wall out of sheer frustration. "Your fingerprints were all over the car's interiors."

"Small wonder. My fingerprints are the same as Allan Turner's."

Markley grinned evilly. "That's impossible. No two men have the same fingerprints. Besides, my man Cooper identified one of the corpses in the lab that you were seen in as belonging to Turner."

"Yeah, he did, didn't he?" The Skyman felt adrenalin

flooding his body, anger regenerating his strength. "I've been waiting for a chance to talk to you about him."

"Oh, I'm sure you have. Divide and conquer, huh?" Markley loosened his tie. "Here's the theory I'm working on: you're working for that Bruhner guy from Germany."

"The man in the armor with all the scars?" The Skyman winced as he involuntarily recalled the speed and strength of the man.

"That's the one and you know it." Markley paced the cell in front of the Skyman. "Somehow, Bruhner found out about Turner's invention. He sent you to steal it."

Skyman smirked. "This should be good. Why did he ask me instead of doing it himself?"

"You could do it more quietly. I watched you break into the Kendall mansion two weeks ago. I know you can move pretty silently."

The Skyman's mouth fell open. "Two weeks? Two weeks I've been here?" He shook his head, his thoughts only on Fawn Carroll, an inquisitive woman who wound up getting caught up in his game of being a "mystery man." Guilt gripped the Skyman's heart in an icy clutch and squeezed slowly.

"Now if I may go on," Markley said, warming up to his narrative, "you rented the room under Turner's name. Pieces of material for your costume was found in the bathroom and the fingerprints in the apartment matched those found in the stolen auto. Anyway, at some point after his uncle was kidnapped, you stole Turner's car, put the Stasimatic Ray Emitter into the trunk, broke into the lab, and blew open the safe. That's when Turner died, probably trying to stop you."

Skyman dropped his head in frustration. "No, Cooper told you that. He's a double agent."

Ignoring the accusation, Markley continued, "There were three dead bodies after the safe was blown. One was a fireman, one was Allan Turner, and the third was Agent Steve Kraddock." Markley leaned in close. "If it wasn't for due process, I'd be expressing my feelings about murdering a federal law enforcement agent, to say nothing about that man being a member of my team." Markley grabbed the apple and flung it against the wall, transforming the fruit into pulp. "Besides, Turner was a very smart young man. He wouldn't be caught dead in a ridiculous costume like yours.

Hell, you don't even sound like that milksop."

The Skyman strained to remain in his chair. "Of course Turner would be caught dead in this uniform because he's not dead to begin with because he's ME! And YOU are so bound and determined to use me as a scapegoat for your wrongheaded theory that you are ignoring the real facts of this case!" The Skyman tried to calm himself. "Here's what really happened."

From taking the Stasimatic Ray device – because "I didn't trust anyone with the prototype" – to witnessing Peter Turner's kidnapping, Allan's failed pursuit, investigating the crime scene, the fire and fight at the lab, and then the break-in at the Kendall estate, the Skyman related the events of his last day of freedom, still omitting any further clues to his true identity apart from his confession. However, he no longer even cared to continue his disguise any longer, not if it would help Fawn. So if he had to …

"Nice tale, kid." Markley shrugged. "But if you think I'm gonna believe some costumed goof over a trained F.B.I. Agent like Cooper, you are so very wrong."

The Skyman put on his sweetest smile. "If you promise

not to ventilate me if I make a strange move, let me have one hand free so I can remove my helmet slowly as you watch. Then after I backhand you a couple of times, just for fun, you'll see that under my mask, I am –"

"Hey, Markley." Agent Cooper stood outside the bars. "I'm gonna grab some lunch. Can I bring you back anything?"

Markley locked his hateful stare upon the Skyman. Without looking up, Markley said, "Naw, I'm okay."

The Skyman looked up at Cooper. Seeing that Markley had his back turned, Cooper grinned maliciously at the Skyman who tilted his head to see the rogue agent more clearly.

"See you later ..." Cooper elevated his flattened palm until it almost touched the ceiling in an imitation of a perfect Nazi salute. "... Skyman."

Then he mouthed with a sick grin, "*Seig heil*," before leaving the holding area, the floor, and then the building itself.

Skyman gritted his teeth. He turned to Markley, "Okay, bring me papers to sign. I'll confess to anything. I'll remove the helmet. I'll dance like we're in an MGM musical. Just let Fawn go. She's innocent."

Markley chuckled. "She's worse than innocent. She's an embarrassment as a field agent and as your accomplice. I can't wait to slam the jail door shut on her myself."

At that moment, several pair of footprints approached the cell from the far end of the outside hallway. Markley turned around just as Miles Rockwell walked up to the bars. The supervisor produced a copy of the key that rested in Markley's pocket and slid it easily into the lock. One turn later, the door opened without even a squeak.

"Everyone out who isn't clapped in irons," Miles hiked a thumb towards the exit. "I've got a special interrogator taking your spot, Markley."

The agent moved towards his supervisor. "And I have a partner who needs a little justice. Give me a few more minutes and I'll get the truth out of him."

"You've had three weeks to –"

Skyman cried out, "Three weeks? You told me two, you jerk."

Markley smiled. "Time flies when you're having fun."

"Shut it, Markley." Miles led his agent from the cell. "Get a coffee and don't come back until you're sent for. That's an order."

Markley almost shook with anger. "No offense, sir, but your order –"

"It's not my order," Miles interrupted. "It comes from the highest authority you can possibly imagine."

The door at the end of the hallway swung open and in walked four bodyguards, one of whom pushed a wheelchair containing the special visitor. Miles turned to see Markley's shocked expression as he recognized the man, the cigarette holder, the wire-rimmed glasses.

Sitting in the wheelchair was the President of the United States of America.

"What suicide mission are you sending me on?"

TWENTY-ONE – An Exchange of Secrets

Miles pushed Markley back so the President

could be wheeled to the doorway of the cell. The man in the wheelchair looked up and stated, "You can leave now. I'll call when we've concluded our talk."

Nodding, Miles left with Markley close behind. The Secret Service men followed until they reached the end of the hallway. At that point, only the F.B.I. men exited the floor. The others took up positions in the hallway to prevent anyone from entering the area, each man's hand resting somewhere near their handguns.

The President wheeled himself into the cell. The Skyman cocked his head to one side, unable to believe what he was seeing. "If you are who I believe you are –"

"Then you're one up on me," The President stated with a grin, "because I have no idea who you are." His expression turned serious. "Young man, it seems you've caused quite a bit of trouble."

"Actually, sir, I've been doing my best to minimize it,

221

however unsuccessfully." The Skyman found his easy smile returning as he rattled his metallic bonds. "I would stand up if I could."

"So would I." The easy smile faded as the President took a long pull on his cigarette. "They say I'm a pretty good judge of character. Plus, I have a great interest in one of the scientists. He's working on something that could spell the end of the war."

Under his visor, the Skyman's eyebrows shot up. "War, sir?"

The President nodded. "I fear its inevitability. You know there's a madman in Europe who subscribes to some kind of 'Master Race' garbage ... thinks he's part of a twisted heritage that allows him to do away with anyone that doesn't share the same ancestry or his bigotry. He's rounding up and murdering Jews, gypsies, homosexuals and the handicapped." The last word stuck in the President's throat.

The Skyman nodded towards the wheelchair. "Accident?"

"Polio. Son, I am not ashamed of what's happened to me, but for the sake of every American, possibly everyone

222

in what's remaining of the free world, I must not appear in any way weak. Hitler's venomous propaganda tears into people who if they possess any physical flaw, they are singled out for ridicule. Thus, I must never be seen as flawed or infirm. My glasses are the only concession I'll make to that bastard or else I'd roll right right into a wall."

The two men shared a chuckle. Then the President continued, "As I said, there's a scientist from the midwest who is helping develop a weapon that will change the face of warfare forever. Unfortunately, so are *their* scientists. We've got to get ours done first. As for the other scientists that have been captured, we'll need every genius we can muster … just in case."

"I have a personal concern about one of the kidnapped men, myself," the Skyman confessed.

"Peter Turner? The one who disappeared just before you showed up?" The Skyman nodded and the President smiled. "Met him once when I was campaigning in '36. Good man."

"I think so too," the Skyman said softly. "The best."

The President shifted in his wheelchair. "So tell me what you know."

From the theft of the knockout ray to Cooper's farewell salute, the Skyman quickly retold the story he'd just related to Agent Markley, however with the same omissions concerning his civilian identity.

The President pondered the story, weighing the Skyman's version of the events. "That's not how Agent Cooper reported it at all. However, if he's working for Bruhner, I can see how he bamboozled his immediate supervisor. Markley trusted Cooper as he trusts all his men." The President turned to consider the Skyman, specifically his masked face. "Just as you are asking me to trust you."

Without hesitation, the Skyman said levelly, "I'll unmask for you right now, if you'd like. If I can't trust you, sir, who can I trust?"

The President tilted back his head to laugh. "And your offer just earned you that trust, young man. No, keep the mask on." The smile left the Chief Executive's face and his eyes reflected the inner strength needed to lead the 48 States. "Not all wars are fought on foreign soil. There is a war on good people being waged every day on the streets of this great nation. I need soldiers I can rely on to wage that fight

224

so I can concentrate on other matters more global in scale. Can I trust that once you find Peter Turner that you won't hang up the outfit in your closet and let it collect dust?"

"Just as you can trust me to keep your secret, Mr. President. But the police –"

"The police can't do it alone. Sometimes, it takes people who will work beyond the rules of the system, writing their own script as the need arises. It takes a special kind of courage and integrity to operate that way, often without profit or advantage as a result."

Skyman nodded. "My rewards aren't anything any man or woman can give me."

"Then why do you do it, son?" The President leaned forward. "What drives you to put on this costume and do what you do?"

For a moment, the Skyman relived that nightmare moment when the airplane carrying his parents slammed into the Earth, killing them both instantly. He remembered the reports of substandard materials utilized, the profit of their use going directly into some manufacturer's pocket. The Skyman pushed those images from his mind's eye and spoke honestly the first thought that entered his mind.

"I do it because it's the right thing to do, sir."

Without a heartbeat's hesitation, the President called out to his nearest bodyguard, "Summon Miles and tell him to bring a key for these cuffs." As the footsteps faded down the hallway, the President turned back to Skyman. "I've read police reports on shadows, bats, lamas, avengers, hornets, whisperers, and bronze men, all seemingly working for the common good. And here I am, encouraging another flamboyant do-gooder."

"Yes, you are," the Skyman agreed with a grin, "and I'm rather sorry now that I wasn't old enough to vote for you last time."

"With any luck," the President said with a smile, "I'll never give you another chance."

Miles burst into the hallway, the Secret Service men close on his heels. Even before he crossed the threshold of the jail cell, he had the key for the Skyman's cuffs out and ready to use. A couple of seconds later, the adventurer was free and rubbing his wrists to restore circulation.

"The Skyman and I have reached an understanding," the

President told Miles. "I want every resource at our disposal to be given to this young man until we learn what became of Bruhner and his plot."

"Will do, sir. Anything else?"

The President grinned. "Now that you mention it, yes." He reached into his inside jacket pocket and withdrew a slip of paper, one that was folded over a couple of times. The President handed it to the Skyman with a slight smile.

Skyman opened up the paper, giving it a quick study. "I'm not familiar with this telephone exchange."

"That's because very few people have it," the President explained with a wink. "If you have anything – and I mean anything – that you need, you call that number and I'll make things happen. My apologies for your incarceration, Skyman." Almost as if cued, a Secret Service man guided the President's wheelchair out of the cell. "Miles, keep me posted. Happy hunting, gentlemen."

With that, the President of the United States of America took his leave. The Skyman and Miles stared at each other until they heard the door close at the end of the hallway.

Miles asked the Skyman. "So what's our first move?"

The Skyman rose slowly to his feet. It felt good to stretch after these sessions. Knowing he wouldn't be interrogated again made the feeling even better. "First of all, I want Fawn Carroll freed."

Miles stated, "I took the liberty of sending Markley to do just that. He'll have her here in five minutes or less."

"Good," The Skyman said with a mean smile, "he should find that task particularly unpleasant. Next, I may need an agent I can count on."

"I have just the man in mind. What else?"

The Skyman crossed his arms. "I want Agent Cooper brought here. Can I borrow a bright light and a rubber hose?"

Miles frowned. "Did I hear him say he was heading to lunch?"

"Yeah, you did. And whatever he's having, what do you want to bet it's steamed?"

TWENTY-TWO – When Like Minds Meet

After he exited the holding cells, Foster Cooper left the evidence impound area with the keys for Allan Turner's automobile. Less than five minutes later, Cooper merged the stolen vehicle into the highway traffic that moved towards the opposite side of town.

With a speed born of constant practice, Cooper reached into his jacket pocket and pulled out what appeared to be a tiny radio, albeit one with a very ornate latticework of stainless steel that wrapped around the small box. He pressed a button and felt the steam building up inside.

Five seconds later, Professor Perkins' voice came through with the clarity of water from a brook. "Y-yes?"

"This is Cooper. The Skyman is about to break, I believe, and my infiltration might be compromised. Tell Herr Bruhner that I'm bringing Allan Turner's invention with me. If it's not in Dr. Turner's plans already, perhaps it can be taken apart and studied."

"Y-yes, sir. Is there anything else?"

"Of course there is," Cooper said with genuine anger. "Have Lange meet me at the intersection of Upper Eleventh and Washington. We will transfer the device and leave Turner's car for the authorities to find." He smiled cruelly. "Did you get all of that, moron?"

Perkins began his reply with a stutter that had gotten worse in the last month. "Y-y-yes, sir. I will tell Herr Bruhner immediately. Will that be all, sir?"

"Yes. Cooper out." He thumbed the radio back into its usual dormant state and dropped it back in his pocket. The radio – in fact, all of Bruhner's inventions – worked so efficiently, Cooper believed he might become an acolyte in the First Church of Steam after all.

Just as Cooper parked Turner's vehicle, Stan pulled up in his own. In less than a minute, the Stasimatic Ray device rested in the other car's trunk and the former F.B.I. agent was on his way to become a major component of the American arm of the Nazi Party.

Fortunately, Stan was not a man of many words. This gave Cooper time to contemplate his life on the drive back to the base and how he reached this point. He'd graduated the

230

head of his class in college, but was paid the same as any agent who barely knew which end of the rifle to aim. So when he investigated the possible architect of the plan to steal America's top scientific minds and was made a substantial offer to look the other way, Cooper pounced on it.

The same talent for subterfuge and duplicity that helped him find Bruhner was even more appreciated by his new Prussian employer. The man was a brilliant engineer and an equally canny manager of talent. He respected Cooper's skills in manipulation and fact-twisting. As a result, the now-former agent possessed a Swiss Bank account that appropriately reflected Bruhner's appreciation.

Cooper didn't know what possessed him to taunt that costumed clown as he did. But in any case, he told himself that it was good practice because the next time he stepped outside of Bruhner's base, he would be on his way to Germany to collect his reward from Adolf Hitler personally.

* * *

"Okay, what do you mean she's putting on her face?" Miles rolled his eyes as he almost chewed through the bit of his pipe. He placed it in a borrowed ashtray before he did further damage. "That sounds too much like her."

Markley shrugged his shoulders and shook his head. "I have no idea, sir," he said with resignation. "I told her to hurry up and she replied with some words even I won't say."

The Skyman pouted. It had been almost a month since they'd been incarcerated and the trail to Albrecht Bruhner was cold enough to grow icicles. Perhaps Fawn didn't feel the same fire to solve this case as she once did. Maybe she wrote off finding Peter Turner once it sank in that Allan Turner "died."

"Well, she'll come in here when she's ready, I guess." Miles pulled out a pouch of tobacco from his pocket, ready to refill his pipe. "She's a private citizen and has been for well over a year. There's no way I can order her around."

"Who could?" The Skyman found himself grinning, appreciating her fire and zest for life.

At that moment, Fawn Carroll entered the office. If anyone doubted that she had mellowed since becoming a prisoner of the Bureau, all doubts vanished like morning dew when she threw herself at the Skyman and hugged him like a life preserver in the middle of the ocean. "Skyman!!! You're alive!"

Unable to stop grinning, the Skyman studied Fawn closely. Her hair was a little longer, of course, and she probably lost a few pounds too. Then again, her keeper was Cooper and he could only imagine what indignities she suffered to prevent him from taking advantage of her helplessness. Probably the same kind of near-starvation he'd practiced on the Skyman.

Fawn's big brown eyes absolutely glowed at the sight of the Skyman. "So what's new, hero?" she asked. The thought of kissing Fawn crossed his mind at that moment as he wondered if she shared that notion as well.

"Are you two done?" Markley grumbled. "Some of us might like to get some serious law enforcement done here."

Fawn and the Skyman disengaged, still grinning like high schoolers. The Skyman cleared his throat. "Well, we have a lot of ground to regain. They've had most of a month to build some of ... Doctor Turner's inventions." The adventurer silently congratulated himself for catching his potential *faux pas*.

"Any ideas?" Miles asked.

"Yes," the Skyman and Fawn answered in unison. Their grins returned for a few seconds. Fawn added, "We've had time to contemplate our possible strategies. Right, Skyman?"

"Indeed, Fawn." The Skyman began to pace the office. "So let's start with Cooper. Chances are when he left the building, he left the Bureau too."

Fawn nodded in agreement. "I wonder if he took his car or stole someone else's. My guess is he's in a stolen vehicle because it buys him some time."

"Good thinking." The Skyman turned to Markley and Mills. "Can we check to see if anyone's car is missing from this facility, other than possibly Cooper's?"

"Hold on," Markley offered. "I can see the parking lot from here." He almost jumped towards the window that overlooked the parking lot. "There's assigned parking," he explained. "Cooper's car is still parked where it's supposed to be." He looked outside again. "My guess is every car is where it needs to sit." A thought crossed the agent's mind. "Hmm, maybe all but one." He snapped his fingers and reached for the telephone on Miles' desk.

"Hey, Cindy, it's Reg," Markley said to the building's telephone operator. "Listen, I need a quick favor. Call Jack in the impound bay. See if we're missing anything or anyone and give me the list. Yeah, phone me right back." With that, Markley hung up the receiver, keeping one hand on it for when it rang again.

The Skyman nodded his approval.

Fawn volunteered, "I'll wager Cooper dumps the car as soon as he can. He wouldn't want to take a risk on someone tracking him back to his home base. What do you want to bet he's going to lie low until it's time to flee the country? At least that's what I'd do."

Miles asked, "Where do you think the base might be?"

The Skyman called up the facts he'd reviewed every day for the last three weeks. "If I was Bruhner, I would want to keep a close eye on my hostages, right? How many does he have by now?"

"With Turner, call it seventeen," Miles said. "Got to love those prime numbers."

"Okay, he's going to need a big place that can house his prisoners and his goons." The Skyman rubbed his hands together as he paced. "Plus, it's got to be fairly close. Look at how johnny-on-the-spot Bruhner and his henchmen were on the night of the kidnapping and the fire." He turned towards Fawn. "Our interference that night and the next day – he couldn't have been too far away to react as swiftly as he did."

Fawn stepped in front of the Skyman, interrupting his circuit around the room. "He's got almost two dozen people to transport back to Germany. Plus, Bruhner had to enter this country somehow. With that cast iron girdle of his, either flying or taking a boat would have raised questions. He's not an easy guy to sneak into a party, you know."

"He had his own aircraft?" Markley ventured, his hand still resting on the phone.

"Smart boy," Fawn said with a genuine smile. "With the usual fanatic's optimism, I'll bet it wasn't exactly an autogyro that made it from Berlin."

Miles decided he'd waited long enough and refilled his pipe. "Let me ask this question: how do we know Bruhner hasn't left the country already?"

Markley spoke with an edge in his voice. "Cooper was

a very thorough guy. How he put together the clues of the case to keep me off his back and on Skyman's proves that." He deliberately avoided looking at the costumed man. "If I know him at all, he didn't leave here without a place to hole up and a plan to get him out of the country."

"Also," the Skyman added, "Bruhner is an engineer. All the ones I've ever met plan thoroughly, to say nothing of hating loose ends and leaving things to chance." It was a trait Allan Turner shared with his uncle, a thought that gave the Skyman a brief smile. "No, Cooper would have been an insider with knowledge of Bruhner's operations. So the engineer wouldn't have left Cooper behind, if only to ensure the guy wouldn't start blabbing when he got arrested. And he will be, mark my words."

"You got that right," Fawn said with equal conviction. "And when we catch him, I'm going to kick Bruhner so hard, his grandkids won't be able to sit down." She smiled. "Something else to consider … let's assume Cooper's aware that he sold out his country. The only place he can be certain he'll find sanctuary is with Bruhner."

The Skyman completed Fawn's thought. "Thus Bruhner

hasn't left for Germany quite yet."

"I'm surrounded by so many clever men," Fawn said in her best Southern Belle accent. "A girl could just get the vapors, she could."

At that moment, the phone rang. Before the bell could finish sounding, Markley pulled the receiver to his ear. "Markley here." He listened, grunting occasionally to signify his understanding of whatever he was told by the other person on the line. Finally, he said, "Okay, thanks. I'll pass it on," before hanging up.

"Cindy just said Cooper just left Impound. The only things gone are Allan Turner's car, the keys to start it, and that device he was hiding in the trunk."

"The Stasimatic Ray." The Skyman stroked his chin as he thought aloud. "But it doesn't have the range or precision yet to be effective as a weapon. What good does it do them right now?"

Fawn remembered the demonstration in the Turner lab. "If Bruhner takes the device home, he'll have enough leisure time to solve the problems Turner didn't have a chance to." She imagined an airplane shining a ray that could knock out

238

entire regiments before a shot could be fired. *Those brave guys would be easy pickings for the enemy*, a thought that left Fawn shuddering.

In between puffs where the flame from his match disappeared into the bowl, Miles said, "So we – believe Bruhner is still here – in America – possibly in town – so how do – we find him?"

Silence filled the room. Each person looked to the other, hoping someone else had the answers to too many unresolved questions.

Then slowly, a smile crossed the Skyman's lips. Fawn, Miles and Markley watched him quizzically. "Okay," Fawn said, taking a step towards the Skyman, "you know something we don't?"

"Nope, not yet," the Skyman said with a sly grin, "but we have the facilities to learn. Or should I say the utilities?"

"Just let Fawn go. She's innocent."

Brian K. Morris

TWENTY-THREE – The Light of Freedom Dimmed

Peter Turner stared directly at the work in
front of him, but his focus was at a point somewhere between
there and infinity.

Stan Lange handcuffed the scientist into the usual chair
that overlooked the work area, but the thug suspected Turner
no longer had the will to move under his own direction.
Every day, Stan gave the scientist his crutch and then led him
from his bed to this chair where he was cuffed to the metal
arms except when he managed to feed himself. Then it was
back to the bunk where he fell asleep almost immediately.

*I guess a few sessions in the "steam room" will do that
to you,* Stan reasoned. He would have to admit that he rather
enjoyed dragging people into Bruhner's personal chambers.
It proved amusing to watch the evolution of the Steam
Master's victims from rebellious to frightened to completely
broken physically, mentally and spiritually.

And it worked every time, regardless of the so-called
intellects of the victims. When he returned in triumph from

241

Germany, Stan considered installing one in his home turf, just for giggles.

To his credit, Turner held out longer than most people. But it wasn't so much the pain of the steam that broke him as the sound of that newsreader talking about his nephew dying. Only whatever higher power that might exist could tell if Turner would recover, assuming he learned the truth, that the boy took it on the lam.

But until then, the scientist would simply sit in his chair and watch the workers go about their duties, constructing Turner's winged creation for Bruhner and his Nazi masters. The guy didn't talk, didn't react to any loud noises – of which there were many – nor did he reply when someone asked him a question. Turner was pretty much a dead man. Only his body hadn't gotten the news yet.

Looking out into the hangar/work area, the kidnapped scientists worked alongside the drifters picked up in the downtown area. A little domestic cash accompanied by reminders of lean times from only a few years before, and Bruhner had a reasonably dedicated workforce who didn't care where the money came from. They now had reasonable housing, great food and good money in exchange for not leaving until the work was done.

And the hardest worker was Albrecht Bruhner himself. He could lift more than anyone thanks to his steam-driven armor and he certainly had the most motivation to succeed. After all, these Wing aircraft meant riding back to his home as a conqueror-to-be. Who could say no to that?

Former F.B.I. agent Foster Cooper entered the work area. "How goes it, Stan?"

The hired muscle's only reply was to shrug. Stan wouldn't admit it openly, but Cooper made him nervous. He and Roove switched teams for money, just like any professional, but at least they couldn't claim to have been on the side of the angels like this guy could. The thugs might have been made men, but at least they weren't turncoats.

Cooper moved to Stan's side, watching the workers move as if inside an ant colony constructed from concrete, cinder blocks and steel. In the midst of the activity stood Bruhner, his bulk effortlessly moving some of the larger pieces of equipment as well as other objects that would take three or more men to transport. As the twin aircrafts took shape, he almost seemed to work faster and demanded that his vassals struggle harder to keep pace with him.

Two men died at Stan's hands last week when they accidentally learned who supplied their money and thought to rebel. Five more died from the exertion of fulfilling Bruhner's wishes. Right now, they were in storage and would be disposed of later.

"You know what I'm looking forward to most?" Cooper asked. "No longer having to say 'please'. I'm so sick of that word." He smiled at Stan. "So what's on your shopping list?"

The man shrugged again. "I just want to work for a mob that'll give me whatever I want. I guess I'm just waiting for payday."

Glancing out into the work area again, Cooper saw four men strain under the weight of a device he'd never seen before. It was taller than any man in the building by at least a foot and wrapped with piping of various diameters. Stan noticed that Herr Bruhner stared at the machine with an oddly fearful expression.

One of the workers stumbled, forcing the other laborers to compensate for his awkwardness. While the device didn't touch the concrete floor, the sight of the men treating this machine with less than total reverence appeared to drive Bruhner into a frenzy.

Closing the distance between himself and the machine in a jet-propelled instant, Bruhner picked up one corner of the device and then backhanded the offending worker with all his might. Both Cooper and Stan could tell the man was dead before his body struck the ground.

"Get busy with connecting the engines," Bruhner ordered. "Leave this to me." As the men hastened to obey their command, the Master of Steam picked up the machine easily and carried it into the closest Wing with no more effort than any other man would lift a shoebox filled with feathers. He turned back towards the others before they moved beyond earshot. "And clean up this garbage." With a nod, he indicated the corpse on the floor.

Stan and Cooper watched Bruhner disappear into the aircraft. The former agent whistled before saying, "Remind me not to cheese off the boss."

Stan smiled slyly. "Only if you'll remind me to ask him if he'll make me one of those suits."

Cooper chuckled as he surveyed the work area. The pair of Wings were amazing aircraft. Each one appeared to be a flying wedge of scarlet metal. A sizable cockpit and fuselage, both painted in blue, rested under the massive airfoil. Two propellers clung to the rear of the Wing but didn't appear to be large enough to push the massive aircraft down a runway, much less keep it in the air.

"So what's the plan for these things?" Stan asked. "Bruhner's been too busy to do more than just bark orders the last three weeks for us to have a chat."

"He'll let us know. But who'd have thought he'd not only get one Wing ready for test flight, but a second one too?"

"He definitely makes things happen." Stan glanced over at Peter Turner. "Hate to leave good company, but I'd better get zombie boy back to his cot. It'll be time for dinner soon." He sighed. "At least the veg can still feed himself."

Stan tapped the scientist on the shoulder. Turner rose to his feet, as always, without challenge, without comment. His eyes stared at something a universe away that only he could see.

Meanwhile, inside the cargo bay of one of the Wings,

Albrecht Bruhner fastened the final length of tubing from his machine to the exhaust vents. Instead of using any tools, Bruhner tightened the connections with his machine-augmented hands.

He then turned a series of valves on the back of the device. He could hear fluid pouring through the copper-lined pathways inside the machine to a pair of mixing chambers. Next, Bruhner turned a flywheel that only his massive strength could move. The music of steam flowed through the device like its own lifeblood. A gauge reported the pressure building inside the machine, leaving a thin red needle teasing the edge of the overload zone.

For the first time in the better part of a month, Bruhner allowed himself a moment to feel proud of his handiwork. In nearly two years, he'd stolen America's greatest intellects and mobilized an army of workers who unwittingly labored on the instruments of their country's inevitable defeat.

For a moment, Bruhner imagined himself at the *Krolloper*, hearing his name called by *der Fuhrer* himself. Bruhner would walk respectfully towards the new leader of the world and bow his head as a medal attached to a crimson ribbon was placed around his neck, signifying him as a hero to the German Republic.

The Prussian glowed with pride. He left Germany a scarred nobody in whom only Adolf Hitler had any faith in his mission. Now, Bruhner would return as a hero.

Once the engines were installed, his armor charged one last time, and his special ally entered the building, Bruhner would become the Steam Master of the Heavens. The very thought of Adolf Hitler officially conferring that title on him before an audience of the Nazi elite filled him with a heat that rivaled the steam that insulated and empowered him.

* * *

"Oh boy, it's Soft Food Day. I'll be back to pick up your plate in fifteen minutes," Stan told Peter Turner as he did every breakfast, every lunch, and every dinner. "Eat hearty."

Stan's footsteps echoed off the stark stone walls of the dormitory. Once Stan strolled out of sight, Turner mentally counted to ten, his senses fully extended and alert as the light of intelligence returned to his expression.

Slowly eating the soft corn meal and overcooked garden vegetables on his plate, Turner fought back his tears of fury.

248

On top of all his losses, the very idea of his inventions being used to attack America made his stomach churn. But he couldn't fight back. He had no weapons, his physical strength was ebbing due to a lack of nourishment and exercise, and he had no allies that he could rely upon. Even Carson served his shift without resistance or complaint now and the two hadn't talked since Turner began his pretense a week earlier.

But what else could he do?

After his last bout in the steam chamber, which brought Turner perilously close to truly dying from the heat, Turner decided to fake his chronic fatigue. It was tough maintaining the facade every waking hour of the day, but the doctor clung to the hope that rescue was at hand. Someone had to be looking for him, he was certain of that.

Oh, poor, poor Allan, he thought. Although he knew it was as impossible as Orson Welles being named Ambassador to Mars, Turner halfway expected Allan to burst into the building, an army at his heels, ready to save everyone and put Bruhner's plans to rout.

But in lieu of that miracle, all Turner could do was bide his time and wait for something, anything, he could do to foul up the plans. He allowed his features to go slack, his eyes to lose any hint of will or intelligence.

If nothing else, perhaps an opportunity to sabotage the special engines would arise once they were over the ocean. Right now, it seemed to be Turner's best chance to be reunited with his nephew, albeit in the Afterlife.

TWENTY-FOUR – Water, Water Everywhere

Markley laid the last wooden crate on Miles'

desk. "And they want them back when you're done."

"I'll return them personally with a pretty pink bow around each one," the Skyman announced as he rose from his chair. After a full lunch in Fawn's company, the man felt virtually rejuvenated after nearly a month's imprisonment. Just being able to speak to someone other than Markley felt like a stroll through paradise. The fact that his company was someone as intelligent and sweet and downright gorgeous as Fawn Carroll almost made up for the indignities he'd suffered and the frustrations of losing Bruhner's trail.

Almost.

"You?" Markley smirked. "You'd scare the nice secretaries there out of their curls. I'll do it, okay?" The agent wiped his hands on his jacket. "So what are we looking for?"

"Yes," Miles said as he dropped his unlit pipe into his shirt pocket. "What are we doing with the water bill of every user in the city?"

The Skyman explained his reasoning earlier. Apparently, the G-men needed a reminder of the long shot they were pursuing.

"It's really quite simple, but it'll be a bit of work. We know that the hideout is close, probably within the city limits because of how quickly Bruhner and his henchmen could appear on the scene in reaction to our intervention on the night of the kidnapping and fire."

"Makes sense so far," Markley admitted. He removed his jacket and hung it carefully on the back of a chair.

"It gets better," the Skyman said. "We know that there's going to be at least 21 people under one roof – Bruhner, Cooper, one or two muscle-for-hires, and the seventeen kidnapped scientists. They're going to use quite a bit of water for washing, cooking, any number of things."

Miles removed his own jacket in anticipation of the work to come. "What about phoning the grocery stores to see if they're selling extra Wheetabix and where they're delivering it?"

Fawn spoke up, "Those Nazis are probably smart enough to either have their food deliveries sent to a dummy address or brought in from out of town. Perhaps the goons buy supplies in smaller, less suspicious quantities. Too many aspects we can't track easily."

The Skyman smiled proudly at Fawn. "Right you are. But water, that's the one thing they have to have and can't haul in the quantities they'd need just to stay alive."

Markley nodded. "Makes a lot of sense. So now, what do we look for?"

Producing several pieces of paper from her purse, Fawn distributed them to the men in the room. "When I called to get these water bills from the local utility –"

"Excuse me." Miles looked at his former employee with a degree of incredulity that almost made Fawn laugh out loud. "But you aren't an agent any more or did you forget?"

"I didn't forget," Fawn confessed, "but I might have permitted them to … misinterpret my current standing with the Bureau. As I was saying, when I called, I asked for a list of average usage per household based on the number of sinks, bathtubs, and water closets, multiplied by the number of users, billed every month for residential accounts and every 60 days for commercial accounts."

"Well, isn't that interesting?" The Skyman found himself smiling at Fawn again.

"No, it isn't," she replied, "but thanks for asking. Let's dig in, gents."

The four investigators each claimed a crate to sift through. A quick scan of the water usage based on the meter readings, eliminated most of the residential users with just a quick scan. The quartet read each sheet of paper in silence, ensuring the bills remained in the order they were given.

After a half hour, the Skyman picked up a crate that held primarily large users and commercial accounts. After a few minutes of reading, he eyed a bill that captured his attention and wouldn't release it. He compared the dollar amount on the bill to the slip of paper Fawn gave him earlier. He cleared his throat. "I think I have something here."

The other three put down their water bills and surrounded the Skyman. "What did you find?" Fawn asked.

"The usage for this particular building is way out of line for – I know this address. It's a deserted Army base on the west side of town."

Markley borrowed the bill and read the address. "Yeah,

254

I remember hearing about this place. It was a training facility up until just after the Great War. Did a lot of work with biplane pilots. Built planes too for a while."

"Airplane facilities?" Miles asked.

"Yep," confirmed Markley. "My older brother trained there, wound up in a few dogfights over France." He looked at Miles. "The place is big enough to house a couple of platoons, but like I said, it's been deserted for almost twenty years. You know, Army budget cuts after the Great War and all that."

Fawn took the bill from Markley's grasp. "Not deserted enough, obviously. But who turned on the waterworks for them? Who owns the building?" She read the payee's name at the top of the sheet. "Nelly, Incorporated? Never heard of them."

Miles pulled a fountain pen from his pocket and a sheet of blank paper from a desk drawer. He wrote down the name and promised, "I'll check into this Nelly company."

Shaking his head, the Skyman said, "But this doesn't make sense. If there's not quite two dozen people living and working at those facilities, why is the water usage off the charts? They're using enough for four or five times that many people."

"Maybe," Fawn ventured, "they brought an army with them from Germany."

"Or hired some workers," Markley stated. "I mean The New Deal hasn't exactly worked its wonders on everyone. There's still people walking the streets that –"

"That's it!" The Skyman slammed his fist into the palm of his other hand. He turned to Fawn. "Remember back in the apartment, I made a comment about the streets of downtown being so deserted? That there didn't seem to be any low-lifes walking the sidewalks at night?" He paused to allow his theory to sink into the others' consciousnesses.

"Really? It makes sense." Miles continued to scribble as he spoke. "The down-and-outers usually congregate in a business district. More chances to pick up work, restaurants that might toss out leftover food, that's where I'd go to pick up some cheap labor."

"Not so cheap." The Skyman studied the bill again. "Between food, water, and some kind of pay, no doubt, someone's putting out a lot of dough. I'll also bet they aren't paying in gold or Krugerrands. Those might be a little hard to convert." He looked up at the others. "What if he's got a source of income here in the States? A partner as it were?"

"Unfortunately, Hitler's message rings true for a lot of Americans, sorry to say." Fawn frowned. "You don't have to be a Nazi to be a bigot. There's some headline-catchers who think eugenics theory makes as much sense as gravity."

"Okay," the Skyman interrupted, "we've got a location that needs investigation. What's our next move?"

Miles sat down behind his desk. "I can call the local police to assist us."

Fawn tugged on the Skyman's cloak. "Can we afford to wait? We never found the original drawings that you saved from the fire. What if they're working on something?"

"I was hoping you wouldn't mention that." The Skyman turned to Miles. "I can go out there and scout. If I see anything, I'll give you a call."

Miles shook his head. "I'm not waiting for you." He pulled his telephone closer.

"Neither are we," Fawn announced, then turned to the Skyman. "Before you ask, I'm going with you," she added in a tone that eliminated any thought of discussion.

"Fine," the Skyman decided. "Get us some reliable wheels and I'll meet you outside. I have to run to the kitchen for something." With that, he raced from the office.

Fawn rolled her eyes. "Men and their stomachs."

Miles barely had the receiver to his ear and the first number dialed when Fawn began snapping her fingers impatiently. "Come on. Unless you gassed up my car while I was your reluctant guest, I'm going to need a vehicle with a siren."

Instead, Markley tossed his key ring at the woman. "Take mine, but don't change the radio station." He frowned. "But why a siren?"

Fawn grabbed the keys neatly out of mid-flight. "Because I don't know when I'll get the chance to use one ever again."

* * *

"C'mon, c'mon, pick up." Cooper whispered into the steam-powered two-way radio in his left hand. The other gripped the steering wheel of his car tightly as he moved across one lane of traffic into the next.

258

After more than a dozen rings, the man on the other end of the wire said, "Hello?"

"It's Cooper. The boss is calling you in. We're about to take a vacation."

"I knew this day was coming," the other party commented. "I just need to get my bag. Where would you like me to meet you?"

"The boss says leave your car there. I'm coming to get you so be outside waiting."

"What about your compatriots?"

Cooper gritted his teeth. It almost pained him to admit, "I'm not with them any more. As soon as the boss leaves his, um, office, he'll be topped off and ready to fly."

"I'll be ready." The line went dead, leaving Cooper to drop his communicator on the seat and concentrate on pushing the speed limit.

"I could do nothing to assist a program that kills thousands of people."

TWENTY-FIVE – Hotly Pursuing

By the time Fawn pulled Markley's car up to

the office door, the Skyman was outside waiting for her. He walked a little stiffly as he moved to the driver's side of the vehicle.

Fawn looked up at him from behind the steering wheel. "What are you waiting for?"

"For you to scoot over."

"Why?" She crooked a thumb towards the passenger side. "Ride shotgun, climb in the back seat or pry the trunk open. No matter what you pick, we're burning daylight waiting for you to make up your mind." She gunned the motor to emphasize her point.

The Skyman grumbled under his breath as he ran around the car. His door was barely closed when Fawn squealed the tires and burned rubber to exit the parking lot.

Pushing himself back up into the passenger's seat, the Skyman told Fawn, "Please don't kill me before we go up against the heavily-armed bad guys, alright?"

261

Fawn barely blinked as she focused on the road ahead of her. "Then don't do anything stupid like treat me like a girl, okay?"

Smiling gently, the Skyman nodded. "It's a deal, Fawn." *Yeah*, he thought admiringly, *you're definitely no mere 'girl,' that's for sure*. "Hey, call me wacky, but do you want to talk about a plan for our heroic arrival?"

Fawn grinned. "Well, Wacky, I figure you'll go in like Gary Cooper, guns a'blazing, mowing down any bad guys you see. We rescue Kevin and the others, you duck out of there just as the police arrive, ready to fight crime another day." She checked the traffic carefully before running the yellow light before her. "I figure you can fill in the details as you go."

The Skyman grunted in what Fawn wouldn't mistake for agreement when something ahead of them caught his eye. "Fawn, do you see that black sedan ahead of us? Get closer to it, would you?"

Fawn pressed harder on the accelerator and narrowly maneuvered the vehicle between two other cars in two

262

different lanes. With driving skills she picked up as an F.B.I. agent, she closed the gap between her car and the one the Skyman pointed out without drawing unwarranted attention to herself. With tires squealing in protest, the sedan turned onto a road that led towards the western edge of town with Fawn not far behind.

"Well, I'll be!" A grim smile crossed the Skyman's lips. "See anything noteworthy?" When Fawn didn't reply immediately, Skyman pointed towards the rear bumper of the car ahead of them. Fawn's jaw dropped as she gave the Skyman a quick look of amazement.

Although a little had dropped off in the last month, the license plate numbers were obscured by a considerable quantity of dried mud.

"It couldn't be!" Fawn's expression turned into something Skyman couldn't recognize. Before he could comment, she accelerated, closing the distance between their car and the sedan.

Inside the other vehicle, Cooper looked into the rear view mirror and recognized his former supervisor's car. "Oh, brother! We've got a tail."

"Can't you shake them? I believe that's what you call it, right?"

Cooper reached into his jacket. "This is pretty much a straight shot until the final turn to the base." He took advantage of the straightness of the road to slow down just a little. He squinted, finding the silhouettes of the driver and the passenger to be oddly familiar.

Handing a .38 to his passenger, Cooper asked, "You know how to use this?"

The man took the firearm between two fingers with the same enthusiasm that he'd pick up a dead mouse. "I've seen how in the movies."

Cooper's right foot touched the brake as his left pressed the clutch all the way to the floor. "You've got about a minute to figure it out. If they lay me out, plug them, whoever they are." Before the man in the shotgun seat could ask what Cooper planned to do, the car already moved onto the shoulder of the road, stirring up a cloud of dust as it rolled to a halt.

Sure enough, the second vehicle followed suit. Once both autos put on their parking brakes, Cooper jumped out through the open driver's side door.

Fawn and the Skyman exited their conveyance. Their grim expressions were met by Cooper's sardonic grin.

"You two escape?" Cooper asked in his "official" tone. "Okay, put your hands up and –"

"Be quiet, Cooper!" The Skyman moved quickly to face the former agent. "You're going to answer some questions and you'll do it fast."

"You bet, Skyguy." By the time Cooper uttered his last syllable, he'd already hurled a right cross that would have shattered most men's jaws, had it connected.

However, the Skyman – or rather Allan Turner – had been the Harnell University Boxing Champion for two years running. He expertly blocked the incoming fist with his left hand. The Skyman's visor prevented Cooper from seeing the confident look in the young man's eyes as he launched his own counter-blow that connected hard against the ex-Fed's nose. Blood and surprise covered Cooper's features. The latter turned immediately to rage as he abandoned his F.B.I. hand-to-hand combat training and threw himself at the Skyman.

Dodging the oncoming man with a flourish of his blue cloak, the Skyman kicked Cooper hard. The added momentum propelled Cooper into the hood of Markley's car, driving the air from his lungs. As he refilled them painfully, the Skyman already had Cooper by the collar and turned him around.

The costumed man's fists struck Cooper in the face again and again. After taking a step back, the Skyman drove his left hand deep into Cooper's gut before following it up with a right uppercut that actually lifted the man off the ground. Cooper landed on his back, his arms and legs akimbo and his head reeling.

While the Skyman dispatched Cooper, Fawn moved cautiously towards the passenger side door of the agent's vehicle. Opening the door carefully, the rider stepped out casually and greeted Fawn with a leer.

For once, Fawn was rendered speechless.

Liberated from his opponent's attentions, the Skyman rushed to Fawn's side. His boots dug into the dirt of the roadside as he saw Cooper's gun in the man's right hand.

"Surprised to see me?" Braden Kendall asked, his smile

266

and his aim never wavering.

"A bit," the Skyman confessed. "But who better but the host of the party, and trusted acquaintance, to maneuver Peter Turner into the place where he'd be kidnapped?"

Fawn stepped away from the Skyman, waiting for Kendall's guard to lower just long enough for her to ambush the junk magnate. "But you were doped up too, just like Dr. Turner."

"However, I came around pretty quickly, you obviously didn't notice. Bruhner helped me work out the dosage. I knew how much I could drink before I'd pass out. This way, it looked like someone broke into my home, drugged up my liquor cabinet, and used me as a pawn to capture Turner. Well, I was used all right ... and paid marvelously for it." He laughed like a Saturday morning serial villain.

"Of course." The Skyman turned to Fawn. "I should have seen it. Stupid villains love to leave clues to prove how clever they are, or aren't." Fawn shook her head so the Skyman continued, "Don't you see? 'Nelly Industries' ... swap around the letters in 'Nelly' and you get ... *'Ellyn'*."

"At least you gave that girl favorable consideration for

something in life," Fawn said contemptuously.

Kendall growled angrily, "I'll thank you to leave that little parasite out of our discussions. She's just a reminder to me that one should choose one's life partners to be less sickly, less clinging, and generally more worthy of you and your station. In fact, I'd love to talk more, but it seems I have a plane to catch."

Kendall swiftly turned his pistol away from Fawn and towards the Skyman. He pulled the trigger twice, each slug slamming into the hero's midsection. The costumed man crumbled to the ground, clutching his guts.

Without thinking, Fawn dropped to her knees, checking the Skyman's wounds and fighting back tears of panic and worry.

Cooper felt a sharp slap against his cheek. He blinked his eyes again and again until Kendall came into focus. "Come on, we have to go," Kendall announced. "I'll drive."

Helping Cooper to his feet and into the back seat of the car, Kendall moved himself behind the wheel and slammed the door shut before locking it. But he didn't need to worry about either Fawn or the Skyman rising to their feet before he peeled out and left the pair behind in a cloud of loose rocks and dirt.

"I do it because it's the right thing to do."

TWENTY-SIX – Into the Skydome

Fawn **Carroll whispered to the unmoving**

figure in her arms. "You had to get yourself shot. Why? *Why?*"

After the roar of the sedan's engine vanished into the distance, Fawn further inquired, "And why isn't there any blood, you dope?"

The Skyman's initial response was a bright, cheerful grin. He rose – reluctantly – from Fawn's arms, brushing his uniform and cloak free of the road dust.

"Because of this." The Skyman reached into his tunic and removed a metal serving tray, the one he'd taken from the F.B.I. Commissary while Fawn procured their vehicle. "I was hoping my 'advantage' would last long enough to be used inside Bruhner's hideout, if they took my body for that Nazi to gloat over, but I won't complain."

He showed off the metallic tray, now adorned with two deep indentations from the gunshots, before tossing it casually towards the grass that grew alongside the asphalt

271

road. "It's a little uncomfortable to wear, even without the dents."

Fawn shot the Skyman her filthiest look. "You idiot! Didn't you realize the metal on that tray wasn't thick enough to stop a bullet, even with any padding that circus suit might have?"

"Really?" The Skyman looked genuinely surprised. "I'm glad I didn't talk to you beforehand about my plan. If I knew any better, I'd probably be a dead man. Talk about being too smart for your own good."

"You yap too much, flyboy." The corners of Fawn's lovely mouth turned downward in severe disappointment. "I can't tell you how glad I am that you're alive. However, those two clowns escaped."

"Get behind the wheel and I can cheer you up pretty quick," the Skyman announced.

"But what good will driving do? They're probably a mile ahead of us now." She closed the door and started the car's engine.

Once he was seated, the Skyman explained with a grin. "I guess we now have verification that Bruhner's secret ally

272

was Kendall, so that's a plus. I bet he's the one shelling out the dollars for supplies and workers in exchange for some Krugerrands. Silver Certificates for solid gold, if you will."

"Makes sense." Fawn coaxed the car to move a little faster. "Go on."

"We know Cooper's a traitor too. If Kendall confessed that he's in with Bruhner, and if he and Cooper are travel buddies the pieces start to fit pretty tightly, eh?"

Fawn aimed a perfectly-manicured finger in the air. "And the fact that Kendall isn't hiding his role in this scheme any more means that he's probably fleeing with Bruhner now that the plan has reached fruition."

"And since this road pretty much leads to the place that's using all the water –"

Without waiting for the Skyman to finish his statement, Fawn pushed the accelerator almost all the way to the floor.

"My heavens," Fawn said with a grin, "we are so smart. Don't we make a pair?"

The Skyman wisely neglected to comment, save for the tiniest of smiles.

* * *

Cooper didn't bother to close the hangar door and Kendall certainly wasn't going to dirty his hands with manual labor. The latter reached into the back seat to pull out a well-worn carpet bag.

Stan jogged up to greet them. "Herr Bruhner just finished up his recharge and he's moved everything into the Wings. The scientists are gathered and ready to go while the workers await their final reward." The thug grinned as if to give his statement the proper finish. "I believe we'll be in the air in just a few minutes."

Kendall looked at Cooper, the millionaire's gaze surveying the length of the road leading to the base. "Will you stop that? He's dead already, okay?"

"Who's dead?" Stan instinctively moved a hand towards his shoulder holster.

Cooper clapped Kendall on the back. "Our man here pumped a couple of slugs into the Skyman. He and his girlfriend were in hot pursuit and he got the jump on me when Kendall here shot the guy down like the dog he was."

"It was nothing," Kendall lied, recalling the look Fawn Carroll leveled at him as she held the man in her arms. It was

274

one thing to cripple a man financially, drive them into such financial despair that they took their own lives. It was quite another to murder an unarmed man and see the soul-crunching results. "Now can we get going?"

"Sure thing, killer." Stan motioned for the two to follow him. "We're ready to fly."

* * *

"So you'll wait there and just observe the building until Markley and I can bring reinforcements, right?"

With her thumb off the radio transmitter button, Fawn almost laughed out loud. She turned to the Skyman. "Miles is such a cut up. This guy's funnier than all the Marx and Ritz Brothers combined." She thumbed the microphone button. "Yeah, you betcha. Agent Carroll, over and out." She hung up the microphone before Miles could object to her stated status.

"You really enjoy making waves, don't you?" The Skyman couldn't fight the smile off his face so he didn't even try any more.

Fawn looked at him seriously. "If you want to surf, you need waves. It's the difference between enjoying the water and just sitting on a blanket, soaking up some other man's sunbeams. Now what's the next move?"

Pointing at the open hangar door, the Skyman said, "They're either very lazy, very not-so-worried about us interfering, or very ready with an ambush. I'm going in to find out which."

"Good plan," Fawn agreed. "I'm right behind you."

"But Miles said –"

"I'll write Miles a note," Fawn said with that tone that promised a punishment worse than any mere death for disagreeing. "If they built even one of those weapons, or swatted the bugs out of the Stasimatic Ray, we're all in a pickle. Race you to the door."

With that, Fawn moved quietly and with stern purpose towards the open hangar door, her high heels making no sound on the concrete driveway. The Skyman pursued her and swiftly caught up, racing on his silent rubber boot soles. The pair entered the hangar and ducked down behind Cooper's car.

"So now where do we go?" Fawn asked.

The Skyman frowned. "Did you think to look at a

blueprint of this place?"

"You're the costumed vigilante with no respect for breaking-and-entering laws," Fawn accused. "Isn't that *your* department?"

"It's only my third real day on the job. Give me some slack, will you?" He cocked his head to one side, listening intently. "Before we turn into Nick and Nora, how about we go join the grownups in the living room?" With that, the Skyman moved quickly along the nearest wall. Fawn followed without a moment's hesitation.

"I'm glad these megalomaniacs love the sound of their own voices," Fawn observed in a whisper.

The Skyman put a finger to his lips and Fawn nodded in reply. They moved behind a series of crates, deciding what might have been Bruhner's heavily-accented voice and which was an echo decaying as it bounded off the concrete walls.

Beyond the crates, the pair could see machines that once helped produce airplanes that aided in the war over the skies of Europe at one time. However, to remain hidden, they couldn't see the rest of the hangar's contents.

Fawn found her attention drawn to the next open area as she noticed the sound growing louder, interrupted by the occasional burst of applause. By now, Fawn could make out what the man was saying and the Skyman recognized the voice as belonging to Albrecht Bruhner. With a shared nod, they moved stealthily towards the rear of the hangar.

As the Skyman and Fawn hugged the shadows on the edge of the work area, the pair could see three distinct groupings of men standing just outside the next room which appeared to be some kind of dormitory.

Of course, Albrecht Bruhner was the most prominent. He stood atop a metal table, one of the few in the room that might not groan in protest of his weight. His armor shone in the light that poured in through the skylights as he raised his arms in triumph.

"– and you will receive your reward for your hard efforts, as well as the gratitude of a nation ready to reclaim its place at the forefront of global affairs."

As the applause started up again, this time accompanied by several whoops of joy, the Skyman continued to scan the room. Standing around the Prussian in a circle were his henchmen: the thug Stan, the traitor Kendall – who appeared to be uncharacteristically apprehensive – and the crooked ex-Fed Cooper.

Standing before Bruhner was a group of a couple dozen men. They were mostly unshaven, their work clothing varied in obvious quality, but each man hung on the Prussian's every word.

"And of course," Bruhner continued, "I could not have accomplished my mission without your help." He indicated the workmen with a sweep of his hand. "When we return to this country in triumph, your temporary sacrifice will be acknowledged and you shall be heroes of the new empire. The paltry gifts that we've given you of money, clothing and good food shall be mere tokens compared to the glory that comes."

And to one side stood sixteen men, each one with their heads bowed, obviously cowed by their armored jailer. The Skyman glanced over at Fawn who held her fingertips to her ruby lips as her eyes went wide in disbelief at the sight of Dr. Kevin Carson. The scientist was emaciated and his beard more shaggy and untrimmed, but it was all she could do to not shout out with joy at the sight of her former charge.

However, Peter Turner didn't appear to be among the captives, which troubled the Skyman.

Albrecht Bruhner raised both metal-covered hands into the air and smiled like a benevolent father. "So once we load the last of our cargo, some of us shall be off." He pointed to the workers. "I would ask you to make yourself comfortable in your dormitory. Our enemies approach, but you have seen what I have done in such a short time with so little. Fear not our challengers for you shall be placed beyond the touch of the law on this day, this I promise you.

"So, *auf weidersehen*, my friends, until we meet again in a better world." With a wave of his right hand that looked suspiciously like a Nazi salute, Bruhner stepped off the table, landing with a thud that the Skyman and Fawn could feel through the concrete floor.

Stan and Cooper herded the scientists in one direction, towards the front of the building, while Bruhner led the workers back to their dormitory.

The Skyman and Fawn moved closer to the hangar door, concealed by a large metal crate that had *Kendall Industries* stamped on the side. The Skyman pointed to the stencil and smirked. Fawn replied with a gesture that was as unladylike as it was appropriate. The Skyman couldn't help but grin in agreement.

Daring to poke his head from around the corner of the box, the Skyman received the latest in a series of surprises he didn't need to see ... the red and blue twin Wings.

He dropped back behind the crate, so pale that Fawn couldn't help but notice.

"We are –" The Skyman then followed up with a word that the last time he used it, his uncle took a bar of soap to his mouth. "They built the Wing," he whispered. "Two of them, in fact."

Fawn shook her head in confusion. "Those big gliders?"

"More than gliders, Fawn. The wings and propellers are just for stability. The real secret is the propulsion system. When properly calibrated, the Wing can move at about 500 miles per hour."

Fawn blinked. "For those of us whose high school teachers thought science wasn't girlie enough for us, isn't that impossible?"

"Forty years ago, so was manned flight." The Skyman grinned for a moment before turning serious again. "The Wing can fly just about forever, uses no petroleum except for lubrication, and can carry immense payloads. One Wing would be invincible in the air. Two would be ... I don't want to think about it."

The Skyman moved to a kneeling position again. "We can't wait for Miles to get here. You and I have to destroy both aircraft before they take off ... for the sake of the world."

Fawn nodded once in resolute support.

With his jaw set firmly, the Skyman thought, *My uncle Peter would have wanted it that way.*

TWENTY-SEVEN – Goodbyes and Parting Gifts

Using his enhanced strength, Albrecht Bruhner carried three heavy crates at once into the dormitory by himself. Stan followed with a hand cart, loaded with four cases of the best whiskey Kendall's money could buy.

Opening the crates with just his hands as easily as most people would tear apart an envelope, Bruhner smiled at his guests. "Eat, drink, and celebrate. I insist! Then once it is all gone, you are welcome to leave for a new life, your pockets filled with cash. Again, I thank you for all you have done. *Auf weidersehen!*"

The workers didn't even wait for Bruhner and Stan to clear the doorway before they tore into the food and alcohol.

Walking back into the hangar, Bruhner asked Stan, "You are clear on what to do? Forgive me for my concern, but so much is at stake at this point."

"No problem." Stan pointed to the second Wing, the one

farthest from the hangar door. "I take the brain trust with me and start flying east at the heading you gave me. Then I wait until you run your errand and catch up with me. Then we open up the throttles to see what these babies can really do." Stan unconsciously rubbed his hands together in playful anticipation.

Bruhner nodded. "Excellent. You'll see that at worst, I shall only be an hour behind you. At half-throttle, you'll still make excellent time, I promise."

"Good. Now I hate to be the doubter, but the planes are going to work, right?" He noticed a thin coating of sweat on his palms, one that he wiped off quickly on his sports jacket.

"The plans were foolproof," Bruhner announced with the certainty of gravity. "I supervised the construction of each plane myself. You will have a certain amount of learning to do, that's true, because of the size and the new technology. But just watch the gravitometric gauges as I advised and you will be fine."

Unconsciously, Stan patted the pistol under his left armpit. *And if the Feds somehow catch me, they won't take me alive. Made too many enemies to go to prison.* "I won't let you down, boss."

"I have every faith in you," Bruhner said sincerely. *I paid enough for your loyalty*, he thought. "Go ahead and raise the hangar door, then perform the pre-flight checks. I want to be in the air within ten minutes."

While Stan jogged towards the second Wing, Kendall approached Bruhner, his carpet bag firmly in hand. "Excuse me, herr Bruhner. I'd like a quick word."

"Quick it must be," Bruhner said with forced patience as he continued to lumber towards his goal. "We have a date with destiny. What is on your mind?"

"That Cooper fellow told me that I am to ride with that criminal, Lange." Bruhner nodded. "Well, I do not deal with underlings. I will be in your aircraft."

"I need you to accompany Stan," Bruhner explained, "because he can use some company." The Prussian added with a smirk, "I understand you're quite the cold-blooded killer now. You should have plenty to discuss."

Kendall cleared his throat. "I am not going to carry five million dollars in bearer bonds aboard a locked aircraft with a common criminal."

Bruhner laughed. "There is nothing common about any of us, Mr. Kendall. But if it will make you happy, we shall be travel mates. So get into the first Wing and we shall soon be on our way."

Good thing you have talents in creating relationships with the loftiest of society. Otherwise, I'd pull your head from your shoulders and seize those bonds for myself.

As Kendall broke into a run to enter the first Wing, Bruhner stopped at his goal with a smile. He looked down at Peter Turner who sat in a metal chair, tied to it at the wrists and ankles by thick, thoroughly-knotted cords.

Bruhner knelt beside the scientist who stared blankly ahead. "Dr. Turner, since we have your drawings, I am afraid I have no more need of you, except as an example to the others on maintaining their usefulness to the Third Reich."

Turner continued to stare, his breathing even.

"I am not fooled by your act, Turner. No man has ever survived so many sessions in my steam chamber. My guess is that you are made of more steely stuff than your colleagues. But a complete mental collapse that allows you to feed yourself?" The Prussian chuckled. "Good bye, Dr.

Turner." With that, Bruhner walked towards the first wing.

"Have a nice flight," Turner said in a clear, strong voice. "And start looking over your shoulder."

Bruhner laughed as he boarded the Wing.

* * *

"I need to get aboard one of those Wings."

Fawn shook her head. "Would you like the Moon on a silver platter while we're at it? What's taking Miles so long?"

"I don't know," the Skyman said, moving out from where he and Fawn concealed themselves. "However, we can't wait for them. Follow me."

Racing from one concealment to the next, the two moved back towards the dormitory, hoping a plan would reveal itself and fast.

* * *

Inside the first Wing, Bruhner completed his list of pre-flight preparations. The Wing hummed with power, almost as if it was eager to take to the skies to prove itself.

While inside the other Wing, Stan completed his own checklist. He thumbed the microphone button. "Calling Wing One, we are good for takeoff." He added with a malicious grin, "The device is primed and ready."

Back in the first Wing, Cooper tied down the Stasimatic Ray machine. Once the final strap was tightened, he called towards the cockpit, "The ray is secure. I'm on my way."

Clutching the precious carpet bag on his lap, Kendall attempted to make conversation to cloak his nervousness. "So how does that device work?"

"No idea," Cooper admitted, wishing this conversation never began. Being in Kendall's presence made the former Fed uncomfortable. He knew he could be duplicitous, but he also recognized when he was in the presence of a master of the craft. "The only guy who could tell us never surfaced after we faked his death. But herr Bruhner will take it apart once we get to Berlin."

"Everyone needs a hobby, right?" Kendall asked with a smile.

Cooper shot Kendall a look that told the scrap metal magnate that he wasn't in the mood for chat. Without another word, the former Fed made his way to the cockpit, ready to leave America behind. He wondered for the merest of moments why he wasn't more disturbed by the notion before shrugging off the feeling.

"This is Wing One," Bruhner announced into the radio proudly, "we are cleared for flight." And with that announcement, the aircraft shuddered and began to move forward.

* * *

The Skyman and Fawn watched the first Wing move towards the hangar door almost noiselessly. Even the propellers spun silently, save for the air passing around the rapidly-turning blades. The Skyman was elated to see the design working as expected, but heartbroken, knowing the purpose for which it would be used.

Soon, the second Wing moved into position, ready to roll outside. It waited patiently for its twin to clear the door and then move towards the airstrip.

The Skyman turned to Fawn. "I just remembered there's an access hatch near one of the landing gear. If I can reach it, I can make my way into the –" His voice caught in his throat and beneath his visor, his eyes went wide with astonishment. The Skyman grabbed Fawn's arm and sprinted across the room, no longer caring if anyone saw him.

Fawn looked past the Skyman to see a man bound to a metal chair at the end of the workroom. Immediately, she sprinted to catch up to the Skyman. As they grew closer, they could see that the man was Peter Turner. Naturally, he was thinner than the last time they saw him and he had several days of extra beard, but it was definitely Allan's uncle.

Turner looked up. The strange man in the odd costume didn't ring any bells with him, but he immediately recognized the woman. "Fawn? Fawn Carroll?"

"Yes, Dr. Turner. Are you alright?" She glanced over to Skyman who began working with the knots that held the ropes, and thus Dr. Turner, in place.

"I am," Turner said quickly, "but you have to get out of here and alert the authorities. Those two aircraft –"

"We know, we know," Fawn said quickly. She looked over to the second Wing and noticed that its cargo bay door was slowly lowering.

* * *

Inside the second aircraft, Stan adjusted the controls one last time on the machine. He couldn't quite see where he was aiming, but he'd gone over the procedure with Bruhner

290

enough to feel confident in his labors.

The machine began to pulse as the hose leading outside stiffened while it filled with atmosphere. Stan glanced around the machine to see a vortex of air form and extend itself towards the back of the Wing, snaking along the hangar floor towards the dormitory.

The grayish man-made whirlwind began to move across the floor of the work area. Stan turned another wheel and the vortex filled with a yellowish-brown gas.

Stan smirked. *The boss sure has a thing for his mustard gas.*

* * *

"Oh, great." Fawn turned back to the Skyman. "Can't you work any faster?"

Turner squinted, trying to see into the rear of the Wing. "Bruhner kept that machine in his recharging chamber. I think it had some sentimental attachment for him."

"I read the files on Bruhner," Fawn said quickly, wishing she'd commandeered a knife along with Markley's car. "The British got ahold of the prototype when they won the war. They gave it to the Americans who tore it open. I guess it was really a piece of junk, wouldn't have worked anyway." She quickly explained the machine's purpose, to deliver a gaseous payload of death with terrifying accuracy. She didn't bother to relate the obvious, that the two-foot wide vortex of compressed atmosphere was relentlessly making its way towards them, filled with one of the deadliest weapons known to science.

Fawn grimaced. "However, it seems he's had time to make some improvements."

TWENTY-EIGHT – To Fly Towards the Sunrise

"**Y**ou'd have to be a Boy Scout to undo these

knots," the Skyman declared as his powerful fingers probed and tugged at the ropes that held his uncle tightly while the vortex moved closer and closer.

A heartbeat later, the knots opened up and the ropes fell free of Turner's wrists. *Fortunately*, the Skyman thought with a smile, *I used to be a Scout.* A few seconds later, the bindings around the doctor's ankles dropped to the floor and Fawn pulled Turner to his feet, a fraction of a second before the tunnel of wind engulfed the chair.

Shouting above the noise from the micro-tornado, the Skyman called out to Fawn, "We still need to get aboard. Get going, I'll follow." He turned to see the deadly air tube moving around the chair, having missed its intended target, and snaking towards the dormitory.

"Go!" commanded the Skyman as he raced to get ahead of the vortex.

Peter Turner grabbed Fawn's arm. "There's an access –"

"– Door in the wheel well, I know." Fawn pulled herself free. "Wait here for the authorities." She ran across the floor, heedless of how high her skirt rode above her hips. This was life-and-death and no time for propriety.

Peter Turner saw a tool box sitting by a nearby table. Limping along on his crutch as quickly as he was able, the doctor made his way to grab the metal box. His face twisted with pain as he dragged his bad leg behind him, determined to get aboard that Wing with the tools.

Fortunately, with the first aircraft still moving towards the hangar door, the second Wing hadn't changed position yet. Fawn jumped onto the landing strut, aware that if the plane built up any speed, the wind would tear her free and send her to a – *Don't think about it, Fawn!*

A quick survey of the interior of the wheel well revealed a latch that Fawn grabbed and yanked with all her might. The door opened up and she leaped through the opening. Looking around in the light coming in behind her, Fawn saw the various pulleys and mechanisms that would keep the Wing in the air and allow it to land safely. She pulled herself onto a walkway, which was actually more like a crawl-way, ready to pull the door shut when the plane began its acceleration.

I'm on a plane, she thought as perspiration began forming on her brow and upper lip. *I'm on a plane, I'm on a plane – I SAID DON'T THINK ABOUT IT!!!* She inhaled sharply, wrestled the flashbacks into submission, and worked to get the butterflies in her stomach to fly in formation.

Her reverie was disturbed by the sound of a tool box flying into the access area, followed by a crutch. A moment later, Peter Turner pulled himself painfully up onto the walkway. Then as the plane began to move forward, the two shared the same thought ... *Where's Skyman?*

* * *

The subject of Fawn and Peter's shared concern ran as fast as he could to put the tip of the whirlwind behind him while he desperately looked for something in particular ...

Factories such as these were murderously warm in the summer, even with all the skylights and the doors and windows open. Thus, pushing hot air around the room made the environment slightly more bearable on the assembly lines. To do that, large six-foot tall fans were placed in strategic points to create artificial breezes.

Skyman raced towards the nearest fan, kicked away the chocks that held it in place, and pushed it with all his might towards the ever-advancing column of mustard gas.

Inside the dormitory, the workers continued their revelry. A partyer closest to the doorway happened to look out to see the undulating column of solid air approaching, a mustard-colored viper slithering towards the hapless men.

Suddenly, a man-sized fan found itself in the air column's path. Then a figure in red, white and blue tumbled behind it, somersaulting with a power cord in his bare hand. In one swift, economical motion, the Skyman pushed the plug into the socket before landing on his feet.

The fan blades immediately began to whirl about. In just a couple of seconds, the steel blades sped up in their dervish-like orbit, pushing their winds against the snaking air-tube. As if challenging the fan's superiority, the column touched the grill, preparing to invade the interior of the device.

However, the gleaming steel blades sliced the column effortlessly and the fierce winds they created rapidly diluted the deadly gasses. Like a scarf unraveling, the column swiftly dissipated.

Seeing this, Stan hastily closed the dispersal machine down, curing the Skyman's interference.

The partyers, unaware of how close to death they'd just come, watched the costumed adventurer step out from behind the fan. Across the distance of the work hall, the Skyman leveled a finger at Stan as if to say, "You're next!"

Feeling the icy grip of fear gnaw at the base of his spine, Stan slammed a fist onto the button that closed the cargo hatch. Without waiting for the gate to completely seal, he raced past the captive scientists who sat along the length of the hold, each man cuffed to a metal strut welded to the wall and sitting so close to his neighbor that they were almost sitting on each other's laps.

"Make a sound, try to help that guy," Stan warned them all with a wide-eyed expression they'd never seen before, "I'll have a bullet in the kneecap for you." In seconds, he dropped into the pilot's seat, secured the safety harness over his chest and began to pull back on the throttle.

Seeing the Wing move away, the Skyman turned around to smile at the workers who witnessed his feat of daring-do.

"Excuse me, I've got a plane to catch." With a brief wave, he began to sprint flat-out towards the departing Wing.

In college, just a few short months ago – a veritable eternity, given the events of the last month – Allan Turner set athletic records that Olympians would have trouble attaining. But Allan Turner hadn't been deprived of sleep and food for a month, nor had the young man set those records while running in boots as well as wearing a padded uniform with a long flowing cloak.

Inside the Wing, the forward movement and a series of odd vibrations in the yoke were the only clues that the airplane was operating. Stan guided the aircraft outside and onto the runway, eager to take to the skies. He marveled at the precision of the controls and smiled that someone added the steering wheel from an automobile. It gave the already quirky airship more of a playful feel.

The Skyman felt his lungs and legs burning from the exertion of running so fast, so far. Ignoring the discomfort, he pumped his arms even harder, straining to reach the access door. He could only assume Fawn and his uncle already stowed away since he could see the open hatch mocking him, deriding his efforts. The Skyman put on one final burst of speed, his teeth gritted and the man refusing to consider failure as an option.

Inside the Wing, Stan pulled back on the yoke. He felt the usual resistance of the wheels pushing against the runway before they lost contact with the tarmac. Once in flight, he looked out the side window, enjoying the feeling of almost falling away from the Earth as the Wing cleared a nearby grove of trees.

A red light flashed on the console. It seemed that one of the rearward hatches was still open, one that didn't show up on the pre-flight checklist. An easy enough fix, Stan pushed a button directly under that light and it went out. No alarm, no problem and he returned his attention to getting used to this amazing aircraft.

Fawn and Peter Turner shared a panicked glance after they saw the hatch close by itself. Even with her training, she wasn't looking forward to tackling whoever was flying the Wing as well as whatever backup they might have had.

Then a hand gripped the bottom of the walkway, followed by another. Soon, the Skyman's head bobbed into view. Relieved, both Turner and Fawn helped pull the costumed man up to safety. Without pausing to catch his breath, the Skyman asked, "You ready?" A nod later, the three made their way to the hatch that led to the cargo bay of the Wing.

The yoke of the Wing handled more smoothly than even those of the smaller aircraft he'd flown back before his Mob days. And the engine operated so quietly that if he couldn't see the ground moving below him as he gained altitude, he would barely know it was on.

Consulting the compass on the control panel, Stan eased the Wing into a due east flight path. On the radio, the regional airport transmitted again and again for his call letters. The thug resisted the urge to utter what few German obscenities he knew. That kind of mischief could get him shot down, assuming any sort of American military plane could catch up with him once he opened this baby up.

Stan was so busy with exploring the controls of the Wing that he didn't see or hear the trio enter from the cargo bay behind him. A couple of the scientists looked up to see the Skyman raise a finger to his pursed lips, requesting their continued silence. Others nudged their neighbors in astonishment at seeing Peter Turner again.

However, the most surprised of the prisoners was Kevin Carson who grinned at again seeing his friend, Peter. Then he caught sight of Fawn Carroll at the very moment she locked her eyes with his. Carson's heart pounded so hard with elation that he feared it might shatter his rib cage.

Skyman smiled at Fawn and whispered, "Go have your reunion. We can handle this."

As quickly and silently as she could, Fawn almost dove onto Carson, hugging him more tightly than she'd hugged any man before. Tears of indescribable joy rolled down her face and Carson's as they each shook with sobs and barely repressed laughter.

Once The Wing reached the proper elevation, Stan placed his hand on the throttle, ready to pull the levers back and leave America behind. But a sixth sense of sorts that he'd developed back in his street crime days stayed his hand. He turned around in the pilot's seat to see two men standing behind him, just watching his actions.

Stan laid eyes upon the one in a painfully familiar

uniform. "*You*! Just what does it take to kill you? *Who are you*?"

"I am THE SKYMAN," the costumed man said, cracking his knuckles, "and you're sitting in my seat!"

TWENTY-NINE – Death on The Wing

Stan **Lange laughed. "Nice Halloween costume."** He swung around in the seat to resume his duties as pilot. "But you might have noticed that I'm flying The Wing and it's a one-seater. Taking a punch at me might not be your best idea today."

Calmly, Peter Turner walked over to stand beside Stan. He smiled as he leaned over. "I'd like to point out that I know how to fly an airplane. In fact, I helped design The Wing so I probably – no, I do know more about its operation than you ever will."

"I still have my hands on the stick, Turner." Stan stared through the windshield of the airplane as the Skyman moved to the thug's other side. "In fact," Stan added with a smile, "if either of you try to yank me out of this chair, we go straight up in the air. Sound like fun?"

Turner pondered Stan's statement. "Not really. But if I was to provide a reason for you to release the controls ..." With that, Turner leaned over and spat in Stan's smiling face.

First, the smile gave way to the most furious scowl any man could hope not to see. Second, Stan's hands instinctively moved from the controls and towards Turner's throat. Third, the mobster felt his harness being unbuckled while another hand gripped his shirt.

One violent pull later, Stan found himself on his feet, facing an angry Skyman. Before he could put his fists up to protect himself, the mystery man threw a haymaker that would have knocked out any ordinary man. However, Stan didn't rise in the ranks of the criminal underworld by not being able to absorb a punch.

Stan moved in with a left hook that the Skyman easily blocked. In reply, the Skyman leaned over and drove a right into the crook's solar plexus. He followed that blow up with a series of punches to that same area, turning Stan's immediate hope of taking a full breath into a luxury.

Then came a left to the eye, a right to the jaw, and then another right, this time as an uppercut. Stan vaguely enjoyed a momentary feeling of flight before darkness claimed him.

From the pilot's seat, Turner whistled. "Wow! I'm not a violent man, but I enjoyed seeing that."

The Skyman disarmed Stan and removed a set of handcuff keys from the crook's shirt pocket before tearing off a strip of the thug's shirt and securing his wrists and ankles securely. "Stick around," the Skyman advised his uncle, "I promise there will be more."

Fawn entered the cockpit. Her eyes were red, but her step was light as if she'd been relieved of a huge burden. She looked down at the unconscious crook. "Just like a man, keeping all the fun for yourself."

Skyman handed Fawn the key ring. "Here, go make some new friends." As Fawn moved back into the cargo hold, the Skyman turned to Turner. "Sir, there's quite a bit you need to know to catch up."

Turner shook his head. "No, let's focus on here and now. I can catch up when we're done. So let's figure out our first priority."

"I'd say it's to find Bruhner and stop whatever he's planning to do."

At that moment, the radio crackled to life. The Skyman reached over and turned up the volume. From the speakers in the console came the sound of Albrecht Bruhner's voice.

The man spoke in even, measured tones. However, since the words were German, neither the Skyman or Turner could understand what he said.

* * *

Inside the first Wing, Albrecht Bruhner flew along the southern edge of Lake Erie towards Cleveland, Ohio. Flying under 10,000 feet, he keyed his microphone and spoke with a smile.

"This is Albrecht Bruhner and I am steam's master. This is your only notice, America.

"I fought your mongrel breeds in the trenches of the Great War. A mishap tore me from the combat and the victory that should have been Prussia's. Virtually paralyzed, disfigured, and in constant agony, my family left me and I had nothing left but my hate.

"That is until Adolf Hitler learned of my plight. He gave me the encouragement and the funding to bring my dream – and his – of a better world to live in. However, it is a world where many of you have no place.

"When I return, I shall bring to your lands a taste of the gas that crippled me, scarred me … and I shall rain death upon your homes from the sky. Or perhaps I shall first shine the Stasimatic Ray upon you and give you the mercy of dying in your sleep.

"You cannot even fight off an imaginary invasion from Mars. What hope do you have against the indomitable forces of the Third Reich?

"But no matter what the Fuhrer decides for you, the end is near and you may look forward to ... death on the Wing."

Bruhner replaced the microphone in its holder on the console and laughed as the miles flowed by swiftly below him.

* * *

"Okay." Turner gave the Skyman a quick look. "Do you speak German?"

In reply, the Skyman shook his head. "I got his name, Hitler's, that's about it. That and the word 'Stasimatic'." His expression turned grim. "That is what concerns me."

"You know about the Stasimatic Ray Emitter? How?"

Smiling gently, the Skyman replied, "When this is over, I'll explain everything. Just take it for now that I know more than anyone realizes."

307

Fawn entered the cockpit again, this time with Carson in tow. The Skyman noted the difference in age between the two as well as how close they stood to each other. She found herself unconsciously scowling at the sight.

Unable to see past the Skyman's visor, fortunately, Fawn asked, "So how do we find Bruhner? The sky is a big place to hide if you don't know where to look."

After an uncomfortable moment of silence, the Skyman snapped his fingers. "Fawn, I saw a toolbox on the way in. Bring it here, would you?"

"When did I become your valet?" Fawn asked with a familiar edge in her voice.

But before an argument could ensue, Carson raised his hand. "I know that tone. I'll go get it. It's safer that way."

"What's your idea, Skyman?" asked Turner.

"I've got a couple. One is a long shot to help us locate him and the other is something totally stupid and suicidal for when we find him."

Fawn grinned. "My favorite kind of plan."

THIRTY – Anchor's Aweigh!

Several minutes later, the Skyman had a

portion of the control panel open and the wiring exposed. "They did a pretty good job on the electricals," he observed as he tied the exposed end of a wire to a metal stud on the compass.

"Bruhner gave them no choice." Turner bit his lip as he gripped the yoke. "Should I ask how you knew your way around the inside of that panel without a flashlight and a Doctorate in engineering?"

"I'll explain later," the Skyman stated softly. He replaced the compass and switched on the radio. Smiling, he said, "No explosion, no flames, no problem." He tapped on the compass and the wheel swung around so the "N" for North faced them.

"We're not flying north, but west," Turner observed. "You broke the compass."

"Nope," the Skyman said triumphantly. "I turned it into a detection device."

"Really?" Turner couldn't keep the admiration from his voice. "And just how did you do that?"

"I wired our compass so it thinks the other Wing's unique transceiver frequency is magnetic north." The Skyman shrugged. "Unless he destroys his own radio, which he won't want to do, he's telling us where he's at as long as The Wing is in the air. Now all we have to do is catch up with him."

Turner grinned. "Take the wheel, young man. I think it's my turn to be insanely clever." The doctor rose from the seat. "Oh, don't worry. The Wing is so aerodynamically stable, if we were to lose power, it would pretty much drift to the ground safely."

As the Skyman slid into the control seat, both men were distracted by the sound of a pair of slender feminine hands applauding.

Fawn entered the cockpit. "The big brains didn't get fed before they left the house. Could we stop and get a few dozen burgers to go?"

Turner opened the panel around the radio, pulling out the device gingerly. He examined it with caution before

310

tapping it with the handle of the screwdriver. Aware of the puzzled looks being aimed at him, Turner explained, "I had a lot of time in the last month to do some thinking. So I amused myself by conceiving some 'improvements' to my existing designs."

Fawn smiled. "How do you improve The Wing? My vacuum cleaner makes more noise than this engine and doesn't go half as fast. How did you muffle the sound anyway?"

The doctor busied himself with adjusting the radio. "Instead of an internal combustion engine like most conventional aircraft, I devised one whose parts move by interacting with the Earth's magnetic field."

"Like it said on the blueprints," the Skyman joined in. "The Wing maneuvers on the magnetic waves just like a sailboat can tack with and against the wind. However, unlike a boat, we can also go up and down, not just to one side or the other."

Turner looked up and smiled softly. "Very good. That's just how my late nephew would have explained it." He turned to Fawn. "So do you understand the explanation?"

311

"Not one word of it. So what are you doing to the radio, Dr. Turner?"

The older man smiled as he continued his efforts. "Let's just say that given the similarities of the two aircraft, I'm working on a way to make the other Wing drop anchor."

"I just wish," the Skyman ventured out loud, "we could catch up with Bruhner, now that we know how to find him."

Turner glanced at the air speed indicator. "Five hundred –? That's all the faster we're moving? How ridiculous." Turner handed his handiwork to Fawn without asking and then opened another panel on the control board. He stuck his arm into the opening, his tongue moving into one corner of his mouth, and began to fiddle with something he could feel in the depths of the Wing's machinery.

"Idiots," he mumbled, "couldn't take the time to recalibrate the ferronomic compensators with the steering linkage … do I have to get out and push?"

Suddenly, Fawn took a step backwards and the Skyman felt himself pressed deeper into the cushions of his seat. He looked at the air speed indicator as it passed 550 … then six hundred … then 650 … finally topping out a notch above seven hundred miles per hour. The Skyman's jaw dropped as he looked towards his uncle.

But Turner kept his gaze completely on the task before him. "That's the best I can do on short notice, okay? Try and work with what you have. I'm busy."

The Skyman grinned at Fawn. "Speaking of what we've got to work with, could I convince you to grab a wrench so you can play a game of Skittles with me?"

Fawn, an ex-F.B.I. agent who managed to survive a fall from an airplane, now found herself partnered with a costumed lunatic and a mad scientist inside an airplane that ran on magnetic waves, trying to catch a Nazi madman who wore steam-powered armor.

"Sure, why not?" One corner of Fawn's perfect mouth rose in a sardonic smile. "It'll be the most normal thing to happen to me in weeks."

* * *

Aboard the other Wing, Albrecht consulted his map and smiled with glee. In less slightly more than an hour, he'd passed Chicago and began banking over Des Moines. With just a nudge from the yoke and a few more minutes, he could fly over either Detroit or Indianapolis.

He envisioned a fleet of Wings, each carrying a payload of bombs that could rain down upon these major American cities. Railroads, highways, factories, all could be afire and the country placed in a state of terror in around an hour's time at this aircraft's amazing speed.

And with the American scientists on their way to Berlin, the victory of the Third Reich was as inevitable as flowers in the spring and beer parties in October.

Meanwhile, Bruhner could almost feel the hatred in the air between Cooper and Kendall. Among the many positive aspects of The Wing was that the Steam Master would have to endure their sniping and constant insults for only a few more hours. Despite having confidence in their switched loyalties, Bruhner still wished for a better class of traitor, certainly quieter ones.

Adjusting his course in the hopes of intercepting Stan's Wing as quickly as possible, Bruhner pulled back on the throttle and savored the mild vibrations that ran through his chair and the yoke. He looked down below to see the landscape change more rapidly than he'd ever seen before. If

314

the armor didn't help regulate his breathing, Bruhner would almost think his breath was being taken away by the glory of his amazing aircraft. *After all, finder's keepers as the Americans would say.*

"Calling Wing One, this is Wing Two. Come in Wing One."

Bruhner's expression changed instantly from near-euphoria to near-panic. He recognized that voice and it sent a chill through him, something he hadn't felt in years.

Forcing an element of calm into his voice, Bruhner picked up his microphone. "Skyman, is it? You are certainly the most persistent individual I've ever met. I do not intend that statement as praise, by the way."

"Coming from you, Bruhner, that's the nicest back-handed compliment I've ever received." Bruhner heard his opponent take a deep breath, ending it with a sigh. "As much as I'd like not to, I feel obligated to offer you the chance to land and surrender to the F.B.I."

The master of steam looked through the windshield frantically. The voice sounded as clear over the airwaves as if the costumed dolt was breathing over his metal-covered shoulder. "And if I don't?"

"Oh, there's no second option," the Skyman explained, an edge in his voice. "You will spend the rest of your days rusting in an American jail cell, whatever your decision. You have my word on that."

Bruhner sat straight in his seat and secured his helmet to his armor. If this Skyman was going to defy him in the skies, then he would meet this challenger as any knight would, fully armored and ready to battle for what was right and true, the Aryan ideal.

Although he had no guns and no bombs, Bruhner could still joust with that ridiculously attired madman. While he didn't have a lance like a knight of old, he still had his Wing and he could out-fly any man. He would drive this Skyman into the ground and then bring this Wing back for Adolf Hitler's approval.

"So what are you waiting for, Skyman? Do you fear to face me?"

"Like fun I do. Heads up, steam punk!"

At first, the other Wing was just a dot over the western border of Ohio. But as Bruhner watched, the dot hurtled

316

across the clear skies towards him in a suicide run as if shot from a cannon.

However, at the very last possible second, Wing Two pulled up ever so slightly, barely avoiding Bruhner's aircraft. The wake of the other airship left the Prussian battling the yoke but with his augmented strength, it proved little challenge to keep this Wing in the air and flying eastward.

"You missed," Bruhner taunted, concealing the trepidation he felt at the sight of the much faster aircraft. *Invent amazing machines, survive fires and gunshots, escape from his own law enforcement agents, steal back his own equipment, was there nothing this Skyman couldn't do?*

"That was just a warning shot, Bruhner. The next time you see me, I'm coming in to get you."

That did it! Bruhner began to laugh so loud that Cooper and Kendall stopped arguing long enough to share a concerned look. Had their benefactor been driven mad?

"At ten thousand feet above the ground?" Squinting into the sun as it moved across the western sky, Bruhner caught the other Wing finishing its banking action and heading directly towards him again. *All this mouse needs to do*, he strategized, *is keep beyond the reach of your claws until the sun sets. Then I cloak myself in darkness and fly by my instruments until I cross over into Spain. From there, I will seek the sanctuary of Nazi occupied lands.*

Ready for aerial battle, Bruhner's chuckling turned into a growl. "Your so-called ethics will not allow you to take my life and you won't risk the lives you carry on board with you." In German, Bruhner added, "A man who serves a higher cause shall never know defeat. Heil Hitler!"

The Wing turned around in the skies over Akron, prepared to meet the enemy.

* * *

"Go to heil, you Nazi jerk." The Skyman looked at his uncle. "How's The Wing handling for you?"

Peter Turner held the yoke steady as he approached Bruhner's Wing. "It's like flying with the wings of an angel. I'm smarter than I gave myself credit for."

"And more humble too, I see." The Skyman placed a hand on Turner's shoulder. "Are you ready to test your theory?"

Turner snorted. "Nope. Are you ready to test yours?"

318

"Of course not. Good luck to us all."

As the Skyman walked purposefully towards the back of the airplane, Turner said, "Good luck to you too, Skyman."

Waiting for the costumed hero in the cargo bay was the mustard gas transmission machine. Fawn had removed the straps that secured it to the floor and wrapped them around the device several times. A towing chain used to move Army vehicles was looped through the straps by Fawn herself while Carson secured the other end to a steel support that ran the length of the aircraft's ceiling.

The Skyman gave the chain a good hard tug as if to verify Fawn's handiwork. He looked around the hold at the handful of scientists who watched him fearfully. While still looking like whipped puppies, they all – except for Perkins – gave their best efforts to assist Fawn.

Pulling his hand from the chain, he hoped no one else saw the sweaty hand print left there.

Looking down, he saw the men had pushed the mustard gas device to a point just on the other side of the cargo bay door hinge on the floor. Everything was in place.

Turning to Fawn, the Skyman said, "Once this starts, things are going to happen fast. You'd best find a new best friend and hold on to them tight."

"Sounds good." She looked at him fearlessly, compassionately. "Be careful. Come back to me."

The Skyman grinned. "Is this where I ask you for a kiss? You know, for good luck?"

Fawn returned the smile. "Let's discuss it when you return. In the meantime, it can build interest, just like a bank. For now, call it incentive."

His heart pounding, the Skyman turned towards the cockpit for a long, and hopefully not final, look at his surrogate father. "Doctor Turner, are you ready?"

Turner turned around in the pilot's seat and gave a thumbs up. "We're coming in fast. Good luck, son."

Rubbing his hands together, the Skyman said, "Let's make herr Bruhner's day a lot less pleasant."

Dr. Turner rotated a dial on the radio transmitter before he cried out, "Anchor's aweigh!"

THIRTY-ONE – With Nothing To Lose

The second **Wing soared past its sister ship,**

deliberately missing by a matter of a few feet. Inside, Albrecht Bruhner flinched as he once again battled the resulting turbulence. Furious at the cat-and-mouse game being played, the Prussian seized the microphone. "If you cannot risk your passengers by crashing into me, Skyman, then I have already won. Now I am bored with this game. Follow me to Germany, if you dare." He then slammed the mouthpiece into its housing.

"Don't pop open the champagne yet, Bruhner." Dr. Turner's contempt came through clearly over the radio. "Prepare to be boarded. But first ... a surprise."

Inside his Wing, Turner flipped a switch with a grim smile.

By way of response, the pitch of the first Wing's miracle engine changed. Bruhner looked out through the windshield to see the other aircraft banking somewhere over eastern Pennsylvania.

Looking down at the air speed indicator, the dial moved from a shade under five hundred miles per hour to 475 ... then 450 ... four hundred ... three-fifty ...

Panic seized Bruhner's heart. He worked the controls frantically to increase the output of the engine, but the ship proved unresponsive. Meanwhile, the airspeed gauge showed The Wing slowing down steadily. Soon, the ship wouldn't be moving swiftly enough to sustain their lift.

"Good glory!" cried Kendall, still clutching his carpetbag. "What the blazes is happening?" Cooper looked concerned, but remained quiet.

One hundred fifty ... one hundred ... seventy-five ... by now, The Wing should have been tilting downward towards the ground. However, it remained parallel to the Earth, slowing down as if it was in an American cartoon and the Law of Gravity no longer applied.

Inside the second Wing, Dr. Turner explained the science to Fawn, "To extend our boating analogy, the Wing's engine can also hold itself in place in relation to the Earth's magnetic waves. It's like dropping an anchor in the middle of a body of water. The water continues to move around the

322

boat, but the vessel itself doesn't go anywhere.

"Also, all electrically-based machines give off some form of radio signal. I found the sympathetic one to the other ship's engine and now I control it remotely. That is what happens when you give a man lots of time to think and the motivation to make it happen."

Fawn patted Turner's arm, "Would you please stop explaining things to me? Are we in position yet?"

"Almost." Turner rested his hand on a lever, counting down in his head. When he reached zero, he pulled the lever and looked back at the cargo hold along with Fawn.

The cargo bay door opened slowly, tilting downward. The sight of the ground rushing below them made Fawn gasp and dig her fingernails deeper into Turner's arm. She fought down the images of her freefall from a year before while her heart hammered inside her chest.

Now, the air inside The Wing began to move as if the plane was haunted by poltergeists. Everyone inside the aircraft held onto something as the outside winds entered. When the cargo bay floor reached a 45-degree angle downwards, the mustard gas dispenser began to slide slowly down the ramp.

With a quick salute and a smile that was braver than he truly felt, the Skyman walked the ramp, keeping pace with the machine. Beside him, the towing chain played itself out as he broke into a run. Soon, the machine fell free of the Wing and plummeted towards the ground and the Skyman dove out after it, his cloak flapping behind him.

Once in the air, the Skyman executed a half-roll in mid-air and then pulled himself towards the metal links. Once the chain pulled taut, the Skyman slammed feet-first into the machine. Gripping the chain tightly, he rode the box just like a cartoon mouse atop a pendulum. The winds tore at the man, but he wrapped his arm around the chain, clutching it with all his athletic might.

Turner wrestled with the controls for a second, doing his best to keep The Wing level. He turned back to see Carson standing near the ramp at a point where he could see the Skyman who jerked his thumb upwards with a free hand.

"Pull up, Peter!" Carson shouted. In reply, Turner gently brought the yoke back until the Skyman raised his fist in a brief salute. Carson called out, "You got it! Stay level!"

With that, Turner gently pushed the throttle forward, killing some, but not all, of the Wing's propulsion. He almost wished he could see Bruhner's face when the mad Prussian realized what was about to happen.

Turner would indeed have enjoyed the sight of bewilderment that reddened the Prussian's face as the second Wing grew nearer. The master of steam saw the Skyman, blue cloak flying majestically in the wind, riding his own murderous creation directly towards the cockpit on a tow chain. Terror gripped Bruhner's heart. He disengaged his safety harness and hit the secret control that shot a little bit of steam from a vent on the back side of his armor, bringing him immediately to his feet.

And it was fortunate that Bruhner acted as quickly as he did. He barely turned his bulk and stepped past the pilot's seat when the giant metal cabinet entered the windshield with a horrendous *CRASSSHHHHH*!!! Bruhner pulled his arm up to protect his eyes from the spray of broken glass and pieces of twisted metal that sprayed the inside of his airship.

When Bruhner pulled his arm down again, Cooper was at his side, pistol drawn and ready. He didn't need to turn around to know that Kendall was, no doubt, pressing himself against the bulkhead, trying to stay as far from any danger as he could.

Clambering inside from around the mustard gas dispenser with the winds outside pulling at his cape, the Skyman entered the cockpit. Hopping over the damaged metal of the control panel, the hero grinned at Bruhner as he shook the loose glass from his shoulders. "Hey, Bruhner! We've got laws in America against littering so I thought I'd return your junk."

Raising his pistol, Cooper readied a shot at the Skyman. However, Bruhner's hand snaked out with surprising speed and crushed the firearm without thinking.

"You fool," the Prussian growled. "If your bullet pierced the machine, this room would be filled with deadly mustard gas. Besides, you shot him once at close range and his uniform isn't even stained."

"Gentlemen," the Skyman said with authority, "I place you both under citizen's arrest and insist that you accompany me back to your home base where you will surrender to the Federal Bureau of Investigation for what I hope are many

326

months of brutal interrogation."

Albrecht Bruhner and Foster Cooper turned towards each other … and then began chuckling.

Cooper tossed up his hands and shrugged. "I figure my ex-bosses will not be terribly charitable to me if I went back." He pointed over his shoulder at Kendall who watched the drama before him like it was a stage play. "And him, he's aided and abetted himself into a ten-by-ten at Sing Sing for about as long as it takes for Hell to freeze over."

Bruhner chuckled. "And I'll be put before a firing squad for all that I've done so you are correct that there's only one outcome to our encounter. The next stop is Germany after I regain control of The Wing." With that pronouncement, Bruhner lumbered towards the cockpit, his eyes fixed on the caped intruder that stood between him and the yoke.

Well, that certainly didn't go as planned, the Skyman thought to himself.

A strange smile crossed Bruhner's face, one that didn't find a reflection in his eyes as he marched towards the controls. The Skyman moved backwards, aware that he had nowhere to find sanctuary aboard this aircraft.

Moving past the Skyman, Bruhner freed his gas machine from the control panel with as much effort as it would take an ordinary man to lift a child's doll house. After setting it down on the floor behind him, the Prussian gripped the straps that surrounded the box and pulled until they snapped like blades of grass.

"*Danke* for returning my … 'junk' as you put it. Now I have a weapon I can use from this Wing. How kind of you."

"Don't count on it. It ends here, it ends now!"

Cooper looked at the Skyman. The steely set of the hero's jaw and the determination in his posture sent a near-Arctic chill down Cooper's spine, despite knowing that the adventurer faced an armed traitor with nothing to lose and an Aryan super-being with no regard for human life.

For a moment, Cooper gulped nervously and wished he could call for reinforcements.

THIRTY-TWO – In Final Combat

The Skyman instinctively crouched into a classic boxing position, both fists up and ready to attack. His feet moved swiftly back and forth, left and right, providing Bruhner with a moving target.

Ignoring the Marquis of Queensbury rules, Bruhner took a step closer and threw a jet propelled punch at his opponent. But Skyman dodged the metal-covered fist.

Skyman countered with a left feint, hoping to find an angle of attack on the Prussian's helmet that would allow him to sink a fist into that mad grin. But Bruhner kept his left hand up as steely protection.

Meanwhile, Cooper ran over to Kendall and seized the pistol that he gave up not even an hour earlier. The scrap metal millionaire appeared to be glad to surrender the weapon. The ex-Fed aimed down the sights of this handgun, making sure the Skyman was covered at all times. If the young twerp would step far enough away from the control panel and the mustard gas machine so he could pull off a shot ...

Bruhner swung his fists again and again. With the pulleys and gears of the suit amplifying the Prussian's natural strength and speed to parahuman levels, the Skyman wondered how long he could continue to dodge, to duck and weave, until fatigue – or a bullet from Cooper's gun – left him vulnerable.

Sensing the tide of advantage shifting in his direction, Bruhner pressed forward, forcing the Skyman back, back, back, away from the gas dispenser and closer to where Cooper stood waiting, his weapon drawn.

Ducking under a right that would have turned his skull into a fine red mist, the Skyman grabbed a corner of his cloak. Thrusting himself closer to Cooper, the Skyman threw his cape upwards like a bullfighter obscuring his prey's vision.

Trained to hold his trigger finger immobile until he could assess the difference between friend or foe, Cooper didn't expect the Skyman's fist to emerge from around that cloak. An explosion of light and fire that could drown out a nova erupted in his left eye. Before he could clear his vision, the Skyman danced out of Bruhner's reach and launched a vicious kick against the side of Cooper's right knee, forcing it to bend at an angle nature never intended for it to do.

As that injured knee gave way, the Skyman was already behind Cooper, using him as a meat shield against Bruhner. Shaking his head to clear the fireworks from his brain, Cooper felt his right arm, his gun hand, rise again as the Skyman's hand wrapped around his own.

Sliding his index finger over Cooper's, the Skyman aimed the pistol at the steam-powered warrior and pulled off a single shot. Unknown to anyone aboard that plane save for the Skyman himself, Allan Turner trained on the Harnell University rifle squad so he knew how to quickly line up a firearm's sights. Confident that Bruhner would build armor that could resist gunfire, the Skyman intended to bounce the bullet off the helmet and stun his foe.

But a quick move from the master of steam pulled his headgear out of the bullet's path. Instead, the projectile bounced off the armor's collar, denting the metal and compromising the seal between the steel and the human flesh beneath.

Suddenly, steam erupted from the collar like Old Faithful. Bruhner's arms flailed wildly as if they could push the gas back where it belonged. The Skyman shoved Cooper to one side and then moved forward, keeping himself low to the floor, eager to stay beyond the reach of those rapidly-moving gauntlets.

Bruhner stumbled backwards, unmindful and unaware of his surroundings, blinded by the steam that now surrounded him like a cottony cocoon. He screamed obscenities and pleas for rescue in German. However, no one could save the man who once claimed to be steam's master as he stumbled backwards, blinded and in terror like a man who saw his life's blood emerge from a gaping chest wound.

Suddenly, a gunshot rang out, almost deafening in the close quarters. The Skyman stiffened as hellfire spread from his right shoulder. He looked down to see a darker patch of red spreading along the fabric of his tunic.

Whirling around, the Skyman looked into the barrel of Cooper's pistol. The ex-agent's left eye had already swollen shut and was turning purple from the earlier punch. Skyman could hear his assailant's teeth grind against each other as

332

Cooper's finger tightened against the trigger.

In one fluid move, the Skyman reached up with his left hand and turned Cooper's wrist inwards, almost folding the tendons upon themselves. Cooper cried out in surprise and pain, but not before he got off one more shot.

The bullet tore through the ex-agent's neck, sending blood everywhere. Then it rebounded off a support beam just inches above Kendall's head, eliciting a most girlish scream from the millionaire.

Ktangggg! SSSSSSSSSSSSSSS!!!

Leaving Cooper to slump to the floor, the Skyman turned towards the cockpit and gasped. The bullet had torn into the gas dispenser's compromised guts. Bruhner stumbled backwards, colliding with his dangerous creation.

The ivory cloud that surrounded Albrecht Bruhner slowly turned brownish in color and his movements became even more frantic.

Skyman instinctively held his breath. *Mustard gas*!

Bruhner screamed again and again, gurgling as the chemicals tore into his flesh and the tender linings of his lungs, almost as if finishing business that was two decades late in completing. After a few horrifying seconds, Bruhner disappeared completely into the yellowish mists.

The Skyman surveyed the interior of The Wing. Shaking his head and avoiding the spot where the deadly gasses flowed, the Skyman moved slowly towards the cockpit, his left hand pressing firmly against his wound.

Smiling, he saw the end of the tow chain resting over the top of the control panel. The Skyman reached for the link – or links, one might think – to the other airship. However, he knew he'd never have the strength to shinny up to the other Wing thanks to his wound.

Looking up into the other airplane, the Skyman saw Kevin Carson standing as close to the edge of the cargo hatch as he dared. A look of relief came over the scientist's face as he mimed a tight orbit around his own waist with both hands.

After a moment of confusion, the Skyman realized what Carson was trying to tell him. After pulling the chain free of the machine, the Skyman looped the metal links around the side of his belt again and again, then around his good arm. He slumped against the control panel, light-headed from his blood loss.

Skyman looked up again and saw Carson calling out excitedly towards the bow of the airship. What little slack in the chain slowly vanished and the Skyman's feet lost contact with the floor as the first Wing slowly resumed its forward movement in the sky.

"Please don't leave me!"

The Skyman looked back to see Braden Kendall hobbling closer, still with a death grip on his valise. "Please, Skyman," the millionaire pleaded, "you've got to take me with you. I beg you to save me. You can't leave me here."

Skyman thought of Ellyn and Kendall's role in betraying his country before saying with sincere contempt, "Just watch me."

Immediately regretting his words, the Skyman reached out to Kendall with his good hand just as the chain went taut and the hero found himself outside The Wing, dangling thousands of feet above the Earth.

But before the heroic young man cleared the window, he cried out in pain as something clamped just below his left knee, squeezing the the leg as if it was trapped in a vice.

Skyman looked down to see a silver gauntlet wrapped

tightly around his leg and digging into his flesh. Evil laughter rang in the hero's ears.

"No one leaves this Wing alive," cautioned Albrecht Bruhner who stood just beyond the veil of chemical death. And for a moment, the Skyman feared the Prussian spoke the truth.

THIRTY-THREE – Destiny Beckons

One summer, Allan Turner found himself
fascinated by some small fireworks his uncle Peter brought
home one Fourth of July. Resembling certain Christmas
presents he'd received from his parents, a cylinder with the
ends twisted shut, Allan pulled the ends apart on one novelty
after the other, awash in the wonder, the unique *pop!* and the
resulting confetti.

Now holding onto a chain with one hand, suspended ten
thousand feet above the ground while he bled freely from a
shoulder wound and an insane half-man/half-machine
attempting to pull him back inside a damaged experimental
airplane, the Skyman felt certain that the resulting stresses
on his body wouldn't result in a rain of confetti.

As the other Wing pulled at the chain wrapped around
his belt, the Skyman summoned up enough strength to kick
Albrecht Bruhner in the face, the neck, even one that
bounced off the dragon emblem on his chest. The Prussian
grunted, but refused to let go of his prey. The Skyman risked

a glance downward and what little he could see of the man's flesh no longer resembled anything human, thanks to the bath in mustard gas and steam he'd just received.

The Skyman kicked out desperately again and again and again, each blow weaker than the one before. With one more effort left in him, the Skyman lifted his right leg as high as he could and slammed it against his enemy's face with all his strength.

Blood oozing from every pore, Bruhner stumbled backwards into the cockpit, barely able to breathe. His own body betraying him, he saw the architect of his misery rising, moving away from him. Fumbling at the controls at his belt, he readied one last burst of steam through the same jets that helped him rise rapidly from the pilot's seat just a few minutes before. He would soar through the heavens like a dragon and slay his foe for the glory of the Third Reich!

Following the Skyman's demise, Bruhner planned to climb the chain and destroy Turner along with that mouthy wench, as a gift for Mr. Cooper, before commandeering the vessel and finally taking the remaining scientists to serve the Nazi cause.

Brian K. Morris

Bruhner heard the reassuring *hsssss* as the gas that gave him strength and life vented towards the nozzles on the back of his suit. With a barely-audible "Heil Hitler" on his lips, Bruhner launched himself through the shattered windshield.

However, the Skyman's accidental gunshot already drained most of the steam pressure from Bruhner's armor. The resulting thrust barely allowed the Prussian to clear the window before Gravity seized the engineer and pulled him relentlessly towards the Earth and to his doom.

Fighting against going into shock, the Skyman barely heard Bruhner's screams. Nor did he feel the chain moving upwards more rapidly as Carson and most of his fellow scientists pulled on the links, bringing their rescuer to safety.

Opening his eyes for a moment, the Skyman looked up to see Fawn standing next to the scientists, close to the cargo door's edge, encouraging them to keep pulling. Her eyes were still wide with potential panic and she gripped a support strut so hard she feared leaving indentations. But she was there, defying her own fears and the Skyman couldn't have thought more of her courage, or of her, than he did at that moment.

Once aboard, Dr. Turner closed the hatch with the flip of a switch. Immediately, Fawn examined the Skyman's wound and smiled softly. "You're going to fly with just one wing for a while, but it looks like the bullet passed completely through. You'll be fine once you get a couple of raw t-bones inside you so you can catch up on the blood."

Fawn pressed her silk hanky to the Skyman's wound. He placed his hand atop of hers. When their eyes met, he smiled and whispered, "Thank you, Fawn. Can I take a rain check on that good luck kiss? I'd like to be fully aware so I can appreciate it."

She grinned broadly. But before she could give her usual smart-aleck reply, from beside a porthole at the rear of the Wing, Peter Turner cried, "The other ship is moving. The mustard gas machine must have damaged the other Wing's controls. It's no longer under my command."

The Skyman forced himself into a sitting position and soon onto his feet. If Fawn had anything to say about her patient moving, his determined expression squelched any debate. He moved gingerly towards the pilot's seat.

"I need to put better insulation inside the control panel,"

Turner muttered as he moved The Wing forward and turned it around 180 degrees to pursue its twin. "I should also think about a set of separate radios, perhaps a series linked together, along with a hand-held remote. But what kind of range –?"

"Can we brainstorm improvements later?" the Skyman asked. "Kendall and Cooper are still aboard the other Wing and there's a couple dozen jurors somewhere who'd like to sentence those two traitors to thirty days in the electric chair."

"Right." Turner called out into the microphone, "Wing One, this is Wing Two. Stay back from the controls and let me attempt to take control again."

"Go to blazes," Kendall growled. "Cooper is dying and my destiny lies in Germany. By the time you can call out any armed aircraft, I'll be halfway to Europe and living an amazing life that no man could dream of." He chuckled. "You know, this plane almost flies itself. When I return from Berlin, perhaps I'll see that you're allowed to work for me."

By now, Turner swung the Wing completely around in the sky and followed a trail of dark smoke that emerged from the back end of the other aircraft. "Kendall," Turner shouted into the transmitter, "step away from the yoke. Let me help you land The Wing."

"They can talk me down in Berlin," Kendall growled. "Then keep your eyes to the skies. Imagine a fleet of Wings, each one with the Swastika on its belly and my imprint on every moving part. Now if you'll excuse me, goodbye, Peter."

Skyman grabbed the microphone. "What about Ellyn? How do you think she'll feel, being the daughter of the biggest traitor since Benedict Arnold?"

The speaker was quiet for the longest of moments. Then in his quietest, calmest voice, Kendall said, "To blazes with her also. I regret every penny I spent paying others to raise her. Now if you don't mind, I have a date with Etern--" And then the radio went dead.

Fawn joined the Skyman and Dr. Turner in the cockpit. "I don't like that bleached bimbo one little bit," she said sadly, "but for all her money, she could never buy her father's love."

"Braden Kendall sold his soul long ago," the Skyman

observed. "But whatever Hitler paid for it, he should ask for his money back."

The smoke coming from the other Wing grew even darker as it crawled across the skies of New York State. Peter Turner observed, "I fear Mr. Kendall is putting too much faith in another piece of scrap metal. I don't think he's going to remain aloft very much longer."

"Couldn't happen to a more deserving guy," Fawn observed, her heart breaking a little bit for Ellyn, from one woman to another.

* * *

Braden Kendall pulled on the throttle controls until they were all the way back, just as he'd observed Bruhner doing. His eyes swept over the console, but he couldn't tell one dial from another. Otherwise, he'd have seen that The Wing was impaired and flat-out could barely fly at half her potential speed.

But by now, he didn't care. Glancing down at the carpetbag on the floor by his feet, Kendall continued to rant, unaware that no one could hear him. "I shall possess the wealth of a Carnegie – no, of a Midas! I will build the new

343

Wings myself and sell them to Hitler personally. I will demand that the able-bodied of the conquered nations be my hands on the assembly lines. Soon, the blood of all lesser men and women shall be the lubricant upon which the gears of conquest grind."

Kendall was only vaguely aware of the waves of heat that struck his face from the damaged console before him or of the smoke that grew thicker and darker in the cargo hold behind him. Ignoring the Wing's danger signals, the millionaire droned on to an audience of no one as he left the eastern coastline behind.

Behind him, most of the lights in the cargo bay had shorted out and the dense oily smoke blotted out the light from those bulbs still surviving. But as long as The Wing remained in flight and it could get him out of this country and into a nation with no extradition laws with America, that's all Kendall cared about at the moment.

Meanwhile, a figure stirred below the worst of the smoke. Foster Cooper was too determined to allow his fatal injuries to claim him yet. He pulled himself along the floor, his blood on the deck making it difficult for his fingertips to find sufficient traction. His lungs burned, he couldn't feel his throat, and all he could see was that accursed Kendall at the controls of the Wing.

The ex-Fed wiped the blood from his eyes as his hands made contact with a metal box. *The engine ... that impossible magnetic engine ...* Cooper thought in his blood-deprived delirium. *Won't ... won't succeed ... must redeem ... myself ... can't die ... a traitor ...*

Unable to see, barely able to think, Cooper attempted to pull himself from the floor by gripping something cold and metallic and drawing himself up to his knees. As if being given a reward, he felt a powerful *hmmmmmmmm* that seemed to fill the marrow of his bones. Soon, the noise transformed into a banshee's tortured wail as the ex-agent rose to a kneeling position.

The wind rushing in through the shattered front windshield tore at Kendall's eyes and made it hard for the millionaire to breathe. But even above the constant white noise of the air stream, the drone of the machine inside the cargo hold demanded to remind Kendall of its presence.

Kendall spun around in the pilot's seat, trying to see

through the billowing black cloud, but couldn't make out anything or anyone. With the throttle back as far as it could go, the millionaire assumed the noise came from the amazing engine that Peter Turner devised, the one that would encourage Adolf Hitler to welcome him with open arms.

The former Bureau agent struggled to right himself, to die on his feet as befitting someone with his record of service. He didn't want Miles to see him kneeling like some weakling ... to justify his actions in another life ... to be found wanting ...

Something nagged at the back of Kendall's mind, just like seeing a face at a party that he should recognize but didn't, or remembering his daughter's birthday.

Then it hit him. "The Stasimatic –"

At that moment, the last of Cooper's blood drained from his shattered body as did his strength and his life. He collapsed onto the Stasimatic Ray device, accidentally striking the activation switch in his final action on this Earth.

The unfocused rays exploded from the lens of the device. From inside the cockpit, Kendall felt his heartbeat skip and his nerves sent out contradictory signals, like feeling the burn from an ice cube. Then he passed out, falling forward onto the yoke of The Wing while the throttle remained wide open.

As the Skyman, Fawn and Dr. Turner watched helplessly, the other aircraft tilted its nose towards the icy Atlantic and slammed into the ocean's surface at a couple of hundred miles per hour. Immediately, the aircraft shattered into countless fragments, most of which sank under the surface of the water immediately. A couple of minutes later, the rest of The Wing disappeared beneath the waves completely, leaving no trace that it ever had existed at all.

The Skyman leaned against one of the walls of the cockpit and slid down its length. He placed his face in his hands and muttered, "If only I'd – no man deserved to die like that."

Fawn dropped to her knees and pulled the Skyman into her arms. She held him tightly, avoiding his wound, and remembered Kendall and how little he thought of Ellyn.

"You're entitled to your opinion," she whispered as he returned her embrace.

347

"Poor, poor Allan..."

THIRTY-FOUR – Debriefed and Relieved

Standing just outside the former Army base,

Agent Reginald Markley watched The Wing approach from just over the trees, an impressive enough sight. But when the airplane came to a complete stop fifty feet overhead before slowly lowering itself onto the tarmac, both he and Miles Rockwell whistled, each man thoroughly impressed.

Then a door opened on the side of The Wing and out walked the scientists in single file. A team of doctors and policemen helped the men back into their old dormitory. However now, it was set up with medical supplies and some hot food for the men. A half dozen telephone lines ran into the room so the men could contact their families and give them the joyous news, that they were free at last.

Miles and Markley debriefed Dr. Turner, Fawn and the Skyman personally. Once they were done, the Skyman asked, "Are you finished with me? Now that you've patched up my shoulder, I've got some errands to run."

Extending his hand, Miles shook the Skyman's

thoroughly. "Thank you for all your help. I look forward to working with you again. And sorry about the arrest."

Fawn whispered, "And the coercion and the starvation and the renegade agent and –" A gentle nudge from Dr. Turner's elbow ended the addenda, but couldn't convince the woman to suppress her smile any more than he could hold back his own.

The Skyman shook Markley's hand. "I don't care what Fawn says about you. You're a good man, Markley."

"That's okay," Markley added with a grin, "I don't care what she says about me either." He then turned to Fawn. "I still think the field is too dangerous for a woman." The agent inhaled deeply, then exhaled slowly. "But you did a good job and I'm kinda proud of you. If you ever need a favor …"

Fawn turned to Miles who surveyed Markley with a smile that told the world just how impressed he was with his agent's integrity. He caught her eye and gave her a wink, which she returned with a grin.

"Well, it's been fun," the Skyman said, "but tomorrow's a school night somewhere and I need my beauty sleep." With a quick wave, he sprinted to The Wing. He called over his shoulder, "Fawn, Dr. Turner, I'll be in touch," before entering the aircraft and locking the door.

Climbing into the pilot's seat, The Wing was airborne in less than a minute. Feeling the weight of the world sliding from his shoulders, the Skyman pulled back on the yoke and enjoyed a view of the city at night from a couple of thousand feet up. He smiled and thought, *Okay, so where do I hide this thing until I find a hangar for it?*

"Penny for your thoughts, masked man."

The Skyman almost jumped out of his uniform at the sound of Fawn's voice. She leaned against the wall of the cockpit, smiling broadly at the costumed hero.

Dropping back into the pilot's seat, the Skyman said with his own grin, "Young lady, you are harder to shake than a cold. How did you get in here?"

She leaned on his good shoulder, sharing the extraordinary view. "Did you know there's an access door by the wheel well?" She smiled. "For a smart enough guy, you certainly have a lot to learn about women. You take a girl to a party, you're expected to escort her home, you know."

The Skyman grinned. "Tell me your address and I'll drop

351

you off." He sighed. "It's been kinda fun, in a crazy, dangerous way. I hope we can do this again sometime."

"I suspect we will. But now you have one more lesson coming." She moved so the Skyman could see her more clearly. "I need to teach you something about me."

"And that is?"

She wrapped her arms around his neck. "I always pay my debts." With that, she locked her lips to his.

As the Skyman lost himself in the softness of Fawn's kiss, he thought, *We definitely will do this again. Hopefully with fewer Nazis.*

* * *

The next morning, Dr. Peter Turner threw away the eggs that were still in the icebox after a month. *They must have been raised by dead chicken*s, he observed.

Early this morning, Miles brought Turner to the apartment that his nephew rented. He felt uncomfortable being in the same room where the young man worked on a personal project that remained a secret to this day, a plan that would never see fruition.

Aside from some clothing in a cigarette-scarred dresser,

there was very little of Allan Turner in this room that Peter could find. The knowledge made staying here for a few days a little easier, but at the same time less comforting. *The young man wanted to make an difference in the world ... and now he'd never get his chance.*

Peter Turner's thoughts found themselves drowned out by a knock on the door. *Maybe Miles or Markley forgot to ask me a question, as difficult as that concept is to absorb.*

The scientist turned the knob and opened the door. A man in a raincoat and slouch brimmed hat stood in the dimly-lit hallway. The stranger lifted his head and smiled. It was the Skyman. "Mind some company?"

"I'd rather talk to you than to myself." Turner motioned for the Skyman to enter. "So what brings you here?"

"Believe it or not, I need a change of clothing. Plus, we need to have a talk." The Skyman removed his outer garments and dropped them on the sofa. He then reached for a spot on his helmet, just under the back of his jaw, and worked a hidden latch concealed under the fabric.

"Talk about what, Skyman? And how is it you have clothing here? I'm afraid I just don't – OH MY GOD!!!

ALLAN!!!"

And for the first time since Allan's parents died, the two held each other and wept unashamedly, but for a much better reason this time.

THIRTY-FIVE – Bookends and Loose Ends

"So it wasn't Allan Turner after all." Miles spoke into the phone's mouthpiece while puffing happily on his pipe. "We finally got some arrest records from Philly and one surviving fingerprint says the deceased was a low-life named Marco Roove."

Miles away, in her hotel room, Fawn Carroll waved a section of newspaper at her freshly-painted toenails. "That's bad news for Roove, but good news for Allan, I hope." *And me.* Fawn smiled. "I guess it's now just a matter of waiting for the man to turn up. So how's that Stan fella doing after we gave him to you?"

"He's singing like a duet with Caruso and Crosby since we dropped a hint that being a good boy could keep him from doing the 50,000-volt Charleston. He's given us enough that we can prevent another network like Bruhner's from being set up ever again."

"Good man." Fawn touched up a couple of spots on one of her pinky toes. "Keep him uncomfortable for me, would you?"

"It's a deal. And I'll send him your love." Miles grinned. "So Fawn ... can I talk you into coming back to the Bureau? It turns out Dr. Carson gave you high marks for protecting him and as far as he's concerned, you brought in the F.B.I. and Skyman to save him and the entire western world from the Nazi menace. On paper, your career just got a jump start." He chuckled. "Markley would say that's not bad for a girl. Come to think of it, he did."

"I can't say I'm not flattered, Miles. However, I was kinda kidding someone a month ago when I said I was a private detective. But the more I think about it, it's a way to take what the Bureau taught me and put that knowledge to good use."

Miles put his feet up on the corner of his desk. "Mark my words, Miss Carroll. You're going to miss all that red tape. Just remember the door's always open."

"I appreciate that more than you'll ever know, Miles." Fawn pulled the cotton from between her toes. "No, I think I'll stay local for a while. D.C.'s got nothing for me except when the cherry blossoms come out."

"Oh?" Miles couldn't keep the disappointment from his voice. "What's that college town have that we don't?"

Fawn's eyes stared into another world as a contented smile crossed her lips. "Well, there's the Skyman." She caught herself. "I mean there's this guy, man."

At the other end of the telephone line, Miles Rockwell clamped both hands over his mouth to keep Fawn from hearing his laughter.

* * *

Allan shouldn't have been surprised when the other party picked up the receiver during the first ring. "Yes?"

Altering his voice slightly, Allan said, "This is the Skyman. I'm glad you made it home safely, sir."

"There's a lot of people who can return home safely tonight thanks to you, young man. So to what do I owe the pleasure of this phone call?"

Allan shuffled his feet uncomfortably. "Sir, I'm not used to asking for favors. However, I have a shopping list of sorts if I'm to get myself off the ground, so to speak."

The President of the United States of America chuckled. "I didn't give you this number just to talk sports results. I've

357

got a pen and I'm ready to write ..."

* * *

F.B.I. Agent Markley's expression never changed, even after radio newscaster Tony Trent objected to the new government-issued script pages. "I understand, Mr. Trent. I appreciate the power of the First Amendment which gives Little Annie Rooney and Ella Cinders the right to say whatever they want."

Markley pulled a dozen sheets of paper from a briefcase and handed them to the radio reporter. "But for you and me, there's only one higher power than the man who wrote these pages. That higher power gives harp lessons after you die, if you know what I mean." His expression turned grim. "But everything on these pages is true and the President is a man who appreciates the power of a favor, mostly when he's getting one."

Wrestling with his conscience along with his professional ethics, Tony finally relented. "Okay, I'll do it. But I'm probably going to have to wear a big, ugly mask to hide my face after this." He sighed. "Never a dull moment, darn it," Trent whispered before walking into the studio to take his place behind the microphone.

Across the country, scores of radios tuned in to hear Tony Trent's familiar introduction before launching into the news of the day.

"Today, a spokesman for the Federal Bureau of Investigation issued a statement that the case of the missing scientists has been cracked. The mastermind behind this plot, Prussian engineer Albrecht Bruhner, died in an airplane accident a couple of days ago."

In Urbana, Illinois, Dr. Kevin Carson nursed two fingers of brandy in his upstairs study as he listened to the broadcast. He took a sip, hoping this time, it might calm the slight tremor in his hand.

"Evidence points to a connection with certain members of the American underworld, one of whom is in Federal custody. Also, diagrams for other sophisticated weaponry were saved from Bruhner's diabolical plan to steal American technology for Nazi benefit."

In upstate New York, while listening to the broadcast in his rented room, Allan Turner congratulated himself for keeping his uncle's blueprints inside his Skyman uniform the entire time as just one more incentive to remain alive, as if he needed any more. If he went, so would they, most likely.

Allan grinned as he watched his Uncle – and temporary roommate – take a pencil to the Wing schematics, jotting down notes for improvements to the already-impressive aircraft.

"The complicated plot was foiled by a freelance law enforcement agent, designated in F.B.I. reports only as 'The Skyman.' This Skyman also put young Allan Turner, Dr. Peter Turner's nephew, into hiding until the all-clear could be sounded. The recent graduate from Harnell University is said to be alive and well and eager to resume his normal life."

Across town from the Turners, Fawn Carroll hugged her pillow and laughed out loud with relief as tears of joy ran down her cheeks.

"In other news, Braden Kendall, the man who made millions of dollars by finding new purposes for other people's scrap iron died yesterday in a tragic accident. After turning all his cash assets into bearer bonds, authorities say it looks like he tried to leave the country on vacation when he lost control of his aircraft over the Atlantic Ocean. Mr.

Kendall is survived by a daughter, Ellyn."

In a dimly-lit mansion, Ellyn Kendall stared out of her bedroom window as the sounds of Tommy Dorsey emerged from her Victrola. She spent the day crying for inheriting a business she knew nothing about and for losing the contents of her bank account, stolen by the stranger that sired her. She wished Allan Turner was there to comfort her, but she wouldn't learn of his renewed existence until tomorrow's newspaper arrived.

Perhaps tomorrow, she'd use her key to open up Daddy's locked desk upstairs. Surely, there were some clues to what he did in there.

"And finally in tonight's news, the Federal Government announced another round of selling off deserted military bases. In fact, one such previous sale was declared to be null and void, but the property – a former airplane manufacturing facility – was immediately resold to a private party."

Allan Turner promised himself to enjoy this one last night in the rundown motel room before he took possession of Bruhner's former hideout tomorrow morning, thanks to some wheel-greasing from the Feds. Meanwhile, his Uncle

Peter could stay with him until his laboratory home at Harnell University could be rebuilt.

As Tony Trent signed off from his radio broadcast, Allan contemplated recent events. For the most part, the Skyman proved useful and he looked forward to taking to the skies again from his Skydome, the name he gave the former Army aircraft manufacturing and training center. He also couldn't chide his uncle for tinkering with The Wing. Allan had some ideas to improve the Stasimatic Ray that he ached to evolve beyond the design stage.

With the Skydome, Allan Turner – as well as his costumed alter ego – now had a quiet place to train, to create, and to live out his dream of public service. How ironic that the nerve center of a Nazi plot that could have taken over the world would now be used as the secret base for the Skyman, a modern day swashbuckler who vowed to protect the helpless, preserve the law, and have fun doing it.

While the dark days loomed beyond the horizon as they always did, Allan Turner asked himself how life could get any better than it was right now.

And the Skyman replied with a grin, "Wait and see."

362

Final Interlude

He **didn't have enough strength to even open**

his eyes. His heart beat irregularly and his lungs moved as if laced with hellfire. The worst kind of biting cold invaded the marrow of his broken bones and he ached for the caress of his mistress, Steam.

But while he still lived, thanks to his amazing armor, he would find a way to avenge himself against the costumed interloper.

"The guy looks like a dog mauled him." The voice was male and didn't sound very educated.

He smelled greenery that mingled with a musty odor, like a rot that slowly ate away at the walls in a shed. He was lying on his back on some kind of table, his feet dangling in mid-air.

A second male voice rejoined, "Yeah, but look at all this shiny metal on him."

Yes, he thought, *the life-sustaining armor that once I fill it again, shall bear my standard. I shall resume my work, my goal being to bring America and that accursed Skyman to their knees.*

"Yeah, kinda reminds me of one of them knights of the Round Table whut married a refrigerator." The voice chuckled at his own joke.

Laugh, you ignorant savage. When die ubermensch *assume their rightful –*

"You start diggin' the grave in back. I'll get to peeling that metal off him. It ain't like he'll need it any more."

What???

"Sounds good. Hey, I hear there's a guy in upstate New York whut pays pretty good for scrap metal."

And Albrecht Bruhner, the former Master of Steam, couldn't even open his mouth to scream.

Brian K. Morris

Author's Notes

We all remember where we were when we
received our first kiss. We can recall where we were when
we heard about President Kennedy's assassination, the
Challenger's destruction, the attack on the Twin Towers, etc.

Of course, I can recall clearly where I first saw the
original Skyman, a far more pleasant memory.

It was on the brilliant cover of the even more brilliant
History of Comics Volume 2 by Jim Steranko. Swinging on
a cable behind The Ray, this figure in red, white and blue
piqued my interest.

Then I read *The Return of The Skyman* from ACE
Comics (1987). Behind the Ogden Whitney cover lay a
time-spanning tale by Mort Todd with artwork by Steve
Ditko and Rick Altergott. Ultimately, Skyman survived the
issue's villain, Shreck, only to fall to the parade of failing
comic book distributors who left ACE with too many unpaid
bills to warrant a second issue.

A couple of years ago, Ron and Mort Todd attempted to

revive the ACE line. At that time, I'd just begun my freelance writing career, having just published my second book, *Santastein*. I also did interview transcriptions for several publishers including the amazing Michael Ambrose (whose *Charlton Spotlight* should be on everyone's pull list). I'd just typed up a tape Ron Frantz sent in, which tickled me to no end as I'd been a huge ACE Comics fan during my comic book retail days.

(In fact, Ron and I found out we'd "met" each other at the 1987 Chicago Comic Con. He was in a room away from the main action on the floor – just what *did* you do to earn this isolation, Ron? – and I think we kinda nodded to each other as I passed through in search of new material. But being a completist, I had everything he'd already published so out the door I strolled. Wotta maroon I was.)

One day, Ron called me to thank me for my work. This led to a conversation and a quick friendship. We began calling each other frequently to gab and share tales of our past adventures in fandom. Ron's were far more interesting than mine, I assure you.

Anyway, as one of our discussions came to an end, he

366

mentioned the ACE revival and the products in the pipeline. With my tongue firmly in my cheek, I said, "What you need to do is diversify your revenue stream by having me write a Skyman novel."

Without a second's hesitation, Ron chuckled and said, "Well, get busy."

So I did. The result is in your hands.

And to my great delight, Roy Thomas (who has put up with me for around a decade as one of his transcribers on his fantastic *Alter Ego* magazine, published by TwoMorrows Publishing) consented to write a forward to this book. I will always be grateful to Roy for his various acts of kindness to me over the years and especially for his generosity of time and praise.

This book has met with numerous unavoidable challenges as it made its way into your hands. However, we didn't give up because that's not what the Skyman would do. I hope you find the results of our efforts pleasing.

The Original Skyman Battles the Master of Steam

The man who started it all...

CONTRIBUTOR BIOGRAPHIES

Brian **K. Morris** has written just about everything.

His articles and interviews have appeared in publications such as *BACK ISSUE Magazine*, *Hogan's Alley*, *Knights of the Dinner Tabl*e, *WHOtopia*, and many others too obscure to mention. He's also contributed to *The Krypton Companion* and the fiction anthologies *With Great Power*, *Malicious Mysteries*, and *Metahumans Vs. The Ultimate Evil*.

His first book release, *Bloodshot: The Coldest Warrior*, was the #1 Hot New Release in Kindle Worlds' Action/Adventure line for October, 2013. His next novel, *Santastein: The Post-Holiday Prometheus*, was released through the Freelance Words imprint to much acclaim. Following the horror/humor book came *Conflict: A Study in Heroic Contrasts*, a short story publication, as well as the first in his new contemporary fantasy series, *.Vulcana: Rebirth of the Champion*

He is currently a writer and editor-in-chief for Silver Phoenix Entertainment (www.silverphoenix.net), working on the upcoming (as of this writing) comic book title *The Haunted Tales of Bachelor's Grove*, horror tales that center around a real-life haunted cemetery in Midlothian, Illinois. He also writes about real-life illusionist Master Ron Fitzgerald; Kadrolsha Ona, the Queen of the Paranormal; as well ass *The History of the Police in America* and an upcoming supernatural western.

Brian lives in Central Indiana with his wife Cookie, no children, no pets, and too many comic books.

To keep up on his adventures, and to purchase his other works, go to **www.amazon.com/authors/briankmorris** and give the **Freelance Words** and **Vulcana** Facebook pages a LIKE for all the latest news and information.

And if you enjoy this book, please leave a review where you bought it. Brian can use the positive affirmation.

Brian K. Morris

Roy **Thomas** has been a professional writer since 1965, primarily for Marvel, DC, and other comic book companies, but also for comic strips, movies, TV, comics-related books, and his own comics-history magazine *Alter Ego*. He is the author of the huge Taschen book *75 Years of Marvel* (2014) and *Stan Lee's Amazing Marvel Universe* and *Conan: The Ultimate Guide to the World's Most Savage Barbarian* (both 2006), and co-author of *The Marvel Vault* (2007).

He served as an editor at Marvel and/or DC from 1965 to 1986, was Marvel's editor-in-chief from 1970-72, and has won numerous professional awards for his writing.

Among the comics with which he is most identified are *Conan the Barbarian, The Avengers, The X-Men, Red Sonja, The Savage Sword of Conan, Sub-Mariner, Dr. Strange, Fantastic Four, The Incredible Hulk, Thor, Daredevil, All-Star Squadron, Young All-Stars, Secret Origins, Infinity Inc., Arak – Son of Thunder, Captain Carrot and His Amazing Zoo Crew!, Shazam! The New Beginning, The Invaders, Avengers West Coast, Captain Marvel,* and *The Amazing Spider-Man.* He co-wrote the 1980s fantasy films *Fire and*

371

The Original Skyman Battles the Master of Steam

Ice and *Conan the Destroyer*.

Since 2000 he has worked with Stan Lee on the *Spider-Man* newspaper comic strip, and he currently writes online comic strips of Tarzan and John Carter, Warlord of Mars. He lives with his wife and oft-collaborator Dann on a South Carolina spread inhabited by numerous species of birds and beasts, and enjoys reading and playing chess and poker when he can find the time, which isn't nearly often enough.

Brian K. Morris

Pat **Boyette** (1923 – 2000) was a highly-respected
artist, writer, and multi-tasker in the comics field for two
decades.

Born in San Antonio, Texas on July 27, 1923, got the
acting bug early in life. Making his first appearance on a
local soap opera, Pat moved into newscasting at WOAI-
AM before entering World War II at a cryptographer.

Resuming his career upon returning to civilian life, Pat
anchored the local television news as well as producing a
puppet show and daytime talk program, among other
duties. By the Sixties, Pat began producing, directing,
writing and composing for a series of low-budget films
beginning with *The Dungeon of Harrow* (1962), *The Weird
Ones* (1962) and *No Man's Land* (1964).

During this time, Pat illustrated a syndicated Western
newspaper strip, *Captain Flame*, for Charlie Plumm. After
leaving film and television, Pat turned his attention to
producing comic book art, primarily for Charlton Comics,
starting with *Shadows From Beyond* #50 (October, 1966).
Soon, aside from numerous horror, romance, science
fiction, and war comics, Pat was the original artist on *The*

Peacemaker, co-created with writer Joe Gill, for the short-lived line of Action Heroes. He also filled in for artist Pat Morisi on *Peter Cannon, Thunderbolt.*

During his stint at Charlton, Pat also worked on the comic adventures of *The Six Million Dollar Man, The Phantom, Jungle Jim, Flash Gordon,* and *Korg: 70,000 B.C.,* among many, many others.

Pat also worked for DC, Warren, Marvel, Atlas, Renegade, Acclaim and Apple Comics as well as his own Wandering Star imprint. A close friend of Ron Frantz, Pat produced a one-page piece of art intended for the first issue cover of *The Return of the Skyman.* However, Ron decided to go with an Ogden Whitney illustration. The cover of this book was taken from Pat's illustration and color guide, with enhancements from Trevor Hawkins, Randyl Bishop and Brian K. Morris.

Pat passed away on January 14, 2000 from cancer of the esophagus. He was survived by a wife and daughter and missed by thousands of comic book fans.

Brian K. Morris

IF YOU ENJOYED THIS BOOK ...

The following titles from **BRIAN K. MORRIS** are available at **amazon.com/author/briankmorris**

The Original Skyman Battles the Master of Steam

BLOODSHOT: The Coldest Warrior

Based on the Valiant Comics character, the nanite-powered warrior investigates the man with the nicest lawn in town whose out-of-date computer may hold a clue to Bloodshot's origins.

It might also mean the One-Man OMD's death.

Available only from *Kindle Worlds*.

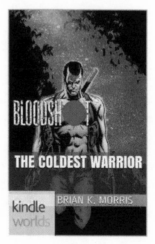

Brian K. Morris

SANTASTEIN: The Post-Holiday Prometheus
Cover by **TREVOR ERICK HAWKINS**

Dr. Victor Frankenstein has a cure for his fiancee's holiday blues. What could possibly go wrong? We take an entire novel to tell you.

Based on the Mary Shelley classic tale of horror, imagine Boris Karloff performing in a script written by Douglas Adams and directed by the members of Monty Python. It would be very, very funny and so is *Santastein*.

Available in print and electronic form from Freelance Words.

ISBN-13: 978-0615987033
ISBN-10: 0615987036

The Original Skyman Battles the Master of Steam

CONFLICT: A Study in Heroic Contrasts

A unique tale told in a unique style, each archtypical character is boiled down to their individual heroic and villainous essences.

The Heroine's deadliest enemy finds a way past her defenses – through her heart, using a kidnapped child.

CONFLICT is the first in a series of short story books where the essences of many of heroic literature's tropes are put on display in a fresh light for a contemporary audience.

Available in print and electronic form from Freelance Words.

ISBN-13: 978-0692251591

ISBN-10: 0692251596

Brian K. Morris

VULCANA: *Rebirth of the Champion*
Cover by **TREVOR ERICK HAWKINS**

An ancient evil finds a way back into this world in order to destroy it. Meanwhile, blogger Angelique Forge accidentally discovers the Armor of Vulcan's Fallen Champion.

There **will** be consequences.

If you crave strong characters, fast-paced action, clever dialogue, and white-knuckle plot twists, *VULCANA: Rebirth of the Champion* is the book for you.

Available in print and electronic form from Freelance Words.

ISBN-13: 978-0692444146
ISBN-10: 0692444149

The Original **Skyman**

WILL return soon

in

SKYMAN ADVENTURE MAGAZINE!

Watch for it in 2017

Made in the USA
Columbia, SC
24 June 2018